IKIRYO

Vengeance

and

Justice

IKIRYO

Vengeance And Justice

An Akitada Novel

I. J. Parker

I · J · P
2017

Published 2017 by I.J.Parker and I·J·P Books
3229 Morningside Drive, Chesapeake VA 23321
http://www.ijparker.com
Cover design by I. J. Parker.
Cover image by Shotei Takahashi
Back cover image by Ohara Koson
Publisher's Note: This is a work of fiction. Names, characters, places, and incidents are a product of the author's imagination.

Ikiryo: Vengeance and Justice, 1st edition, 2017
ISBN 978-1973833031

Praise for I. J. Parker and the Akitada Series

"Elegant and entertaining . . . Parker has created a wonderful protagonist in Akitada. . . . She puts us at ease in a Japan of one thousand years ago." *The Boston Globe*

"You couldn't ask for a more gracious introduction to the exotic world of Imperial Japan than the stately historical novels of I. J. Parker." *The New York Times*

"Akitada is as rich a character as Robert Van Gulik's intriguing detective, Judge Dee." *The Dallas Morning News*

"Readers will be enchanted by Akitada." *Publishers Weekly* Starred Review

"Terrifically imaginative" *The Wall Street Journal*

"A brisk and well-plotted mystery with a cast of regulars who become more fully developed with every episode." *Kirkus*

"More than just a mystery novel, (*THE CONVICT'S SWORD*) is a superb piece of literature set against the backdrop of 11th-cntury Kyoto." *The Japan Times*

"Parker's research is extensive and she makes great use of the complex manners and relationships of feudal Japan." *Globe and Mail*"

"The fast-moving, surprising plot and colorful writing will enthrall even those unfamiliar with the exotic setting." *Publishers Weekly,* Starred Review

". . .the author possesses both intimate knowledge of the time period and a fertile imagination as well. Combine that with an intriguing mystery and a fast-moving plot, and you've got a historical crime novel that anyone can love." *Chicago Sun-Times*

"Parker's series deserves a wide readership." *Historical Novel Society*

"The historical research is impressive, the prose crisp, and Parker's ability to universalize the human condition makes for a satisfying tale." *Booklist*

"Parker masterfully blends action and detection while making the attitudes and customs of the period accessible." *Publishers Weekly* (starred review)

"Readers looking for historical mystery with a twist will find what they're after in Parker's latest Sugawara Akitada mystery . . . An intriguing glimpse into an ancient culture." *Booklist*

Characters

(Japanese family names precede proper names)

Main Characters:

Sugawara Akitada nobleman between assignments

Yukiko his second wife, daughter of Kosehira

Yasuko & Yoshi his children from a prior marriage

Akiko his sister

Tora his senior retainer and friend

Saburo his secretary, another retainer

Genba his *betto*, another retainer

Sadako his daughter's companion

Kosehira his best friend and father-in-law

Nakatoshi another friend

Kobe superintendent of the Police

Characters involved in the jail murder:

Sato a wealthy young rice merchant

Mrs. Kuwada his manageress

Miyagi a popular courtesan

Saeki her brothel master

Ishikawa Ietada a noble client

Morikage another client

Ohiya a drunk

Kagehira a doctor

Characters involved in the case of possession:

Fujiwara Tadanobu a nobleman with a violent past

The Prime Minister his brother

The Crown Prince another relative

Lady Aoi a medium, another relation

Tadanobu's cook and assorted servants and retainers.

Ikiryo

"Living ghost"

Ikiryo is a spirit that leaves the body of a living person in order to inhabit that of a hated individual to harm it.

1

A Prisoner Dies

It was the middle of the night when the jailer heard the groans and shouts coming from one of the cells. He was alone, the others having long since gone home to their families and bed. It was cold, and he huddled under a cloak next to the small brazier. He did not want to get up and check on the prisoner.

He knew who it was. Only one of them was sick. The rich guy. When he had been brought in, they had all stared. He was young, good-looking, and dressed in fine clothes. Definitely not your run-of-the mill jailbird.

They heard soon enough that his offense had been not kneeling and bowing before a high-ranking nobleman. It was a minor offense, and he would soon be released. Their antipathy toward rich young men melted very little at his offense. They did not much like kneeling and bowing either but accepted it as their way of life. This handsome fellow was clearly spoiled beyond his station in life and deserved to be taught a lesson.

Then the prisoner turned out to be a complainer. He kept them running with requests to send messages, with pleas to buy him some expensive foods, with demands for paper, brush, and ink. All were denied, and the jailers became resentful.

Apparently to protest the prison food, he next claimed it sickened him. This went on, though the doctor had shaken his head and said it was nothing.

Another horrible groan and a shout. "Help! Please! I'm dying."

How could he be dying? He had been fine a few hours ago. No, he was just making a racket to spite them. In the middle of the night!

But more voices were raised and doors were being rattled. The shouting had woken the others. With a muttered curse, the jailer peeled back his cloak and got to his feet. "Shut up!" he yelled at cell doors, as he made his way down the row of cells. It was dark, but he could see faces pressed to the grill in each door. "Go back to sleep!" he snarled.

What a noise that man could make! Almost artistic. An actor playing a man at death's door could not sound more convincing. The jailer cursed again.

He finally reached the cell of the troublemaker and peered through the grille. Horrible sounds came from within.

"What the devil do you want now?" he shouted through the grille. Then his eyes adjusted to the darkness inside and the smell hit his nose. He cursed and opened the door. Taking a torch from the wall, he stepped in and peered down at the human being writhing on the dirt floor, a dirt floor that was covered with ill-smelling puddles and stains.

The handsome young man was handsome no more. His face was contorted, his eyes stared sightlessly, and he twitched uncontrollably while screaming with pain.

The jailer jumped back, slammed the cell door shut, and rushed off for help.

Since it was the middle of the night after a day of troubles, help was slow to arrive. The screams became moans and then ceased. By the time a doctor had been roused from his bed and made his way to the jail cell, the young man was dead.

*

The doctor was Dr. Hori who also sometimes served as coroner. The jailers, who had eventually gathered, liked him because he did not give himself airs like other doctors often did. But at the same time, they were a little worried. What if there had been something wrong with the swill they had fed all the prisoners and that Sato had complained about?

Sato was the dead man. Sato Yutaka. He was a well-to-do merchant who had inherited his father's rice dealership. There were bound to be repercussions, especially since this man had not been your run-of-the mill criminal and had claimed that he had been arrested on a trumped up charge. There was always a chance that a judge would have found him innocent.

Dr. Hori eyed the body and the condition of the cell only briefly before asking, "What did you feed him?"

The jailer threw out his hands and cried, "Nothing that would kill him. The same as all the rest, and they're alive. Besides, he didn't touch it. Filled his belly with what his girlfriend brought him."

Hori's eyebrows shot up. "He had a visitor who brought him food?"

"Yes. Nothing was wrong with him when his doctor came."

"He called his doctor? What was his name?"

"No idea. As long as he sent for him and paid him, it was his business. But that doctor said it was nothing. I tell you, he was always complaining. How was I to know he was really sick?"

Hori frowned. "Well," he said, "you'd better inform the police. This man's been poisoned."

2

The Broken Bond

It was spring before Akitada saw the capital again, an early spring that seemed more like winter. Snow had fallen overnight to make the roads difficult, but the world looked both beautiful and peaceful. The roofs of the houses were covered in white and only the roadways stretched black against a white world. A whiter light filled the air, turning the colors of people's clothes brilliantly bright. The air was brisk and the sky a deep, fathomless blue.

It should have been a cheerful sight. The ugliness of the great city's tenements and beggars' huts had been smoothed over with a soft blanket of white and the pagodas and houses of the rich sparkled red, gold, and green against this. Beyond lay the mountains, shrouded in hazy gray.

But Akitada had reason to dread this homecoming.

He would be reunited with his wife Yukiko, a young beauty who had betrayed him with a man at court. He would also greet a child that was nominally his but really the offspring of this unknown lover. To spare her the scandal, Akitada had agreed to raise the child as his own.

He had loved Yukiko once and she had claimed she loved him, at least until one day a year ago when her love had turned to disgust and bitter dislike. Akitada had grieved then, but now he did not know if he had any love left for her. Most men would have divorced their wives under the circumstances, but she had feared the scandal and he owed her father, who was also his best friend, this sacrifice. The truth was he did not want to see her, did not want to share his life with her again, did not want to be reminded of her betrayal by the expected child.

But inexorably their journey had ended. The great gate of the Sugawara residence opened and there were the smiling faces of his people: Genba, a little grayer and heavier than last time, Genba's small wife Ohiro running from the service yard, and even Saburo's mother, Mrs. Kuruda, fat, yet surprisingly agile, coming down the stairs from the main house. There were others, too, grooms, stable boys, maids, all smiling broadly.

"Welcome home, sir," Genba boomed, his eyes moist. "You have a daughter, sir! My heartiest good wishes. We're all overjoyed."

So Yukiko had given birth and the news had somehow missed them. A daughter? Akitada was relieved. For all that he had made a promise to himself to love this child as his own, he was also proud of his family lineage, which was older than Yukiko's, and would have disliked passing his name on to the child of another—unknown— man.

"Thank you, Genba. When was the child born? And is all well?"

"Two weeks ago, and her ladyship is said to be in good spirits. They say she had an easy birth."

"My wife isn't here?"

"No, she preferred to stay at her father's house, though we assured her that you had made all the arrangements."

"I see."

It was not really surprising. She had gone to her parents right after their quarrel and remained there except for a short visit to Mikawa to tell him about the coming child. They had both known that it meant a complete break between them, though she remained in name his wife.

With the arrival of the rest of his family, Akitada prepared himself for this homecoming. Somewhat to his relief Mrs. Kuruda was sidetracked by her son Saburo and her avid interest in his new wife. Saburo had written her, and Akitada had received long letters from her, asking questions and voicing complaints that she had not been consulted and that Saburo was not answering her letters. These he had passed on to Saburo in hopes that he would somehow manage to reassure his mother.

Now, Mrs. Kuruda merely spared him a bow and a quick, "Welcome, sir. All is in readiness. I have seen to everything." She did not really hear his thanks. Her eyes were already on the carriages and wagons being unloaded of the womenfolk. When she saw her son with his new wife Sumiko and the little girl, she muttered, "Excuse me," and dashed off.

Akitada was curious about their meeting, but he had to see to his own children and to Sadako. For Sadako, another new member of his growing family, it must be a particularly trying time. She had traveled in the carriage with his daughter and had passed over the same road where her husband had been killed by highwaymen, and now she found herself a servant in a new, unfamiliar house and in expectation of being inspected by Akitada's wife.

Their carriage had been backed up to the veranda of the main house so that the women could step from it and walk into the house without getting their clothes dirty or their slippers wet in the melting snow of the courtyard. Yasuko was out first, her face shining with joy.

"Father, did they tell you?" she cried. "I have a new sister. I want to see her now!" She started off without another glance at her companion.

Sadako emerged from the carriage and smiled at him. If she was tense, she did not show it. "What very happy news, sir," she said. "My felicitations. Please don't bother about me. You must go see your wife and the new child."

Akitada smiled back. Sadako always lifted his spirits. "My wife isn't here. She is staying at her parents' house."

Her face fell. "Oh," she said, then added brightly, "Yes, that makes sense. But you must go right away. They'll expect you."

Akitada did not go right away. In fact, he procrastinated, making sure first that Sadako and his daughter were settled in comfortable quarters. He gave silent thanks to Mrs. Kuruda who had for once really seen to everyone's comfort.

Then he visited the newly built pavilion which stood ready to receive Yukiko and her child. He saw that no money had been spared in the furnishings and thought that her father must have had a hand in this. After walking around the house and the outbuildings and finding them in excellent repair, he chatted with Genba and Tora. Saburo had disappeared to get his own family settled. He found that he had been right; Kosehira had taken a special interest in his daughter's quarters, sending workmen and goods. The rest of the property was in a better state than it had ever been. Thanks to his remunerative governorship, Akitada had been able to pay not only for the new building but for long overdue repairs to the rest.

Having made sure that all was well, Akitada retreated to his study. There he sat down and looked around with a sigh of contentment. He had missed his home. All looked just as he remembered: his books, many of which had been his father's, on their bamboo shelves, his scroll paintings on the walls, his bedding rolled up in a corner, and the four lacquer trunks that held his clothes, separated by season. He would have to find room for the things he had brought back with him from Mikawa. His desk, also once his father's, was old but still beautiful. On it stood his writing things: brushes, ink stones, water container, neat stacks of assorted papers, his personal seal. He touched them one by one and smiled.

Then he rose and threw wide the doors to the veranda and his small garden enclosure. Snow still covered some shrubs and paths, but a steady dripping from the eaves signaled that it would not remain. All looked tidy here also. He walked out and stepped down on the wet stones. Cold water seeped into his cloth slippers and he quickly stepped back. The trees were still bare, but the buds on the azaleas were already fat. In the *koi* pond, the colorful fish moved about sluggishly. He was transported back to happier times when he shared this house with Tamako, his first wife. In those days, the rooms had been cold and the roofs had leaked, but he had been happy. Or at least happier than now.

Ahead loomed the visit to his current wife.

*

It was getting dark before Akitada arrived at Fujiwara Kosehira house. He was alone, having left without so much as a servant, and on foot. This was no occasion for pomp and circumstance. He meant it to look like the visit of an impatient new father. For that reason, he told the servant, who greeted him with a broad smile and an eager offer to let the family know of his arrival, that he wished to see his wife and daughter first.

His firm demand meant that he was shown to Yukiko's pavilion, where his sudden appearance caused consternation. Yukiko herself sat behind a low screen where she had been looking at an illustrated book by the light of several candles. Near her sat maids and in a darker corner the child's nurse hovered over the sleeping infant.

Yukiko, startled, jumped up. "Akitada! Where did you come from?"

Akitada frowned at this greeting and said, "Dismiss your women."

Yukiko hesitated, then sent everyone out except the child's nurse. Akitada took up a candle and went to inspect the sleeping bundle of his new daughter. He was surprised that he felt nothing: neither anger, nor disgust, nor the slightest twinge of fatherly affection.

Yukiko, suddenly anxious, joined him. "Your daughter, my lord," she said formally, perhaps to remind him of his promise.

Akitada glanced at the nurse and said, "You may leave us." The woman looked at Yukiko and bustled out. Akitada handed Yukiko the candlestick and bent to scoop up the tiny bundle. The child opened its eyes and stared at him. Soft pink lips pursed as if she had her doubts about this stranger. For a long moment, Akitada just held her and stared down at the small face. The other man's child.

Yukiko gave an exclamation and set the candle down. "Here, give her to me," she said, her eyes now flashing with anger.

He obeyed. The child began to whimper.

Yukiko rocked the baby in her arms. "How could you burst into my room in this masterful fashion, ordering my women out, and glaring at an innocent child? Really, Akitada, I had expected better of you."

He countered, "Why must I come here to your father's house to welcome my new daughter?"

"Because there was no point in living at your house. I'm shortly to return to court."

That took his breath away and the strength from his legs. He sat down. "You what?"

She raised her brows. "Surely you knew this? Her Majesty has done me the honor of making me her senior lady. I have only waited here for the birth."

Akitada saw in his mind's eye more opportunities for liaisons. Perhaps she would even return to the arms of the father of her child. And he would be the laughingstock of the entire court. And not just the court. Everyone would know and snicker.

He snapped, "I absolutely forbid it! You will return to my home with me now."

The child had calmed down. Her mother looked at Akitada and shook her head. "You were more reasonable in Mikawa."

"I had no idea then that you would continue saddling me with children that aren't mine."

"How dare you?" She was furious. Perversely, she also looked more beautiful to him than he had ever seen her.

"I thought you wanted to keep your unfortunate affair and its result a secret from the world."

"I still do." She hesitated. "My parents know."

Akitada threw up his hands. "Then I suppose the whole world knows our shame."

She said nothing for a moment. Akitada stared down at his hands, trying to grasp the situation. She knew as well as he that he could not forbid her service at court if it was the express order of the empress. With a sigh of despair, he got to his feet.

"Wait, Akitada," she said, suddenly conciliatory. "Let's not quarrel. I know this is very hard for you, but I really must return to court and you must try to trust me and protect my secret."

A sharp answer was on his lips, but he bit it back. "Do I assume that neither you nor the child has any intention of ever living in my household?"

"I didn't say that. It's only for now, as long as Akiko is as small as she is. It's just more practical because everything is here to take care of a small child. And I have no choice in the matter of my service to the empress. Try to understand."

"I see you have already named her. Without consulting me?"

"I'm sorry. It was Her Majesty's wish that she have her name. I couldn't refuse."

Akiko also was his sister's name. It would not be very strange that his child should have been called after her. In any case, it seemed he had nothing to say in the matter. He had nothing to say in anything any longer. He suddenly hated Yukiko and wished it were possible to divorce her.

Rising, he bowed formally. "In that case, we have nothing else to discuss."

She cried, "Don't go away angry, Akitada." But he was already at the door and did not stop. Sightlessly, he made his way along the connected galleries and somehow managed to reach the courtyard again. As he hurried down the staircase of the main house, he heard Kosehira's voice calling out to him. He did not stop. He simply could not face Kosehira who had also been a cause of the misery of his present and future life.

But Kosehira called again and there was a note of desperation in his voice. "Akitada! Wait! Don't go."

And so he stopped and turned.

Kosehira, on the veranda above him, looked shockingly old. His eyes were red-rimmed. "Come up and talk to me. Your face makes me wish I were dead. Please, for the sake of our friendship. I love you like a brother, Akitada."

Akitada shook his head at these words, but he climbed the steps again and followed Kosehira to his study. They sat down, and Akitada saw that Kosehira wept.

"Kosehira," he said, "don't. It isn't your fault. Don't grieve so."

Kosehira dabbed at his eyes with a moist sleeve. "I wanted her to be happy. She was my favorite, Akitada. I wanted you to have her. I shouldn't have meddled."

This was true, but even at this distance, Akitada remembered how he had lusted after Yukiko. It had been shocking, because even then he had known that he should not feel this way about someone who was still a child. But he had felt old and lonely and so he had reached for what was offered.

He sighed. "You forget that I had a part in this. You did nothing to force me into this marriage. And do not blame Yukiko for being affectionate. She was very young. The young act on impulses they later regret.

Kosehira sniffed and looked at him blearily. "That is generous. But think of what she has done since. How can you forgive that?"

The truth was that Akitada had not forgiven it, but he did not say so. "Yukiko had become convinced that I did not care for her."

Silence fell between them. After a long time, Akitada said, "She says she will not come home."

"No. Express orders from Her Majesty. I could not have foreseen it, but I was also instrumental in getting her a place in the palace when . . . when she first ran home to us a year ago. I tried to make her go back to you, Akitada, but she wouldn't."

Akitada wondered what horror stories she had told about him as a husband. His suspicions were justified when Kosehira added, "Try to accept it. It's probably better this way."

And so his marriage was truly and irrevocably broken. And yes, it was better this way, except of course that until this very morning he had still hoped that some accommodation could be reached between them so they could live again as husband and wife. Now he bowed his head and nodded agreement.

Another silence fell. Then Kosehira said, "I have been very angry with her."

Given the results of Yukiko's actions, this was laughably inadequate. Akitada rose. "No doubt in time you will forgive her," he said tiredly. "I must return home. Perhaps later, when things have settled a bit, you'll join me for some wine and food?"

"Oh. Yes, of course. And you will come here, I hope. Very sorry about all of this, my friend. You've been more than understanding."

3

The Arrest

A murder in the prison was sufficiently shocking that Superintendant Kobe was notified the very moment he arrived in his office.

"A brawl between prisoners?" he asked the sergeant who brought the news. "Surely there is a way to keep troublemakers and violent men separated?"

"No, sir. This man was a merchant and he was in a cell by himself. He was poisoned."

The superintendent became attentive and sat down behind his desk. "A mystery?" he asked.

"Yes, sir. Sort of."

"What do you mean, 'sort of'?"

"We have a suspect."

"Well, that's something. Start at the beginning."

The sergeant did so, only to be interrupted immediately. "Who was on duty during the night?"

"Otsuga. He was alone, sir. He said he thought the man was faking it because he'd done so before."

"How dare he make assumptions like that? It was pure laziness."

"Yes, sir. I thought so, too. But the prisoner had been seen by his own doctor before and found to be fine."

"Strange! Who sent for the doctor?"

"I believe the prisoner, sir."

"Then the poison must have been given to him later. Was something wrong with the food?"

"Well, yes and no, sir."

Kobe raised his grizzled brows. "Explain."

"It is thought that it was in his food all right, but not in what the jailers gave him."

"How do you know?"

"He didn't eat that and they gave it to the dog. The dog's fine. Apparently a young woman visited him. She brought him food."

"Hah! You don't say. Has she been brought in?"

"No, sir. Nobody seems to know her."

"What? Is our jail run so poorly that the guards don't even ask visitors who they are and what their purpose is?"

The sergeant looked embarrassed. "They do, sir. But he wasn't that sort of prisoner. His was a very minor offense and he was about to me released anyway. I expect they relaxed their rules a little."

"What exactly was his offense?"

"He was found guilty of not kneeling and bowing to a senior noble."

"Oh." Kobe pondered this for a moment. A lot of people, especially when they were young and well educated, resented the constant kneeling in the dirt. And most nobles did not make an issue of minor cases. It must be that this particular man had done something else to offend his accuser.

Kobe, no longer young, slender, or agile, lumbered to his feet. "The body's been taken to the coroner?"

"Yes, sir."

"Then let's go!"

*

"Morning, Doctor Hori," said Kobe, when he entered the bare room where they brought the corpses and where the coroner had a look at them to certify cause of death. The body of a naked young man lay stretched on a reed mat, and the slender, elderly figure of the coroner was bent over it. The coroner looked up with a smile, "I've been expecting you, Superintendent. It's an interesting case."

There was no place to sit in this simple space with the hard dirt floor, variously stained with old body fluids that had soaked in in spite of rigorous scrapings. Kobe bent to look more closely at the dead man.

"Young," he said, more to himself than anyone else since the fact was obvious. But to Kobe it meant also a strong feeling of pity. The young were not supposed to die, especially not the ones who had good lives and good futures. This young man was in his twenties, very good-looking, well-built, well-fed, and with the hands and feet of an affluent man. He had not gone barefoot in the streets, begging for pennies. Neither had he lived the sort of rough life that leaves scars. All of which seemed to support the notion that he had defied the burdensome rule of submission.

The coroner said, "Yes. He was rich, I hear."

Kobe sighed and tried to comfort himself with the thought that, being rich, the dead man had at least enjoyed the short span of years given to him. "Who was he?"

"Sato Yutaka. Owned the big rice store on the market and quite a few farms, I'm told."

Kobe was astonished. "He's young for that. And what in the name of all the Buddhas was he doing in jail?"

Doctor Hori got to his feet with a grunt. "My thoughts exactly. You should know that better than I, though I can answer your question about his youth. He was his father's only son and came into the property three years ago when the father died. Nothing against him. He seems to have been a good businessman for all his youth."

Kobe shook his head. "I'll look into it. Something is not right about this case. Apparently he was poisoned by some woman who came to visit him."

"Is anything ever right about murder, Superintendent?"

Kobe growled, "You know what I mean. Most of the prisoners are criminals of one sort or another and nobody bothers to do away with them. What can you tell me about the poison?"

Hori shook his head. "Could be a lot of things, including poisonous mushrooms, but most likely it was arsenic because it was so fast. It was ingested."

"In food, you mean?"

"Or wine."

Kobe turned to the sergeant. "You said he had a visitor, a woman, who brought him food?"

"Yes, sir. But I don't know who she is."

Kobe said, "She must be your murderer. Now go and find out. Question everybody who saw her. Question the other prisoners. Do I have to do your job for you?"

The sergeant blanched. "Yes, sir. I mean, no, sir. Right away." He saluted and ran out.

Kobe stood for a moment, chewing his lower lip. "Things have gotten very sloppy," he muttered.

Dr. Hori cleared his throat. "I hope you don't mean me, Superintendent."

Kobe said, "What?" and focused on him. "No, no. The jail, I mean. And my men. We had a near riot when a drunken sumo wrestler had a birthday party in jail. They lifted the cell door from its hinges and started breaking up the furniture. It took ten men to get chains on him. We rushed him through his court hearing. He paid a fine and is gone. But this! My fault, I'm afraid." He paused. "Well, don't release the body quite yet. Let me look into this more closely."

Hori bowed, and Kobe stalked out, muttering under his breath.

*

Toward midday, Kobe became aware of a disturbance outside his office. Male voices were raised, talking excitedly, and now and then a woman tried to be heard. He was about to rise and see what the unseemly noise was when the door opened and the sergeant looked in.

"We've got her, sir!" he said triumphantly, smiling all over his face.

"You've got her? Already?"

The sergeant came in and closed the door. "Yes, sir. You'll never guess!"

Kobe frowned. "I don't guess," he snapped.

"Well, sir, she walked into the jail as calmly as if she lived there. Carrying another meal."

"Hmm." Kobe began to wonder if perhaps the solution of this murder was not as simple as the sergeant thought. "Bring her in!"

The sergeant opened the door again and shouted an order. Two brawny policemen dragged in a woman whose clothes looked disheveled and whose long hair had slipped from its ribbon and hung over her face. She stood before Kobe, bent double and sobbing.

Kobe got up and looked in some surprise at her clothes: a figured, green and white brocade over rose-colored gowns. Her hair was long and glossy and she was perfumed. A high-class courtesan? That sort of person was rarely involved in sordid crimes. As a rule, their nests were feathered and they had no need to murder people for their money. But then, they also were known to have some strong passions, and the dead man had been handsome.

"Name?" Kobe asked her.

She did not answer, just went on sobbing, perhaps to appeal to their pity. The sergeant finally said, "She wouldn't tell us, but one of the jailers thought she looked familiar. He thinks she's well-known in the willow quarter."

"He may be right," Kobe said, pleased that his guess had been correct. "In that case she'll be identified." Turning to the woman again, he said, "You're accused of having given poisonous food to Sato Yutaka. Do you have anything to say? I must warn you. If you don't speak, you'll simply be locked up without food or water. One way or another, we'll find out who you are and what your relationship to the dead man was."

She made a great effort to brush aside her hair and look up. "I'm Nagano Miyagi. I was his wife."

The moment she straightened and raised her head, Kobe saw she was beautiful, though now her face was streaked with tears.

He considered for a moment. By her name, he guessed that she was well-born. A memory from the past surfaced suddenly. His friend Akitada's youngest sister had paid visits to bring food to a prisoner many years ago. It had been an outrageous thing to do for a girl from a noble house, but she had loved the man. And she had certainly not poisoned him. But the memory was enough to soften Kobe's manner.

He said, "Sato Yutaka died from poison. Since it was not in the jail food, it must be assumed it was in the food you brought him."

She raised her head again. "No! Oh, no! I didn't. I would never . . . I loved him. Oh, who would do such a thing? Yutaka was a good man. He hurt no one. He was the kindest man I've ever known." Her voice broke and she wept again. One of the guards snorted in derision and Kobe glowered at him.

She sounded convincing, but Kobe was too good a policeman to believe her. Some villains he had known had been utterly plausible in their declarations of innocence. "So you claim you are his wife?"

Suddenly she was unsure. "Well, Yutaka bought me out. I live in his house."

"Ah. You worked as a courtesan?"

She nodded. "But I loved him. He was very good to me." She wept again.

So the man who had thought he recognized her had been right. This changed Kobe's attitude. Prostitutes and courtesans were very unreliable women, much given to greed and unstable emotions. This one had played her cards right and achieved what every prostitute hoped and prayed for. She had snared a rich man who bought her out and maintained her in luxury. Had she killed him because he planned to sell her back? Or had she done so in hopes of inheriting his property?

Kobe nodded. “Very well. That’s enough for now. Your story will be checked out.” He turned to the guards. “Take her back and lock her up.”

4

The Plum Tree

When Akitada returned home from his visit to Kosehira's, his mind was full of the changes his broken marriage had wrought in his life. While he was angry with both Yukiko and Kosehira for the misery they had brought to him, he was even angrier at himself. What had possessed him, a mature man with a family, to fall for the wiles of a pretty and lively nineteen-year-old? For Yukiko had seduced him; there were no two ways about it. And he had been foolish enough to fall for it. He had felt flattered and, yes, he had lusted for her, because he had been desperately lonely after Tamako's death. But what had come of this ill-planned marriage? He was now lonelier than ever and had encumbered himself with another man's child and a wife who wanted nothing to do with him.

He was in no mood to start on the waiting paperwork—his reports for the Ministry of Popular Affairs and for the Office of the Prime Minister were due, and he had to look into household expenses and income. Instead he walked out into his garden. The snow had melted off the gravel paths and he went first to his small pond. The *koi* rose to the surface when his shadow fell across the water. How they had grown! He wished he had some rice to feed them. Genba had taken good care of everything. He strolled about to look for changes and to inspect the construction damage that had happened around the new northern pavilion, now doomed to stand empty. Tamako's wisteria had disappeared. His heart contracted with grief at this. The wisteria had been a symbol of their love and his happiness.

He stood there for a long time, remembering, and felt more than ever that his life was over. Tears rose to his eyes and the world blurred.

Suddenly there was the touch of a hand on his arm. "Bad news, sir?"

Ashamed, he blinked his tears away and shook his head. "Nothing unexpected. How are you settling in, Sadako?"

She stood beside him and regarded him with serious eyes. "You have a beautiful home. It's so large that I've seen little of it, but this garden is lovely. It looks as if it has been here for centuries. The trees are so big they hide the sky, and there are so many different plants. It will be wonderful seeing everything come to life this spring."

She had somehow said the right thing once again. Sadako had a way of lifting his spirits. He smiled at her. "Thank you. My ancestors planted the trees, and my wife brought in many of the flowers. She loved this garden, too."

She touched his arm lightly again, perhaps out of pity.

Sadako was a widow and had had a hard life before becoming his daughter's companion. The two got along very well and Sadako had been a big help when Yasuko had been so angry with him over his breach with Yukiko. His smile faded when he thought of what Yasuko would say when she heard that Yukiko was not coming home.

He decided he needed an ally. "It appears my wife Yukiko will not return to this house. She has her duties at court and wishes the child to remain with her parents for the time being. Yasuko will be upset."

She studied his face and said softly, "I see. Yes, she'll be disappointed. But I think you'll have to give your daughter credit. She is old enough to accept what life brings. Could you not take the children for a brief visit?"

Akitada grimaced at the idea. He did not want to see Yukiko again. In fact he also did not want to see her father.

She said, hesitating, "Or perhaps I could take them?"

"Yes. Would you? But not until tomorrow. You must all be tired. Are you quite comfortable?"

"Yes. Very comfortable. Mrs. Kuruda has seen to everything."

He muttered, "Oh, dear! Mrs. Kuruda can be a trial."

Sadako chuckled. "She talks a good deal, but she is quite devoted to the family."

"I know. I must be more tolerant." When she said nothing to that, he began to feel awkward again. "Oh, well, I'm glad you like the garden. Feel free to explore it. And now I must go back and see to some business."

She cried, "Oh, but before you go . . . did you notice the plum tree?"

He looked at her shining eyes in surprise. "The plum tree?"

"Come, I'll show you."

He followed, bemused. And when they reached the tree, an old one that Tamako had treasured, he saw that it bore the first pink blossoms and he gasped a little with pleasure. At that moment, the snow began to fall again, slowly and in large, soft flakes. Beside him, Sadako laughed softly and held out her hands to catch the flakes. "How beautiful!" she cried. "It will not last, but it is beyond beautiful."

The white flakes were clinging to the brave pink buds and flowers, the final battle between winter and spring, and he hoped the cold would not harm the blossoms. His gaze went to the woman beside him, to the snowflakes settling on her long black hair, to her pretty face and smiling eyes, and he felt a great longing to draw her close. But that would never do.

"Thank you," he said stiffly. "This is indeed beautiful. But now you must go in before you get too cold."

And so they parted and he went back to his study where he sat behind his desk, gazing out at the falling snow with a smile on his face.

*

The next day the snow had melted and a bright sun shone. Akitada put on his court robes and made the rounds in the Daidairi, presenting his reports as a returning governor. Somewhat to his surprise, for he had expected some fall-out from the visit of the investigator whom the Censors' Bureau had dispatched to Mikawa the previous fall, all seemed well and there were even hints of promotion and another assignment in the capital. He knew he had Yukiko and her father to thank for this and accepted it with some bitterness.

Business being taken care of, he stopped to visit his friend and former protégé Nakatoshi, senior secretary in the Ministry of Ceremonial.

Nakatoshi was in his office and rose with a cry of joy to embrace Akitada.

"I have been looking for you every day," he said, releasing him to study his face, "and here you finally are! You look tired. Have you not been getting enough sleep or is something else the matter?"

"No, nothing is wrong. Perhaps the journey back with my entire household was a little tiring, but all is well."

"Ah! And you're a father again. My heartiest felicitations! A little girl, I hear. Daughters are delightful. And your lady is well?"

Akitada turned away and seated himself. "Quite well, thank you. She is to return to her duties shortly."

There was a brief silence, and Akitada was again aware of his friend's scrutiny. Then Nakatoshi said, "She has won Her Majesty's favor. A great honor, of course, and one which will be good for your career."

"I prefer to win my own honors."

Nakatoshi sighed. "Yes. I knew you would feel this way but, my dear friend, we must accept the good things life offers us along with the hard challenges. Enjoy your wife's success. I imagine she expects it."

Akitada doubted that Yukiko had any expectations of him. "Well," he said, "I suppose I'll muddle along somehow. The children are growing—Yasuko now has a companion—and so time moves on in the Sugawara household." He thought again of the flowering plum in the snow and his face softened.

Nakatoshi cocked his head. "Tell me about her," he said.

"Who? Sadako? Actually there is a story and it's connected with my last case." He told Nakatoshi about the robbers on the Tokaido highway and the brave woman who lost her husband and everything she had in the world. "There is some mystery about her, but I don't want to press her too much," he said. "She has a fine education that is quite out of the ordinary in the poor widow of a schoolmaster."

"Perhaps he taught her."

"She says not. She was taught as a child, but that childhood she will not speak about."

"How old is she?"

"I'm not sure. In her thirties. It's hard to tell with women."

"Does she have children?"

"No. She was all alone in the world. A pitiful situation for a woman to be in."

Akitada caught an amused expression on Nakatoshi's face and went on quickly, "Anyway, I was quite lucky to find her for Yasuko. She's a very good influence on her."

Nakatoshi nodded wisely. "Excellent. So will you bend your mind to finding out her secret?"

Akitada looked a bit guilty. "It intrigues me, but I think she really wouldn't like it, so I'm not letting myself think about it too much."

Nakatoshi laughed. "Pity!"

Embarrassed, Akitada asked, "But what is new in *your* life?"

"Not much. I have moved up into the hills and decided to make a garden, but it's still too early. My family is well but unchanged. However, there is always the usual gossip in our world. I hear Fujiwara Tadanobu is very ill. He's the chancellor's younger brother and a major counselor."

Akitada frowned. "I don't know him personally, not being in such illustrious company. Wasn't there a rumor that he used his influence unfairly?"

"Oh, he did that on many occasions. Some call him the evil Tadanobu still. Which makes the rumor all the more interesting, for it's said that he is possessed by some vengeful spirit of one of his victims."

"Utter nonsense. Still it seems rather appropriate. Maybe it will teach him and men like him a lesson about mistreating people."

He detested those high-ranking officials who used their power to destroy the lives of those who stood in their way or offended them. The life of an official invariably taught him that rising in rank and income depended on politics, and flattery of the great was mandatory. He had never played this game and therefore had made enemies. If he found himself now in a comfortable position and relatively safe from attacks, it was due to his marriage, and that thought irked him constantly.

Nakatoshi smiled. "I see you haven't changed. You really have to watch your tongue more, Akitada. There are always those who will quote you."

"I know, Nakatoshi, but if you cannot share your views with your friends, what hope is there for any of us?"

"You're safe enough with me, but we're in the Daidairi and the walls have ears."

Akitada looked at the walls of his friend's office. "Oh," he said. "Yes. I'm sorry. It would get you in trouble also. I think I haven't quite adjusted to being back here. One good thing about a provincial appointment: you generally don't expect to have to flatter quite so many people." He heaved a sigh. "Well, I'd better be off. I still have to call on some other friends. But I promise you, I'll be more circumspect."

They embraced, and Akitada walked to the Ministry of Justice, his former work place. Fujiwara Kaneie was still its minister, and Akitada had grown fond of the man over the years. Kaneie was another Fujiwara who did not share many character traits with the rest of his family.

Kaneie greeted him effusively. "Oh, my dear Akitada! How I have wished for you all this time. I'm so glad you're back. Any chance you might return to your old position?"

Kaneie was as always perfectly open about asking Akitada's help. Akitada said, "I have no idea. I just got back yesterday and will probably be reassigned some place."

Kaneie's face fell. He gestured to a cushion and they sat down. Kaneie said glumly, "I keep forgetting your marriage—and now a little daughter. My felicitations."

Akitada thanked him, knowing that Kaneie would have preferred an Akitada with less influence who could have returned to his old position as senior secretary of the ministry of justice. He almost wished the same.

"Well," said Kaneie, "what I meant to say: you'll be promoted. Maybe they'll give you my job. The gods know you're more qualified."

This was embarrassing, even if it was true. Akitada said, "I doubt they'll let me work at anything I'm good at. It's not really their way. Besides you'll still outrank me."

"Well, this place could use someone who knows law." Kaneie brightened. "But never mind my problems. How are your lady and the little one?"

"Both well. Yukiko is to return shortly to the empress's court."

"Yes. I hear Her Majesty has grown very fond of her." He noted Akitada's lack of enthusiasm and added soothingly, "Never mind. She'll be back with you soon enough. They change the attendants so quickly. Whenever another promising daughter is old enough to catch the emperor's eye." Kaneie chuckled.

Akitada knew this well enough, but he also knew there was no hope in it for him. He changed the subject. "Nakatoshi mentioned that Tadanobu is quite ill."

Kaneie put a finger to his lips. "They are keeping it quiet. Just between us, yes. It's pretty hopeless. They've tried everything: the monks, the sutra readings, the soothsayers and their mediums, but nothing stops the angry spirit. Poor Tadanobu gets weaker every day. Nobody knows what else to do."

"I'm sorry to hear it."

Kaneie nodded. "Yes. Pitiful. You know, you might just be the man to find out what Tadanobu has done to anger this spirit. Maybe then the matter can be corrected."

Horrified, Akitada said, "No! Under no circumstances. I never deal with cases of *ikiryo.* I simply don't believe there is a word of truth in such things."

Kaneie stared at him. "How can you say such a thing? You know as well as I how many such cases happen every year."

"Yes, and they make the soothsayers and the temples rich."

"But there have been cases where intervention has worked. Our own senior empress would have died in childbirth except for the prayers and incantations that drove out the spirit that possessed her. She gave birth to our present emperor right after."

"Coincidence. A difficult birth that resolved itself."

"Don't let people hear you say such things. They'll think you're an unbeliever."

Having so quickly forgotten Nakatoshi's warning, Akitada had no response to this. It was true enough. His enemies would welcome the merest rumor that Akitada had no faith in the Buddhas and gods.

"Well, your opinion is safe enough with me, but if you could have done such a service to Tadanobu, your career would be made. He is the prime minister's brother." He paused. "But then you don't need such help, having married Kosehira's daughter."

On this Akitada fled, making excuses about other duties.

5

A Curious Poisoning Case

Akitada's next call was on Superintendant Kobe, who was interrogating a shaking individual. The man knelt in the gravel of the courtyard, sobbing, and answering in monosyllables. Kobe glared down at him and a guard stood by with a whip. The man wore the uniform of a jailer and had clearly felt the whip already.

This was so unlike Kobe that Akitada hesitated to come closer.

But he had already been seen. Kobe shouted, "Akitada!" and started toward him, remembering at the last moment to tell the guard, "Take the bastard away.

I'll get to him later." Then he came to slap Akitada's back. "I had no idea you were back. What a pleasure this is! Come, come! We'll have a cup of wine in town. I'm sick of this place."

As they walked away from the jail and the buildings that housed the police department, Akitada asked, "What did that man do to make you so very angry, old friend?"

"Hah!" said Kobe, scowling again, "That lazy bastard is one of the jailers. He let a prisoner die while he was in his care. The man died an agonizing death while this scum sat by his fire, ignoring his cries for help and later his screams. I ask you, what sort of human being can be that heartless? And that's not all. It turns out that the prisoner was poisoned. A horrible tale. We've arrested a former prostitute who brought him food."

"Yes, I can see why you'd be angry," Akitada said. "But calm down. I cannot think this much fury is good for you." The fact was that Kobe had turned nearly purple just retelling what had happened. He had aged a good deal and looked unwell. Akitada noticed he walked more slowly and was breathing heavily.

Kobe gave him a smile. "There was a time when you accused me of mistreating my prisoners. Remember?"

"Yes. Back then I still believed in the goodness of men," Akitada said bitterly.

Kobe raised his brows. "Is anything wrong? You say that as if you knew of a particularly appalling deed."

Akitada had been thinking of a multitude of cases that seemed to him to prove the evil heart of both men and women. Yes, women also. Women who betrayed men. It was, of course, an exaggeration of Yukiko's treatment of himself. He must try to control his absurd emotions.

He said dismissively, "No, no. I'm just getting older. Life has brought me in contact with too much evil."

"You and me both," Kobe said as they turned into the doorway of a pleasant wine shop. "To tell you the truth, I'm tired of this job. I don't think I'll outlast this year."

It was not crowded and the back of the place overlooked one of the many canals crisscrossing the capital. The weather had warmed. The willows on the banks were still bare, but Akitada saw that the grass and weeds on the bank showed a fresh new green. They sat on cushions near an open door, a brazier filled with glowing coals nearby, and sipped an excellent wine.

Akitada eyed Kobe with concern. His old friend did look tired and worn, but he said nothing.

Kobe had cheered up a little. "They make a fine shrimp dish here. Will you join me?"

Akitada was not very hungry, but sharing a meal companionably and chatting about Kobe's latest case was far preferable to telling the superintendant about his broken family. Still, such personal matters must be gotten out of the way and so he agreed and asked, "How is dear Sachi?"

Kobe's head sank. "I worry about her. She's very frail. She makes me so happy, Akitada. I never knew a man could be this happy before." He paused. "Oh, forgive me. Of course, you and your ladies are exceptions to my own dim views on marriage. How I used to envy you! Lady Tamako loved you very much indeed. I recall her anxiety when you fell off the mountain that time." He chuckled. "And now you have a lovely new lady. How is she?"

"Very well. We have a new daughter."

Kobe clapped his hands, startling the waiter who had been about to serve the shrimp dish. "Wonderful! A new father again! And at your age! And here you were in such despair only a few years ago. You thought your life was over. We all feared for you, you know."

Akitada smiled, a little bitterly. "I'm grateful for my friends," he said quietly.

Kobe was helping himself to shrimp and sampling. "Mmm," he said. "I really like this. Mind you, I don't come here very often. Mustn't spend money too freely. Besides Sachi feeds me very well." He patted his stomach. "Too well."

"You're a lucky man." Akitada meant this sincerely. To everyone's shock, Kobe had taken a blind shampoo girl from one of the bath houses into his keeping several years ago. His wives and adult children were outraged and refused to accept her. Kobe had left his comfortable home and found a very modest house for Sachi and himself. He had also left to his family most of his income. This explained why he rarely permitted himself treats. On this occasion, Akitada felt a little guilty and promised himself to bring Kobe back as his guest.

"You know," said Kobe, putting down his bowl still half full, "it must be auspicious that you should have walked in when you did. This promises to be a very interesting case, and I'm not up to it."

It was the second time this day that Akitada had been told of an *interesting* case. He did not really feel any more interest in Kobe's case than in the strange possession of Fujiwara Tadanobu, but this was Kobe, and Kobe was uncharacteristically low, and so he said, "Really? Can you tell me about it?"

Kobe could and did. "The thing is," he concluded, "I'm not at all satisfied that the woman is guilty. It's all too easy to blame crimes on those who work in certain jobs."

That was true, and Kobe had reason to know all about it. His own Sachi had been arrested for murder. That was how they had met. But on the other hand, it was also true that more crimes happened in the amusement quarters and on the streets where the poor and outcasts lived. Prostitutes quite often belonged to the outcasts.

He said, "What makes you think something is wrong?"

"Well, she brought him food, and he became ill shortly after eating it." Kobe said. "But she doesn't seem the type. And she really seems to be grieving. She claims she loved the dead man."

Akitada grimaced and pushed away his empty bowl. "Sometimes the passions of such women run high and they do violent things to the people they love. Women have very different emotions from men."

Kobe stared at him. "You sound as though you speak from experience."

Akitada flushed. "You and I have dealt with enough criminals to have encountered evil women in our careers."

Kobe shook his head. "True. But since I met Sachi, I think of most women as essentially helpless and caring. And I think this one is innocent. Will you help me look into the matter, or are you too busy?"

Akitada said quickly, "You know how it is. I have just returned. I shall be called in to deliver reports and explain them. So yes, for a time anyway, I'll be occupied with much more boring stuff."

Kobe's face fell. "I don't know where to begin with this case, especially just now. But never mind. I understand. Well, I must do the best I can. I wish you could have seen and heard her. If ever there was a grief-stricken woman, it's Miyagi."

Akitada noted the use of the woman's first name. He distrusted Kobe's sudden softening towards the women he encountered in his work and stiffened his resistance. Quite apart from the fact that few deserved such generosity, this sort of thing could jeopardize Kobe's position, which was never very secure. But Kobe looked so unhappy that he said, "There are a number of things you can do that would be entirely appropriate. You should, for example, look into her background: her family, her work, her reputation. Find out what sort of temperament she had. Inform yourself about her attitude toward money. Then there is the victim. How did he come to meet her? What caused him to buy her contract? Talk to his servants. Ask about quarrels and about the way she deported herself. Did she spend his money lavishly? Were there other women that she was jealous of? That sort of thing."

Kobe looked at him with a frown. "You sound as if you'd already found her guilty and were building a case against her. Don't you think there might be things that would exonerate her?"

Akitada nodded. "Quite right. And you'd discover those also."

Kobe shook his head and said no more. They finished their meal and started back, chatting about other matters. When they were close to the jail, Kobe said, "You know, I've missed you very much. I'd hoped we'd work together again someday. But you've returned to another promotion and, no doubt, some new challenging assignment is waiting. Do you think they'll send you away again?"

Akitada's heart softened. He felt guilty. "I don't know," he said. "I've also missed working with you, but you're right. It may not be possible again."

A silence fell.

Then Akitada said, "I tell you what, I have a little time right now. Perhaps I could meet this young woman."

Kobe brightened. "Of course. Thank you, Akitada. I've been trying to make it as easy as possible for her, but jails aren't really good places for women with her sort of background."

A prostitute's background? Akitada wondered again if Kobe was losing his mind. But he said nothing and they soon reached the jail building.

The jailers all stood to attention. Apparently Kobe punishment of the lazy fellow who let a man die had had a good effect on them. Kobe merely glared at them and demanded to see Miss Nagano. The first man gaped at this, but the second said quickly, "This way, Superintendent. I just took her some food. She didn't seem to want it."

Kobe grunted and followed.

The accused woman's cell was very clean. Fresh straw lay in the floor and someone had placed a piece of matting on it for her to sit. She knelt there, looking anxiously at them when the cell door opened. Like Kobe, Akitada was struck first by her fine and tasteful clothes, though these were now wrinkled and slightly dirty. Her hair also was not quite tidy enough, but jails did not offer such amenities as combs or mirrors.

"How are you, Miyagi?" Kobe asked.

"Thank you, Superintendent. I'm well enough."

She had a soft voice, spoke well, and her bow was graceful. Akitada revised his expectations. She was clearly a courtesan of some standing. While not precisely beautiful by court tastes—her face was not round enough for that—her features were pleasing, the eyes large and well-spaced, the nose small and straight, the mouth full and pretty. She had cried recently. She reminded him of someone, but he could not place the resemblance. In any case, it was easy to see why a wealthy young man would have bought her out.

Kobe pulled him forward and he found himself introduced. "This is Lord Sugawara. He takes an interest in solving puzzling cases. I thought he might like to meet you."

Miyagi's eyes were now on Akitada, weighing perhaps how much help he could be to her. He thought she must be frightened by the murder charge and desperate to clear herself. But to his surprise she said, "Oh, please find who killed Yutaka, my lord. Yutaka was a good man. He did not deserve what has happened to him. I am to blame for his death. Oh, how I wish we had never met! He was killed because of me."

Kobe and Akitada spoke simultaneously. "How so?" asked Akitada. "What do you mean?" Kobe wondered.

She looked from one to the other. "I know I did not do it. But that does not matter. It means someone else did this. And they meant to put the blame on me. Yutaka died because someone hates me."

This caused more astonishment. Kobe glanced at Akitada and asked her, "Do you know who might do such a thing?"

Her shoulders sagged. "No," she said. "I would have told you already if I knew. I've been sitting here thinking and have come up with nothing. Perhaps you, since you are men and not in jail, may do better. I'll tell you all I can."

Much against his inclination—Akitada had a great distrust of courtesans—she impressed him favorably. It was difficult to imagine her as a cold-blooded poisoner. Her sorrow seemed sincere, and so did her pleas to find the real killer.

Her story was simple, if astonishing.

6

Miyagi

She was a poor schoolmaster's daughter. After her father's death, her mother had sold her to a brothel keeper in the mistaken belief that she was to become a dancer. The mother could not read and did not understand the contract she agreed to before a judge. Miyagi was fifteen years old. It was her beauty and her dancing talent that had led to the brothel keeper's interest. It was her mother's wish that her daughter enter a profession that would make it possible for them to live. The silver the brothel keeper paid her she accepted as an advance on her daughter's earnings. There were younger children to feed, and she asked no questions, nor did she follow Miyagi's career very closely from the distance of the village where she lived.

The brothel keeper immediately sold Miyagi's virginity to the highest bidder. Miyagi's share of the money, she sent to her mother. After this, her career continued normally in that she was now a courtesan, earning money for the brothel keeper, who paid her back a small portion and provided an occasional dress.

But because of her beauty and her dancing skills, as well as a sweet and friendly manner, Miyagi became popular. By the time she was eighteen, a number of wealthy men had offered to buy her out. She had resisted until she met Sato Yutaka.

"He said he loved me," she said in a broken voice. "They all say that, but I believed him. He was different. He wanted to be with me . . . just to be with me. He hated what I was doing. And he made me ashamed of my work. I got into trouble for turning away customers, and that's when he asked me if I would be his wife." She paused and brushed at her eyes.

Then she looked at Akitada, saw his expression, and hung her head. "I didn't believe it either at first, but I had begun to love him. He was so good to me. He cared about me. I had not been cared for like that for a long time. I didn't want to lose him. Ever."

There was a silence after which Akitada asked, "So he did buy you out?"

She nodded. "You see," she said, her voice breaking again, "by then I was so much in love with him that I would have followed him anywhere."

Akitada suppressed a snort of derision.

Sato Yutaka had paid an astronomical price for Miyagi. The brothel owner had charged for all the gowns she had worn during the four years she had worked for him. Sato had taken her home to a house in the city, and they had lived there together as man and wife until he had been arrested.

Akitada asked, "How did this come about?"

"The constables came to our house with a charge of insulting a high-ranking nobleman. Sato denied it. He argued with them, he begged for more time to clear his name, he asked for details, but they gave him none. The constables brought out their chains and their metal rods. I was frightened and tried to interfere, but one of them hit me. Sato agreed to be chained and go with them. He told me not to worry. He said it would all be cleared up within hours."

It was not.

She waited for several days, then went to the jail. The case against him kept being postponed. He had only been told that the charge had been brought by a captain of the imperial guard. He looked unwell and did not want her to see him like this. When she asked, he complained that the jail food was making him sick. She had seen the food being served to prisoners and gone home to prepare his meals for him. For a while, he was better, but then he had become sick again and had died.

As a defense, her story was worthless.

Akitada pondered all of this. Leaving aside the fact that she looked and sounded believable, he concentrated on the facts. She had brought the food that must have contained the poison, for the rest of the prisoners had eaten the jail swill and remained well, as did a dog that ate Sato's jail food. Either she was lying and had indeed killed Sato Yutaka, or she had been the innocent tool of a murderer.

In the first case, he must establish a motive. Had Sato made a will to benefit her? Was there another reason she might want him dead, such as revenge? Investigating such a motive would involve speaking to people who knew both her and him. The willow quarter was a gossipy place, and Miyagi had been one of its foremost courtesans. But that meant he must guard against professional jealousies among the women, who might well hate Miyagi and might even have sought to hurt her by killing the man she loved and implicating her in his death. Tora was good at talking to the inhabitants of that world.

If Miyagi had been the innocent tool for someone else's murderous plot—a very interesting possibility—then surely that person was a close acquaintance of the couple, or at least of Sato.

In the end, he made no promises to either Miyagi or Kobe. They walked out together and when they reached the forecourt of the jail complex and paused for Akitada to depart, Kobe said, "I feel guilty. It weighs heavily on me, seeing her like this. I'm convinced she's innocent."

Akitada brushed that aside. "You must not blame yourself for the actions of others. If she is innocent, then she or Sato have made an enemy and should have been more circumspect."

"But I should have been here. I should have kept my eyes open." Kobe looked miserable.

"Now you blame yourself for what the jailer did or didn't do. It was night time. You cannot be expected to be in your jail day and night."

"I know. Only just lately I haven't been paying much attention. You see . . ." He paused.

Akitada said firmly, "Your blaming yourself doesn't help. I'll have a talk with Tora. Maybe he can ask a few questions."

Kobe nodded and looked relieved.

"Thank you, Akitada."

7

The Visit

Sadako felt inadequate to presenting herself to Lord Sugawara's wife, the formidable beauty who was a senior lady-in-waiting to Her Majesty. What if Lady Sugawara found fault with her, as surely she must when she asked about Sadako's background, her recent background, for her distant past would quickly send her into the streets where she would have to earn her living as a prostitute. She had been terrified of this eventuality ever since her husband's death.

Lord Sugawara had asked questions about her past, but he had not pressed her and he had been kindness itself in the way he had looked after her, making sure she was not treated as a common servant but as a respectable widow.

Sometimes her thoughts went back to her dead husband. He, too, had been a kind man and she sincerely grieved his death. Never in the daytime, though. Only at night when no one could see her tears. There was little privacy in a noble household.

But here she was, willy-nilly, walking toward the Fujiwara mansion beside Yasuko and Yoshi. She and Yasuko were wearing hats with veils and they were accompanied by both a maidservant and a groom for protection. Even so, they attracted the curious looks and comments of passing young nobles, several in the uniform of the imperial guard. Yasuko giggled and waved and had to be told this was improper. She took it in good spirit, her mind on the prospect of seeing Yukiko and the child.

Sadako had been getting an earful of how wonderful, how gracious, how beautiful, how clever, how talented Lady Sugawara was. Instead of feeling curious to see such a paragon, she was overcome with panic.

This did not improve when they arrived at the Fujiwara mansion and she saw its size and the number of servants. They were taken first to Lord Fujiwara's senior lady. She was not alone; two of his other ladies and several children were also there, as well as two young men. All of them greeted Yasuko and Yoshi with hugs and smiles and were kind to Sadako. This eased her worries a little. It was clear that this was a happy family, something that surprised Sadako who had come to think such a thing a great rarity.

She would have liked to stay, sipping juice and nibbling nuts and listening to the excited chatter of the young people, but Yasuko was impatient to see the baby. Eventually Lady Fujiwara relented and walked with them to her daughter's pavilion, giving Sadako another view of the extensive property as they passed along innumerable covered galleries through gardens where soon the azaleas would bloom.

As soon as a maidservant opened the door of the pavilion, Yasuko dashed forward and threw herself into Yukiko's arms, crying, "Oh, Yukiko! I've missed you so! I'm so happy to be here! You must let me stay with you and my sister. Please!"

Yukiko laughed and released herself. "My dear girl," she said. "Where are your manners? You're waking the baby." But her eyes went past Yasuko, Yoshi, and her mother and rested thoughtfully on Sadako.

As the others gathered about the child–though Yoshi only peered at the baby briefly and then retreated–Sadako hung back and found a place near Lady Sugawara's maidservants. For a while she was effectively hidden as the others talked excitedly. Yasuko pleaded with her stepmother to return to the Sugawara house with the little one. "You're my father's wife; you belong there," she said, causing an uncomfortable silence.

Yukiko broke it with a light laugh and a hug for Yasuko. "But my sweet girl, you know I must return to my duties, just the same as your father does. We have no choice in the matter. But you will come to visit me and see Her Majesty."

"Oh!" murmured Yasuko, her eyes shining. "Could I? Maybe she'll like me and let me serve also. We could be together then."

Yukiko laughed again—she had a charming laugh—and exchanged a glance with her mother who was playing with her grandchild. "We'll see. Perhaps if you learn your manners first." This reminded her. "But you do have a companion now, I hear. Where is she?"

Yasuko stretched her neck, found Sadako and cried, "Sadako, come here. Meet my stepmother. She says if you teach me my manners I may also serve Her Majesty some day."

Sadako rose reluctantly and approached the group, bowing deeply before Yukiko. "My lady?"

What followed was a very thorough inspection by Lady Sugawara that moved from her hair and face to her figure and clothing. "You are called Sadako?" she eventually asked.

"Yes, my lady."

"How old are you?"

The question was blunt, and Sadako, already rosy from the close inspection, colored more deeply. "I'm in my thirty-second year, my lady."

Lady Sugawara seemed satisfied. "I understand you're a widow? Do you have children?"

"I am a widow but I never had children."

"Hmm. Why did my husband hire you to look after his children, then?"

Sadako cringed inwardly, and Yukiko's mother reproached her, "Surely, Daughter, he had his reasons. It seems pointless to question Sadako about them."

"Not pointless, Mother. As his wife and his children's mother I take an interest in their upbringing. Yasuko should have only the best teacher if she wishes to appear at court."

Sadako stood dismayed, her eyes downcast. Support came from an unexpected quarter. Yasuko said, "Oh, Sadako is very talented. We read and write together. She even knows some Chinese, and she writes excellent poems. And she plays her *koto* beautifully. Father bought it for her since you took yours. We have little concerts together. Father and Yoshi play their flutes and I play the lute, and Sadako the zither. Don't we, Sadako?"

Sadako felt like sinking into the ground with everyone's eyes upon her, but she smiled a little as she looked at Yasuko and nodded. Lady Sugawara did not look at all pleased with this testimonial though her mother was very complimentary.

Soon after this Lady Sugawara seemed to lose interest in Yasuko and Yoshi and began to discuss her wardrobe needs for the palace with her mother.

Not sure what to do, Sadako sat and listened, marveling at the unfamiliar terms describing precious fabrics and the color combinations of seasonal layered robes. It seemed Lady Sugawara must replenish her entire spring wardrobe and was in some doubt as to the colors that were fashionable this year because she had been away from court lately. Wisely her mother suggested that she write to some of her colleagues.

Yasuko sat mesmerized and clearly in no hurry to leave, but Yoshi made his way to Sadako and whispered, "Please, can we go now?"

Flushing with embarrassment, Sadako rose during a lull in the conversation, bowed deeply and said, "Forgive me, my lady, but it is time for us to return."

Yukiko stared at her for a moment, then said, "Yes, of course."

Yasuko protested bitterly, but Sadako said quite firmly, "Yasuko, please apologize and thank everyone for the lovely visit."

Pouting, Yasuko did so, adding, "But you promised I could come to the palace, Yukiko. When shall I come? Please make it soon!"

Her good humor restored, Yukiko laughed and said, "I'll write you, little one."

They returned home—Yasuko full of excited talk about Yukiko's beauty and elegance and about her place at the empress's court, Yoshi grumbling about "women's chatter and babies," and Sadako silent and unhappy.

At home, Yasuko hurried to her father's study to share her news and Sadako followed, wondering if this would spell the end of her employment.

Yasuko flung open the door, announcing in a voice that quivered with excitement, "Father! I'm to be invited to court! What do you think about that? Yukiko says if

I please Her Majesty, she may add me to her younger ladies there. Isn't that the very best news?"

Sadako, having reached the open door, saw that clearly it wasn't.

Yasuko's father scowled. "Well, my daughter," he said in a sharp voice, "you'll hardly make a good impression if you behave in this manner. Have you never heard of announcing yourself at the door? Or of walking and talking in a quiet and ladylike manner? They will hardly want an unmannerly child at court. And besides, I shall have something to say to such a plan myself."

Sadako cringed. Her charge had demonstrated to her father that her new companion had failed miserably at instilling ladylike behavior. She bowed and murmured, "I beg your pardon, your lordship. Yasuko was excited by what she took to be an invitation."

Akitada said dryly. "I can see that. She dotes on her stepmother. Please come in." He gave Sadako a searching look. "And you? What was your impression?"

Sadako flushed. She had not liked his wife. "Lady Sugawara is most beautiful and elegant," she said. "And your new daughter is charming."

He looked from her to Yasuko who immediately cried, "You must permit it, Father. It's such a great honor. Please! You let Yukiko go."

"That's altogether another matter," he snapped. "You should have realized by now that I don't approve of everything that happens in the imperial palace. And I will certainly not let a young girl, who is barely out of her childhood, mix in that company."

This astonished both Yasuko and Sadako because it amounted to a criticism of His Majesty Himself. They stared at him.

Akitada caught their expressions, and added quickly, "But you're not of speak of my feelings in this matter to anyone, do you hear?"

They both nodded their heads.

He focused on Sadako again. "Did you find the visit pleasant?"

Impossible to answer that. Sadako said quietly, "I fear, my Lord, that I'm unable to do what her ladyship expects of me. I know nothing of life at court and cannot prepare your daughter adequately. I think her ladyship will expect me to resign my position."

Yasuko said quickly, "Yukiko hated her, but I spoke up and told her how much Sadako knows and what she has taught me. I told her about our concerts and the books we read, and she seemed pleased and stopped questioning Sadako."

For the first time, her father's lip twitched. "I see. Well, I'm glad you did speak up. And if Sadako is willing to put up with us, I have no fault to find in her instruction." He gave Sadako a warm smile that nearly made her cry with relief. She had been so afraid.

8

Akiko

Akitada did not fool himself into thinking that Yukiko had accepted his daughter's companion. The fact that she had bothered to question her meant she had no intention of relinquishing her prerogatives as his wife and mistress of his household.

In a way, this was amusing. Apparently their marriage represented something that she wished to retain. He did not believe that this was due to any remnant of affection she bore him, though it was possible she was fond of Yasuko. It would not surprise him since the girl adored her so very obviously. Few people are inured to such flattery. But there was really nothing objectionable about Sadako's appearance and demeanor, so why the sudden suspicion?

When Yukiko arrived the next day and wished to see him, he was intrigued. He liked the feeling. It meant he had moved on to a certain distance from which he could observe his wife without feeling the pain of loss or the frustration of betrayal. He was merely curious about what she was up to.

She swept into his study accompanied by a maid, and bowed formally to him. "My husband, I came to take my leave before returning to court. I hope you will come to see me there." She gave him a charming smile, half hidden by a graceful hand.

He rose, returned her bow and gestured to a cushion. "Your visit honors me. I trust my daughter is well?"

She seated herself. The maid withdrew to a far corner and knelt there. Yukiko took out her fan and raised it, but her eyes still smiled at him. "Oh, yes. She will be spoiled by my mother and by my father's other ladies. You must remember that we are a very close family. Your daughter is loved by everyone. Of course, you will want to visit her also to make sure all is well. I'd be very grateful if you would show her your approval."

The word "approval" was a bit difficult to swallow, but Akitada reminded himself that this was a child who had had no part in their quarrel. He nodded. "Of course. And she would also be loved in this house, should you decide to trust her to my care," he said a little spitefully.

She played with her fan. "Naturally. When she is out of the dangerous years."

Years? Well, he had known well enough that they would probably never share this house again—or co-habit in a physical way. His detachment still in place, he regarded her beauty with a small regret. Yukiko had been easy to love and had known how to raise his passion to astonishing heights, but the thought of making love to her raised again the hateful subject of her life at court. He bit his lip to contain his rising anger. He had no right to consider her his property when he no longer loved her.

A short silence fell, and then Yukiko said, "This companion you hired in Mikawa—are you sure she is quite proper?"

He frowned. "Of course. Or I shouldn't have done so."

She plucked at her gown and said hesitantly, "It is only that the woman seems to have no family. Father and I tried to find out where she came from, but she refused to answer questions about her past. Do you know her family name?"

Akitada glared. "I know all I need to know. Don't trouble yourself about the matter."

Yukiko's eyes flashed. "So! This is the way it will be. I'm to be your spouse in name only while you make all the decisions?"

Akitada laughed. "Come. Surely that is the arrangement you chose in Mikawa. I'm to give my name to your child and perhaps to others as well, while you are free to do as you wish. Well clearly, I shall look after my own family without troubling you."

She paled, then flushed with anger. "Ah, I see how it is. You have replaced me with that provincial tart. Be very careful to treat me with the respect you owe me, Akitada, or I'll blacken your name at court and end your career."

He shook his head and smiled bitterly. "How little you know me. This career that you seem to think I owe to you means less than nothing to me."

She rose with an angry toss of her head. "Beware, Akitada! You will regret this." And with that final warning, she flung out of his room, her stiff silk gowns hissing her anger. Her maid, looking frightened, scurried after her.

Akitada did not feel good about this open quarrel with his wife. For one thing, there was the presence of the maid. No doubt, maids everywhere became privy to all sorts of embarrassing scenes between their employers, but he felt this to be very improper. And then there was Yasuko who might be forced to choose between him and Yukiko. He was by no means sure whom she would choose.

And lastly there was Sadako. Yukiko assumed that he had taken Sadako as his concubine. No doubt jealousy had had a part in her outburst. She was wrong, of course. The thought had never crossed his mind.

Until now!

*

As if family matters did not weigh heavily enough on Akitada's mind, his next visitor was his sister Akiko.

She came in briskly, asking, "Was that Yukiko just leaving?"

Akitada came back with a jolt from a pleasurable, if uneasy, contemplation of courting Sadako. The thought was still strange to him, and he blushed as if his sister could read his mind. "Good morning, Akiko," he said, and thought of the child who now bore her name and the fact that Akiko must have known the truth.

Akiko came, bending her face to touch his, and said, "Welcome home, Brother. I'm so very glad you're back. One of the servants told us. Servants always know before their masters." She went to sit beside his desk and studied his face. "You look thinner and there is a bit more gray in your hair, I think. Have you been well?"

"Yes. You look well yourself."

Akiko, in middle-age, had gained weight. Her face was rounder and she moved more slowly. She had given her husband Toshikage four children, two sons and two daughters, and had declared herself done with childbearing. Toshikage had meekly accepted this and still doted on her. The friendship between Akiko and Yukiko had been responsible for introducing his young wife to the court and had unfortunately given her a taste for high society. And almost certainly his sister knew about Yukiko's affair.

"Don't look so glum," Akiko told him. "If I didn't know better, I'd think you were angry."

"You always knew how to read my moods," he said sourly.

She opened her eyes wide, pretending surprise. "Why? Surely you have every reason for satisfaction?"

"Let's be frank with each other, my dear. I had a rather strange letter from you in Mikawa where you urged me to return to the capital as soon as possible. Why was that?"

Akiko blinked and clearly did some rapid thinking. "I had certain concerns, but then Yukiko paid you a visit, so I assumed all was well."

"What concerns?"

"I'd better not say. It's rather pointless and would only make trouble when you're just returned and a new father."

They looked at each other in silence. Akiko looked away first. "Have you seen the child? I must pay my visit soon," she said lightly.

"The child isn't mine. Perhaps that lets you off the customary courtesy visit."

Her eyes flew back to his. "How . . . what makes you say such a thing?"

"For one thing the fact that this was a nine-months' birth and my wife and I were not living together at the time of its conception."

"Surely it was early. Yukiko came to visit you." She faltered.

"She came to see me five months ago." He paused for effect. "To tell me that the child wasn't mine."

"Oh!" Akiko covered her face. "Oh, Akitada. I'm so sorry. I'd hoped . . . you used to be so happy together. Oh, that is really too bad of her. Why, it's an insult to our family name." She lowered her hands. "You will divorce her, of course."

"No. We are to pretend the child is mine."

Akiko was speechless.

"What troubles me most is that Yukiko is returning to court."

"You must divorce her, Akitada. This isn't to be borne."

Akitada sighed. "I have given my word and shall keep it, but for all practical purposes the marriage is over."

Akiko had tears in her eyes. "Oh, Akitada. I blame myself."

"Yes, and so you should. You introduced a young, impressionable girl to the sort of life they lead at court."

She wailed, "I had thought better of her. I'd believed you two were in love. But you made her angry and left for Mikawa."

"Yes. I know. Dry your tears. What's done is done. But I wanted matters clear between us."

She dabbed at her eyes and nodded. "You need a distraction. Perhaps another assignment in the provinces? Yes, I think that would be best. Surely Yukiko owes you that."

Akitada thought it tempting. He would not have to deal with Yukiko or her child and he could take his children away from any bad influences. He nodded.

"You may be right. I shall apply for another post. I don't want Yasuko at court. Yukiko has invited her."

"Oh? Yes. I think you're right. The child is much too young. Oh, Akitada, I'm sorry. I had no idea that having friends in the palace could ruin your life. I thought they would help your career."

Her brother sat lost in thought, drumming with his fingers on the desk. "I think I shall ask for an audience with the prime minister himself," he said finally. "They may be very happy to have me out of the capital."

"Not the prime minister. Not a good idea. His brother is dying. He cannot think of anything else."

"Oh! That's Tadanobu, isn't it? I heard about the *ikiryo*. Surely the prime minister isn't still caught up in that superstition?"

"You have very little notion about what the people in power care about," Akiko said a little snidely. "And the fact that you believe in very little yourself hasn't helped your case in the past. Tadanobu is in terrible straights. He cannot keep any food down. I'm told the prime minister sits by his side for days, weeping."

She was right. Akitada bit his lip. "From what I hear about Tadanobu, he must suffer from a bad conscience. The man has made any number of enemies with his ruthless methods and been protected by his father and brothers all along. Someone probably poisoned him." The thought reminded him of Kobe's prisoner. Perhaps giving Kobe a hand might take his mind off his marital problems.

Akiko said, "I don't think it's a matter of poison. I'm betting on an angry ghost. He gets better, but then collapses again. You're right about his past. He was ripe for an attack a long time ago. As for you getting another assignment, why don't you let Kosehira get you an audience with the emperor? He has access to His Majesty."

"No, I'll do this without consulting him."

"Don't be stupid. Why not use the influence you have through Kosehira and your wife?"

"No. Absolutely not. I will not be indebted to either. I must think what to do. Frankly, I'd happily go someplace just by myself."

"Well, if you're just taking a trip, you could go visit Yoshiko and Kojiro. It's been a long time."

Akitada was struck by this idea. Yoshiko was his younger sister who had very unsuitably fallen in love with a commoner. Akitada had cleared her lover of a murder charge and had relented in the end to allow the marriage. Kojiro was quite wealthy, which helped under the circumstances. Since then, they had only kept in touch with an occasional letter. He knew they had moved to Yamato Province and Kojiro had become landed gentry by wisely investing in and managing land. Their long separation had been due to the fact that Akitada had been busy with his career, but on Kojiro's part it had, no doubt, been due to the awkwardness of their different stations in life. They had never come to visit.

But Akitada liked his brother-in-law, and Yoshiko had been his favorite sister. He nodded. "Perhaps. The children should meet their cousins."

"There you are! It's decided."

"But I still have to make my reports to the ministers and ask for leave."

"Well, do it!" Akiko rose briskly. "Now I want to see the children and invite them. Their local cousins also want to see them. Will you come along?"

Akitada joined her, his heart much lighter. Together they walked to the pavilion that had once been Tamako's. Her memory still brought tears to his eyes, but he blinked them away quickly when they heard laughter and came across a charming scene. Yasuko and Sadako were performing some sort of dance on the veranda while Yoshi alternated between playing a melody on his flute and adding a rhythm by hitting the veranda railing with a baton.

Akiko stopped. "Who's that?" she asked in a low voice.

"Sadako is Yasuko's companion. I hired her in Mikawa. It seemed time. Besides by then the children were motherless again." He added the last bitterly.

"I see." His sister gave him a curious look. "She's very attractive."

"More to the point, she seems to have had a very good upbringing, though she doesn't like to talk about it."

Akiko smiled. "Ah, a mystery in your own household."

Akitada said repressively. "I don't intend to pry."

Akiko laughed, and Yoshi saw them. "Father! Aunt Akiko!" he cried, dropping baton and flute and running down the steps. The two ladies on the veranda stopped their dance.

Yasuko cried, "Oh, how embarrassing! We were just practicing the dance of the cranes."

But it was Sadako who blushed, and Akitada's heart went out to her. Surely she expected another interrogation from Akiko, and he was very much afraid that his sister's notion of some mystery would make this a certainty.

When they all met, he smiled at her and said, "This is my sister Akiko who has come to invite the children to her house."

Sadako, her hands shaking a little, bowed deeply. "An honor, my lady."

Akiko said brightly, "It's a pleasure to meet you also, Sadako. Of course you're included in the invitation. Perhaps you can teach my awkward girls that very graceful dance. My brother tells me you're quite a paragon."

Sadako shot him a glance. ""Not at all a paragon, my lady. Yasuko and I were reading about the dance of the cranes in Lady Murasaki's *Genji*, and she was curious to know what it was. I'm afraid it's been so long since I saw it performed that my movements must have been quite incorrect."

"Ah," said Akiko. "You must tell me more." She turned to Akitada. "You can run along now, dear Brother. I know you're eager to get to your reports.

We'll go to my house for the afternoon. I'll see to it that Sadako and your children return safely before the evening meal."

Akitada left a little nervously. He wondered what Akiko would manage to learn. His sister's ability to get to the bottom of secrets was well known to him."

9

A Surprise

Akiko's interest in Sadako troubled Akitada for a while. He was not at all sure he wanted to know Sadako's secret. If she had been hiding some shameful secret in her past because she was desperate to support herself in a world that seemed determined to oppose this effort, then maybe he would not be able to keep her in his household.

Akiko, for all that she had helped undermine his marriage, was highly intelligent. Proof of this: she had accepted the fact that she bore some responsibility and immediately thought how to help him cope. And she had been right. What he needed more than anything was distance and distraction. Perhaps time would resolve the unpleasant relationship, either by dissolving it completely or by Yukiko waking up to her responsibilities.

It was getting dark in the room, and Akitada lit the large candle that stood beside his desk. He took up brush and paper and rubbed some ink for a letter to his younger sister. Then he paused. Would he be welcome after all these years? What if they resented the fact that he had waited so long? But he pictured Yoshiko's face and knew his little sister would always welcome him. About Kojiro he was not quite so sure. There was the difference in class. Kojiro was a commoner, albeit a wealthy landowner. Never mind. He had a great longing suddenly to see both of them again. Perhaps it was a way for him to recapture a little of a past that had been so much happier.

The letter written and sealed, he considered the present. Kobe's prisoner again came to his mind. Much against his inclination, she had impressed him favorably. It was difficult to imagine her as a cold-blooded poisoner. Her grief had seemed sincere, and so had her plea to find the real killer.

Before he could formulate some plan, Akitada was interrupted.

Saburo scratched at the door, then looked in. "You have a visitor, sir." Without waiting for instructions, he threw the door wide and bowed deeply. Akitada watched with surprise as a short, youngish man in a beautiful silk robe walked in. He had a small mustache and chin beard, a fan, and a broad smile on his face.

Akitada's first reaction was displeasure. It was already late in the day. The sun had set, Akitada's stomach growled for his evening meal, and he had had a full day of mostly unpleasant events. Moreover, this person was a stranger. He hesitated to welcome him until he saw the rank ribbon on his visitor's hat.

Then, starting to his feet, he bowed as deeply as Saburo had. "C-could it be Your Royal Highness?" he stuttered.

"It could indeed," said the crown prince affably. "Do you mind?" he gestured to a cushion and seated himself.

"A great honor, Your Highness," said Akitada, then glanced at Saburo, who still stood frozen at the door, "Some refreshments, please, Saburo."

But the crown prince shook his head. "Nothing. Thank you."

Saburo woke, bowed again, and left, closing the door.

"Well, now," said the crown prince, regarding Akitada with a smile, "so you're the renowned solver of crimes and mysteries. I've wanted to meet you for a long time now. You don't come to court very often, do you?"

Akitada flushed. "I'm sorry, Your Highness. I've been posted to the provinces for some time now and have only just returned."

"Yes, yes. And your lovely wife has just presented you with a little daughter, I hear. My felicitations." He smiled broadly.

An awful suspicion crossed Akitada's mind. Could it be that the future emperor was the father of Yukiko's child? That would explain a good deal. But what had she seen in this bland and somewhat foppish man? Still, that was not the issue. When approached by an emperor or his successor, a woman could not very well decline. He found he could also not very well resent it. Perhaps, if he had still loved Yukiko, but as it was, it did not seem to matter.

He choked out a "Thank you, Your Highness," and waited.

"Please do sit down." The crown prince glanced around at the room, noting the many books and the good paintings, and nodded his approval. "I have a request," he said, turning his smiling glance to Akitada. "My cousin is quite ill. On the point of death, in fact. It's a matter that requires a good deal of discretion. I've been told that you're the person to consult."

Akitada's heart sank. He suspected that the prince referred to Fujiwara Tadanobu, to the *ikiryo* case. Perhaps Akitada might have been hard-pressed to refuse the prime minister, but refusing the crown prince was an absolute impossibility.

He said cautiously, "How may I serve Your Highness?"

"Good man," the crown prince said with a nod. "Here's the situation: My cousin's condition has worsened; he has started speaking in strange voices. The family called in soothsayers and mediums and had monks read sutras day and night. Nothing has helped, though the medium did say Tadanobu was possessed by an angry spirit. That's when his family consulted with the Bureau of Divination. The *onmyodo* sent their most experienced doctor. Ki Owaro has studied under the late, great Abe no Seimei and is an excellent *onmyoji.* Ki has determined that the spirit that has taken possession of my poor cousin is someone, a living person, who bears him a grudge from some past event. He suggested that we must discover whom Tadanobu has offended so that this person may be pacified in some way. That, says Ki Owaro, is the only way to save Tadanobu's life. Since nobody knows this person and since Tadanobu cannot speak sensibly, it was decided that we must find someone who can solve this mystery." He ended somewhat triumphantly on this last word and smiled at Akitada.

The term "it was decided" was both vague and, given the crown prince's rank, ominous. Was the emperor himself involved?

Akitada said, "I see. But why have you come to me? I deal mostly with crimes, murder and such."

His highness shifted a little and said, "Well, since we don't know what happened . . ." His voice trailed off and he looked distinctly uncomfortable.

So. Tadanobu's offenses apparently included certain violent outcomes that might involve someone's death.

"I would need to know all about Tadanobu's past." Akitada did not bother with title or surname. A man with such a guilty past deserved neither in his opinion.

"You would be informed, of course, but I doubt that everything is known."

"This seems to be a particularly . . . er . . . outraged spirit. Perhaps Tadanobu's family and friends will refuse to divulge more serious incidents."

The crown prince pursed his lips at so much hesitation. "What another man may consider an outrage may, in fact, have been a justified act," he said with a frown. "You are to investigate all who may conceivably have decided to take such terrible vengeance for whatever they may have resented."

Akitada sighed. "Very well, Your Highness. I'll try my best."

The smile was back. The crown prince got to his feet. "Very good. You'll not regret it if you're successful. But please be discreet. Someone will be in touch."

Akitada rose, bowed, and walked His Highness out to where his entourage waited. The humble Sugawara courtyard was lit by many torches and filled with an ox carriage, outriders, liveried servants, and armed men.

The Sugawara servants peered at them from doorways and gates. As soon as the crown prince had entered his carriage and the visitors had formed an impressive procession and left by the gate, everyone popped out, looking up at him and chattering. Saburo silently appeared by his side.

"Quite an honor, sir," he said.

"Yes, but one I could have done without."

"Indeed?"

Tora came up the stairs, his face alight with questions.

Genba also appeared and shouted, "Back to work, everybody!"

"We'd better obey," Akitada said with a smile. "Come inside, both of you. It appears we'll be busy."

10

More Visitors

They sat in Akitada's study, as they had so often in the past. The shutters were closed against the night air, and an assortment of candles and oil lamps provided light. Saburo had provided wine and food from the kitchen and they ate and drank together, postponing details until later. This cheered Akitada. Tora's eyes were bright with interest, though, to Akitada's mind, he still moved too slowly after the near fatal attack in Mikawa. With Saburo it was harder to detect enthusiasm. His character was more self-contained and he seemed to enjoy dull office work as much as getting out into the streets to investigate crimes.

"The august visit dealt with a case of *ikiryo,*" Akitada eventually told them, setting down his empty bowl. He had been very hungry.

"The crown prince himself!" Tora said. "We're moving up in the world. You mean there's an angry spirit plaguing the imperial family?" He leaned forward as he reached for the wine flask, his face expressing delighted shock. Tora believed in ghosts and all sorts of supernatural events, though in the many years he had served Akitada he had managed to come to grips with his more irrational fears.

"Not the emperor's family. The victim is Fujiwara Tadanobu."

Saburo nodded. "I thought so." He had long since finished his meal, because he never ate very much.

Surprised, Akitada asked him, "You knew? I thought this was being kept quiet."

"Servants talk."

"But we've only just got back. And besides, this happened in the household of one of the ministers. His Imperial Highness insisted that discretion was essential. Do you mean to tell me that it is common gossip?"

Saburo smiled. "It will be soon. As for how I found out, I've kept up with some of the men who serve in similar positions to mine. There's a group of us, majordomos, *bettos,* and secretaries of the first families. We meet regularly for a game or two or to attend a performance."

Akitada shook his head in amazement. "Do I assume that you, too, regale the others with tales of our household?"

Saburo pursed his lips. "I am circumspect, sir."

Akitada thought about his marriage and the child and wondered how much Saburo knew. Silly question; Saburo knew. He asked, "What have you learned?"

"His Excellency, the minister, has had a difficult year. He lost a favorite over the summer. Then one of his small sons died. His income from the estates in the western provinces was halved because of pirate attacks. Then he fell down some stairs while drunk and broke a leg. The leg isn't healing well. There's a good deal of pain, and he's been bedridden ever since. The idea of his being persecuted by some malevolent being started before the fall. The more recent physical suffering made him afraid of dying. I cannot be certain about the possession and when it began. It may be someone has put the idea in his head."

Akitada nodded. Thank heaven, Saburo was not superstitious. His years with the monks had given him some insights that were normally not available to the general population. "So what is the opinion of your, er, friends?"

"They think he's dying and are glad of it. He's a bad man."

Akitada sighed. "Well, I'll have to find some way of dealing with this demand. You can't really call it a request when it is issued by the future emperor. There's another case I'd much rather get involved in. Superintendent Kobe asked for our help. A young woman from the amusement quarter stands accused of having poisoned the man who bought her out." He poured himself another cup of wine.

Tora said, "You mean Miyagi?"

"Yes. I see you're both well-informed about local events. Do I need to give you any more details?"

"If you would, sir." Saburo was clearly interested.

Akitada told them what he knew, then suggested that they also speak to Superintendant Kobe before talking to Sato Yutaka's servants and neighbors and to Miyagi's former fellow courtesans. They exchanged grins, and Akitada guessed that it was already clear who would do what.

From outside came the sound of the night watchman calling the hour. Akitada suddenly felt exhausted. He saw that Tora also looked drawn and worn out. "Let's go to bed," he said. "Tomorrow may bring some solutions to our problems."

After they left, Akitada pondered Tadanobu's possession and his own bad luck. The crown prince had made it impossible for him to leave the capital and visit his sister. More perplexing was what he was going to do about Tadanobu.

The answer appeared early the next morning.

*

Saburo arrived as Akitada was eating his morning rice gruel. Looking apologetic, he said, "Sorry, sir. There's a female, here who wants to see you."

"A woman? Who is she?" Upper class women never called on men outside their families without a male escort and Genba or Saburo should have dealt with ordinary ones.

"She didn't give her name." Saburo shook his head in disapproval. "I doubt she'll leave, sir."

This intrigued Akitada. "Well, then you'd better show her in, hadn't you?"

Saburo disappeared and a moment later opened the door to admit a striking figure.

She was tall, handsome, and dressed in a shocking assortment of clothes in all colors. Her long, black hair hung loose and tangled, mingling with innumerable chains of beads, shells, amulets, and what looked like dead creatures that hung about her neck. She made clacking sounds as she walked.

And Akitada knew her well.

He stared as she approached with a firm step, waving a paper wand in one hand. "Sugawara," she said in her strong voice. "You've grown older."

Akitada got to his feet and bowed. "So have you, Lady Aoi." He expressed neither pleasure nor courtesy. "Please be seated. May I offer refreshments?"

"No, thank you." She seated herself gracefully and looked around.

"Then how may I serve you?"

She studied him. "I recall that I came to serve *you* last time," she said finally. "You wouldn't listen then. I wonder, have you gained more wisdom since?"

She was as irritating as ever. They had met years ago when he had been accused of killing Lord Kiyowara Kane. He had tried desperately to find the true murderer and clear his name, and his suspicion had fallen on several likely people, when Lady Aoi, a shrine virgin and a professed seeress and medium, had walked into his home, much as she had done this time, for the sole purpose of calling him a fool.

He said, "I don't know, Lady Aoi. Have you found it necessary to kill anyone else?"

It had been Lady Aoi herself who had committed that crime. He supposed her conscience had made her come to him to steer him away from the innocent, though he had not guessed that she had committed the murder until it was almost too late.

She did not find his question amusing. "I see you have never really forgiven me even though the emperor did. Never mind. I have come to warn you again, since you seem to have some strange compulsion to meddle where you shouldn't."

"Let me guess. This concerns Tadanobu's illness?"

"It does indeed. I'm told the crown prince has asked you to investigate. I'm here to tell you to stay out of it."

"You must allow me to make my own decisions. Do I assume that you are personally involved in the exorcism?"

"He is my cousin. Of course, they sent for me."

They were all related, these people, and that allowed them to get away with murder and other reprehensible behaviors.

"And have you made any progress?"

Her eyes flashed with resentment. "Yes," she snapped.

"Ah. I've been told that your cousin has deeply angered a lot of people. Have you identified the spirit who possesses him?"

She glared. "You don't know anything about my work."

Akitada nodded. "You're right, but His Imperial Highness thinks I can learn the person's identity and allow the afflicted to make reparations for his offense. Surely such a thing isn't unreasonable?"

She opened her mouth to argue, but thought better of it. Getting up with a rattle of beads and shells, she snapped, "You're still a fool."

And left.

Akitada sat smiling at the door she had closed behind her. Contrary to her intentions, she had managed to make him take a sudden and avid interest in the Tadanobu case. He cared little about stopping Tadanobu's affliction, but he suddenly saw a way of bringing some justice to someone who had been injured by him and had no hope of any. And, given the minister's reputation, it might be possible to straighten out a few others of his past offenses.

Besides the crown prince had asked him to do so, and he surely outranked Lady Aoi.

Akitada decided to go out and ask a few questions.

11

A Wealthy Merchant

Tora and Saburo walked to the jail together. They had already discussed the visit of the medium to their master and wondered about it. Alas, he had not enlightened them.

"This is like old times," said Tora. "I'm glad there was another case waiting for us."

Saburo glanced up at the blue sky through trees that were still leafless but already budding. "Yes," he said, "I need a diversion. Mother has become an infernal nuisance. Sumiko's been in tears several times already. This morning she told me she was bad for me and should leave."

"What did you say?"

"Tried to calm her down and when that didn't work, I left."

Tora glanced at him, amused. "Really, brother, you know nothing about marriage. When they are upset, you take them to bed and show them how much you love them."

Saburo blushed and changed the subject. "How do you propose to start?"

Tora misunderstood. He stopped and looked at Saburo in disbelief. "Surely you know how to make love to a woman? Really, brother, your monkish life must have killed the spark in you. No wonder Sumiko wants to leave. Wives like to be bedded regularly, especially after a quarrel."

Saburo snapped, "I'm talking about our assignment, and there is nothing wrong with my . . . marriage, thank you."

"Oh."

They started walking again.

After a moment, Tora said tentatively, "About this Miyagi. I should talk to the girls in the willow quarter. They'll know things about her."

Saburo suppressed a smile. "Suppose we split up? You go to the quarter and I'll check out Sato's home and place of business."

"Sounds good," Tora said happily.

At the jail, they asked to speak to Superintendent Kobe. A sergeant told them that Kobe was out.

Saburo asked, "How is your lady prisoner?"

The sergeant smirked. "No lady, sir, though she has the clothes. Just another whore who fleeced a customer." He paused for effect. "And then she killed him."

Tora growled, "You don't know that for a fact. Anybody else could have poisoned Sato. You, for example."

The man stopped smiling. "Look here, sir, I get paid to keep people safe, not kill them. Besides it wasn't our food. His own doctor said there was nothing wrong with it or him. He didn't get sick until his girlfriend brought him his food. Mind you, if it had been the wrestler, I could see where there might be a problem. His friends were in and out, smuggling in wine for him. Made him so drunk he attacked a guard and tore the prison to pieces."

Tora looked interested. "That wrestler. What happened to him?"

"Fined and released. Good riddance."

Saburo said, "Right. We'll be back later. Tell the superintendent Tora and Saburo came about the Miyagi case."

The sergeant, who was new since they had both left for Mikawa, raised his brows and said coldly, "If you have information about that murderess, you can talk to me right now."

Tora glowered at him. "Never mind. You've already found her guilty."

The sergeant laughed. "You must be a bigger fool than a man your age ought to be," he said with a sneer.

"She gave him the poisoned food. He ate it and died. End of case."

Tora, insulted both by the slur on his age and on his intelligence, clenched his fists and took a step forward. Saburo caught his sleeve. "Come, brother," he said. "We'll speak to Kobe later. After we have some information for him."

The sergeant laughed again. Tora unclenched his fists and shook his head. "Things have changed here," he said darkly as they walked out.

They parted at the entrance to the willow quarter. It was quiet beyond the gate during these morning hours. Saburo said, "Well, good luck, brother," and walked on alone toward the eastern market where he expected to find more activity.

A few housewives were already headed in the same direction and he asked one of them for directions to the rice dealer Sato. The business turned out to be near the Kamo River and was a sizable compound incorporating not only a shop front where people could buy their rice but also separate living quarters and warehouses to store the precious commodity. At the gates to the compound and beside the door to the shop were pious statues to the rice god and *kinari,* the sacred fox god, both decorated with rice sheaves and pine branches.

Saburo ignored the shop, though it was open for business, and walked into the courtyard. He saw some men carrying rice bales and in one shed a boy was treading a steady rhythm on the rice mill, pounding the kernels to fine flour. These, too, he passed by on his way to the house, presumably the living quarters of the owner. This resembled many homes of well-to-do merchants, being one-storied and solidly built of heavy, weather-darkened timbers.

Saburo was surprised that Sato's business was not closed after his death. There was no sign of mourning either. The workers he could see wore ordinary clothes and went about their chores in what seemed the usual way. And customers had been walking in and out of the shop. It was almost as if this business belonged to another man.

Curious about the reason for this, he walked up to the dwelling place and into the vestibule, calling out, "Ho! Anyone home?"

When there was no answer, he slipped off his shoes and stepped up on the polished wooden floor. Some vague sounds came from his right, and he walked in that direction.

The house was mostly open, with partial dividers between rooms. He could see into smaller spaces under the eaves, and one room must be the principal one because it contained *tatami* mats on the floor.

The noise, however, came from a sunken kitchen area toward the side of the house. This was paved with stone, contained two rice cooking stoves and the usual utensils and bunches of dried goods hanging from the rafters. Two women were busy with food preparations. Because they were chattering and banging pots, they did not hear Saburo approach until he loomed above them and cleared his throat.

One of the women, a plain girl, in a lower servant's rough clothing, screeched in fright. The other was a middle-aged woman wearing black silk much like his own mother. And like his mother, she was clearly made of sterner stuff than the maid. She glared at Saburo. "What do you want and who let you in?"

Saburo said smoothly, "I'm a merchant and came to see who's going to pay me now that Sato's dead."

Her face became pinched. "I'm his widow," she said. "What's the bill for?"

Saburo scratched his head. "His widow? I was told he was unmarried. And he was quite a young man."

She turned ugly with anger. "What's it to you? You've never heard of a wife being older than her husband? Anyway, what's the money for?"

Saburo cast about and finally said, "We provided screens and reed curtains. All the finest quality." Belatedly he thought that this plain house clearly contained no such fancies. He should have stuck with some items used by rice merchants.

To his surprise, she snapped, "I expect that was for that murderous bitch. You can collect from her." She snorted.

So, thought Saburo, Miyagi was living elsewhere. He looked around again. It made sense. Nothing about this place fit his image of a pampered top courtesan. He put on a worried face and said, "But surely he's still responsible for his own debts? Or rather his heirs are."

She put her hands on her hips. "Everything belongs to me now. And you'll not get one red copper from me.

I'm not paying for what he spent on her. Go get your goods back, is my advice!"

Saburo looked crestfallen and nodded. "Yes. Good advice, I think. And where do you think they are?"

"How should I know? Go ask her. She's sitting in jail." She smirked with satisfaction. "I hope they kill her."

Saburo thanked her and departed.

He thought about this astonishing development. On the whole, he thought the woman was lying, but it was indeed not unheard of that handsome young men gained businesses by marrying elderly widows and daughters of the previous owners. Was it possible that Sato had been married all along? To this thoroughly unpleasant woman, at least fifteen years older, and not attractive at all? Perhaps Sato, disappointed at home, had searched out a young beauty in the quarter and bought her out to keep her in a separate establishment. What was more, if the woman he had just met was indeed Sato's lawful wife, she had had reason to poison him. She might be playing a dangerous game to gain control of the property and business.

He left the courtyard by the gate and turned instead toward the shop entrance, taking his place in a short line of customers.

When it was his turn, he said, "I'm with the city administration, checking on merchants' permits. Where's yours?"

The middle-aged clerk eyed him without favor, reached under his counter, and placed a document before Saburo. It was properly made out to Sato Yutaka and gave him the right to sell rice and rice flour at the present location.

Saburo tapped his finger on the name and said sternly, "This Sato is deceased. Who has the permit now?"

This produced the expected consternation. The clerk stammered, "Mrs. Kuwada's looking after the business. You'd better ask her. She told us to open the shop."

"And where is this Mrs. Kuwada now?"

"She hasn't come in yet. Must still be at home. In the dwelling in the back of the compound."

"And how is this Mrs. Kuwada related to the deceased?"

The clerk looked dumfounded. "No idea, but she's always been here. Giving orders." The last was added somewhat resentfully.

"What's her position?"

"She's the manageress, I think. Anyway, the boss lets her run things. He was hardly ever here lately. He lives elsewhere." The clerk smirked a little. "With his new lady."

Saburo's ears perked up. "Ah. His wife, you mean?"

But now the clerk looked dubious again. "As to that, I couldn't say. She's beautiful and finely dressed, but . . . the young men gossip a lot and maybe she was just . . . you know . . . someone he kept for his pleasure."

"So she's been here?"

"Oh, yes. He brought her once. To show her the place. Very nice, I thought her. Not at all haughty. Say, if you're working in the city administration, you can look up who owns the place now."

Saburo nodded vaguely, thanked the man, and left. He had gained nothing. Miyagi's role in Sato's life was uncertain. Few courtesans, even of the first order, achieve the position of wife, and then only after giving the man sons. His sympathies were with Miyagi.

Provided she had not in fact poisoned Sato.

12

Tora Meets an Old Friend

Tora entered the willow quarter with pleasurable anticipation. In his younger years he had spent much time here and it had been here that he had met his wife Hanae who had once been a fine professional dancer. When she became his wife she had put a crimp in his social life with the pretty girls in the quarter, so he was no longer well informed about the courtesans and entertainers. As he strolled about, he also found that some of his favorite restaurants and the biggest brothels and houses of assignation had changed owners and now bore different names on their colorful door curtains and lanterns.

For a while, he wandered about, shaking his head. This world, once his world, had changed as he had changed. He recognized none of the names and saw nobody he knew. A street sweeper was out and a couple of boys, nine or ten years old, employed by brothels to carry messages, chatted in front of one large house. It looked familiar, and after some thought Tora recalled it as the Golden Lantern. He wished Kobe had been in or the sergeant had not been such a bastard. He could have asked what house Miyagi worked for before Sato bought her out. Well, he'd have to find out himself. Surely everybody here knew her by name.

He approached the boys. "Morning, gentlemen," he said with a smile.

For a moment, it looked as though they would run, but then they took in his age and good clothes and decided to talk to him. "Morning, sir," said the taller one with an impudent grin. "We're not open yet."

"I'm well aware of it," Tora told him. "I need some information." He dug in his sash and came up with a few coppers.

The boys eyed these with a sneer. "It'll cost you more than that," the taller one informed him.

Tora snapped, "Listen, you little good-for-nothing. You don't even know what the information is. I can ask anyone around here." He glanced around and saw the figure of an old drunk appear from one of the side streets. "I can ask that drunk over there, and get it for nothing."

They looked at the drunk and burst into laughter. "Him? He doesn't even know his own name anymore." They exchanged a glance and abandoned Tora. Instead they ran to the old drunk, leaving Tora standing with his disdained coppers. He sighed and put them away. Yes, things had changed.

But then, maybe not completely.

Up ahead the two boys were picking up rocks and garbage to pelt the old drunk who wobbled along faster but fell over his legs. The boys' laughter reached Tora. The drunk tried to get up, fell again, and finally started to crawl away. The taller boy, apparently the ringleader, straddled him like a horse and whipped him to greater speed. The drunk collapsed, and the other joined the first in kicking him.

By then, Tora had reached them, seizing both by the scruff of their necks and shaking them. "You little bastards!" he snarled. "How'd you like it if I did to you what you just handed out to that poor old drunk?"

The old man lay whimpering, the gray hair of his topknot undone, his thin, mottled arms and legs like sticks. He seemed to be wearing an odd collection of clothes, notably among them a woman's red robe embroidered with peacocks. This was stained and torn but odd enough to attract the cruel mockery of street kids.

Dropping the boys, Tora gave each a push and said, "Don't ever let me see you do such a thing again."

They scrambled away as fast as their legs could carry them, and Tora bent to help the drunk to his feet. He rose, muttering and clutching at Tora weakly. "W-what .

. . ?" he mumbled, looking up blearily. "W-would you have a copper, s-sir? I haven't eaten all day?" He burped and the smell of cheap wine reached Tora's nose. He was looking down at the man, an unattractive sight if ever there was one. The sunken cheeks were stubbled with gray beard, the thin mouth hung loose, dribbling saliva, and red-rimmed eyes stared back at Tora through a film of mucus.

Tora sighed and reached back into his sash to press a handful of coins into the old wreck's claw like hand. "No wine," he said. "Go get something to eat and then go home and sleep it off. You're no match for the boys in this quarter."

The old man clutched the coins eagerly and gave Tora a toothless smile. "Thank you, honorable and fine sir. May Amida bless you a thousand fold." He burped again. "And may he give you life in paradise for your goodness."

Tora shook his head, put a hand under his arm, and dragged him upright. "Remember," he said sternly, "food. No wine."

The old man nodded vigorously and Tora walked on.

In the next street, he finally saw a sign that he recognized. The Lotus Pod was a wine shop he used to frequent back in the days when he made more frequent visits to the quarter. As he recalled, its owner knew everyone. He walked in, saw it was pleasantly unchanged with the usual clients hanging about the wine tub on the raised platform at the end. It was still early. Later in the day, Kozuke, the host, employed waitresses to serve the crowd that spread all over the dirt floor to the door. The Lotus pod served decent wine at good prices and its host enjoyed joking with the regulars.

Kozuke presided over the tub and the regulars today seemed to be a couple of middle-aged shopkeeper types and a market woman. Kozuke's eyebrows rose when he saw his new guest.

"Tora? Can I trust my eyes? Where have you been? I've been mad at you, thinking you'd gone to the competition."

Tora grinned and climbed to the platform. "Never. We've been ordered to provincial duty these past four years, and before then Hanae kept a sharp eye on me."

His host dipped out a cup of wine and made introductions. "Kuro over there has a fan shop in the eastern market; He's a widower and comes here a lot." This was greeted with laughter and back-slapping for Kuro. "The one beside him with the big belly is Kanjubo. He runs the Golden Perch two streets over. Best fish soup you ever tasted." Kozuke smacked his lips. "And the lady's Mrs. Matano. Mrs. Matano dresses the hair of the most beautiful women in the quarter."

Tora nodded to each and tasted the wine. "Good!"

Kozuke told the others, "Tora works for Lord Sugawara. You know, the one who catches murderers."

They all looked at Tora expectantly.

He settled down on the floor among them, grinned, and said, "You might say I'm here on a case. And maybe you can help me."

"Of course we'll help!" cried his host and the others nodded vigorously.

"I'm trying to find out about a woman called Miyagi–"

He did not get any further. They all cried out in surprise and started talking at the same time. Kozuke shouted, "Hush. Let me tell him." The others fell silent. Kozuke turned to Tora. "Tora, they framed her. The bastards framed her. Sweetest girl there ever was. You and your master must help her."

"I'll do my best. But how can you be so sure she's innocent?"

They all answered again, saying they knew and they were sure and they'd swear to it, and Tora said, "Have any of you met her?"

The woman, Mrs. Matano, nodded vigorously. "I have. I've done her hair many times. She was the sweetest girl in that house. Always pleasant, always grateful, and so well-spoken. You could tell she came from good stock, poor love. That's why she was so popular."

Kozuke said, "Oh, come. The men liked her because she's a beauty."

"That too, but there are lots of others that are beauties. No, she was special. She could've had anyone, but she took Sato. She could've had a great lord. I tell you, Tora, she was in love with Sato. She would never have killed him."

The others nodded. One of the men said, "I knew Sato. He was besotted with her. The whole quarter watched the two of them."

Tora had struck gold. Such things happened in the willow quarter where everyone took a big interest in everyone else. "So, "he said, "I expect there were a lot of the women who were jealous of Miyagi?"

Mrs. Matano looked thoughtful. "Some maybe. But not a one who'd kill her man. They're the kind that find fault, you know, even when there aren't any. Miyagi is really nice, friendly to everyone, and very pretty, and she's smarter than most and talks better. Some of the women come from good families, you know. Gentry that's fallen on hard times. That makes them loners in a house where all the rest are off a farm or from the slums. They aren't liked much and it gets worse when the auntie or the owner of the house shows them preference."

"But you liked her?"

The hair dresser nodded. "She didn't give herself airs. When I first met her, she was shy and very sad. It takes some of the new ones like that. But she settled in soon enough, and then she met Sato, and she was a changed woman. She was happy." Mrs. Matano, sniffed. "Poor girl. Just when everything was perfect for her."

They were all silent in contemplation of so much good fortune destroyed by utter tragedy.

"Who can know when his life will fall apart?" asked the one called Kanjubo.

"No one. It's all in the hands of Buddha," nodded Kozuke.

"If only she'd known," muttered Mrs. Matano. "Or if Sato had never seen her."

Kozuke frowned. "It's not a matter of knowing or not knowing, it's *karma.* It happens because it must."

They all nodded.

"What about that charge that sent Sato to jail. You know about that?"

Kozuke said, "So he didn't kneel down before some great lord. Big deal! That just gets you a fine in court and you're out again. And Sato could well afford it."

Tora cleared his throat. "All the same, if Miyagi didn't poison Sato, then someone else did. I'd like to know who that was."

They considered this and nodded again. Kozuke said, "It's your business to find out."

Tora was about to point out that he could use a little help when the door opened and the drunken beggar tottered in. He cried, "K-Kozuke, one of your best, if you please, and don't spill any." Then he made his unsteady way to them and fell down beside Tora. "M-morning," he muttered, looking at him from bleary eyes. "You l-look f-familiar, f-friend."

Tora scowled at him. "I gave you money for some food, not to buy more wine."

The beggar leaned closer, and Tora held his nose and moved away.

"Smile!" said the beggar.

Tora glared. "Leave me alone. You belong in the gutter where I found you."

Their host cleared his throat. "Ohiya's a regular. He's harmless. You got money, Ohiya?"

Ohiya dug out some of Tora's coins and tossed then to Kozuke. Kozuke picked them up and filled a cup for the drunk.

"Ohiya?" Tora stared at him. "You're Ohiya, the dance master?" But he knew the answer already. The disgusting specimen was indeed the formerly refined teacher of his wife Hanae. He'd been drinking too much even then.

Ohiya tossed back the wine and held out his cup for a refill. He burped. "The same, sir," he said and made Tora a lopsided bow. "You knew me?" He told the others, "I was famous. They all loved me, the women and the men. You should've seen me then." He sniffed and wiped away a tear. "You remember, don't you?"

Tora nodded and grinned at the memory of the foppish dance master with his taste for colorful costumes and pretty boys.

"There," Ohiya cried, clapping his dirty hands. "I knew it. The teeth. Those gorgeous teeth. Oh, I had such a crush on you, Tora." He crept a little closer.

Tora wiped away his smile and scowled. "You were obnoxious even then."

Kozuke got bored with the conversation and said, "Ohiya knows Miyagi."

Ohiya burped and nodded. "I know everybody."

"What do you know of Miyagi?" Tora demanded.

"My mouth is really dry," the former dance master complained.

"All right, just one more." Tora tossed Kozuke a coin and Kozuke grinned and filled another cup.

"Well," said Ohiya, after emptying the cup, "I know her mother, and I know that Saeki sold her." The wine seemed to have steadied him amazingly.

"I already know she was sold. So Saeki owns the brothel? What about her mother?"

"Woman from Fushimi. A widow trying to find a place for her daughter. Brought the girl to the capital and ended up with Saeki. The mother thought the girl could learn to be a dancer there. Silly, really. Saeki's the biggest brothel owner in the quarter. And Miyagi's not like your Hanae. Now *she* was a natural born dancer. Anyway, Miyagi stayed and worked for Saeki. Not what the mother had had in mind, but these things happen." He turned his cup upside down to show how empty it was. "Another?"

"No," said Tora, getting up. "I can get the rest from Saeki.

He left, depressed by the meeting with Ohiya. He had disliked Ohiya years ago, first because he had been Hanae's dance master who had opposed her marriage to Tora. Later, Ohiya's flamboyant life style with a series of young male lovers had disgusted him. Then, when Ohiya propositioned Tora, Tora had panicked. Now the man had become a filthy beggar who ought to be pitied. This turn of events upset Tora who saw neither reason nor justice in it.

But then, most stories in the willow quarter ended this way. Look at Miyagi's fate: first sold by mistake to become a prostitute, she had caught the eye and heart of a wealthy young man, only to end up in jail for having killed him. Fortunes had a way of changing quickly.

13

The Summons

Akitada set out to pay a visit to Nakatoshi, always a source of information about the nobility. But as it was, he had hardly entered the *Daidairi* when he was hailed by a black-robed official whose cap announced him to be of the fourth rank. The man was a stranger, but the fourth rank was well above Akitada's and so he paused curiously as the other hurried up.

He was slightly older than Akitada and not used to hurrying, so he arrived out of breath. As he stood gasping, Akitada bowed and put a smile of greeting on his face.

The other frowned. "Sugawara? I think it must be you."

"It is, but I don't think we have met."

The other man sketched a small bow. "Minamoto Yoritori, secretary to His Excellency, the prime minister. We haven't met, but you've been pointed out to me."

It was getting more curious by the minute. Akitada asked, "How may I be of service, sir?"

"His Excellency wishes to see you. If you are free, please come with me."

It was not a question of being free, of course. If the prime minister summoned, one appeared. Akitada said, "Of course." And they walked quickly in the direction of the prime minister's office. Akitada forbore asking questions and his companion volunteered no information. Minamoto Yoritori bypassed the main gate of the *Daijokan-cho* and turned the corner. There, in the wall, was a small gate, used by servants and messengers. This he opened, walking through, and waited for Akitada to follow.

Finally he thought an explanation was in order. "It is best if you're not seen to visit the prime minister in this instance."

Akitada could not restrain his curiosity any longer. "What instance?" he asked.

"You'll see. Come along now."

They were in one of the inner compounds of the *Daidairi,* the one belonging to the Great Council of State, not the largest or most elaborate but the one treated with the utmost respect by everyone. This was where the prime minister had his offices. Dark-robed secretaries hurried about in the wide hallways, glancing curiously at Akitada and bowing to his companion, who merely nodded. At the end of a long corridor, a pair of armed guards stood on either side of wide double doors. When they saw the prime minister's secretary, they stood to attention and flung the doors wide.

They walked into a large office occupied by three or four people sitting at low desks and wielding their brushes or reading various documents. All were ranking noblemen.

"Your Excellency," said Akitada's companion, "I present Lord Sugawara."

He had spoken to a corpulent man in a green silk robe who sat by himself at a desk on a dais against the back wall, idly tapping his baton on his knee. The man looked up and put down the baton.

"Already? Have you grown wings, Yoritori?"

"I ran into Lord Sugawara at the Suzaku Gate. He was just coming in."

The prime minister made a gesture for Akitada to approach. He walked forward, knelt, and bowed deeply, then sat back on his heels. "I'm at your service, Your Excellency," he said, waiting, curious to find what this was all about. Akitada guessed it might have something to do with the possession of the Prime Minister's brother, but it could equally well refer to his recent service as governor of Mikawa Province.

The prime minister said, "I wanted to meet you. You're a stranger at most official functions, Sugawara."

A reprimand? "I've served mostly away from the capital, Your Excellency."

"Yes. Hmm." The small eyes still studied him, weighing what they saw. "You solve crimes, they say."

"I take an interest in what makes people commit acts of violence against others, my Lord."

"Hmm." The prime minister made up his mind. Glancing at Yoritori, he said, "We'll go to the small room. You may stay."

The prime minister rose and walked out of the room, followed by Akitada. They went to an enclosed area under the eaves. The small space contained only a desk and two cushions. The shutters were closed, but a lamp provided light. The prime minister waited until Akitada had closed the door behind them, then he said, "I'm told you can be discreet."

How to answer that?

Akitada hesitated, then said, "I do not cover up crimes."

The prime minister turned red and compressed his lips. "I beg your pardon?"

"Forgive me, Your Excellency. Since I have no idea what this is about, I thought I would clarify the matter of my discretion."

The other man said nothing for a moment, and Akitada grew nervous again. But eventually the anger receded and His Excellency said, "Yes. Quite right. Let us sit down. Anyway, in this case you need have no such fears. It concerns my brother."

There was plenty to fear in that.

"My brother is very ill," the prime minister continued when they had seated themselves on two cushions. "He is not expected to live."

"I'm very sorry to hear it."

The prime minister's eyes narrowed. "I'm told you had a visit from His Imperial Highness."

Akitada nodded. "That is so."

After a moment's silence, the prime minister asked, "What did he want?"

Akitada bowed a little. "I regret, Your Excellency, but it was a private conversation."

Compressing his lips again, His Excellency snapped, "Don't you mean consultation?"

"No, Your Excellency."

An impasse. The room had grown measurably chillier. After a moment, Akitada said, "I would rather not discuss the meeting with His Imperial Highness. What is it that made you send for me? Your brother's health or the crown prince's visit to my house?"

For a moment, His Excellency looked affronted by the blunt question, then he smiled thinly. "You are very direct. I like that. Such men get things done. The answer is, both. Your name was suggested to me as someone who can be trusted in the matter of my brother's troubles, and I was curious to know why His Imperial Highness takes such an interest. And your answer?"

"As to His Imperial Highness, I cannot say. He indicated that he hoped your brother's life might be saved if some mystery could be solved. I assumed his belief was based on wishing your brother well. Was I wrong?"

Now the frown was back. Akitada knew this sort of verbal fencing was dangerous, but he felt he must establish some level of authority early, or he would learn nothing.

After a long moment's silence, His Excellency said, "I do not know His Imperial Highness's mind, but I do know that people believe there are things in my brother's past that account for his affliction. Such beliefs are dangerous."

Akitada raised his brows. "You prefer to ignore them? Even to the point of having him die?"

The prime minister stared at him. "Of course not. My brother cannot speak for himself. He has not been rational."

Akitada pondered this. If Fujiwara Tadanobu could not be questioned, he was forced to come at the truth from the outside by speaking to the people who had known him or had been with him during the dark times of his past. The task had just become immeasurably harder. And it was significant that not even Tadanobu's brother knew his secrets.

Or wanted to admit to knowing them.

Or wanted Akitada to know them.

After a moment, Akitada said, "I have been told that you employ a medium. She has surely been at his bedside. Isn't it likely that she may have learned things from listening to her patient?"

The prime minister bit his lip. "I see you already know some of what has been going on. I suppose there is much talk?"

Prime ministers did not know everything. Akitada smiled. "Yes, I think so."

"It must stop. People will start to imagine something much worse."

Akitada took a deep breath. "If you'll forgive me, Excellency, but your brother's reputation has long been dubious. Gossip is rarely accurate and tends to exaggerate; he is said to have been an unjust administrator. Apparently no details are known, but people are beginning to make guesses."

The prime minister turned red again. Glaring at Akitada, he hit the dais angrily with his baton. "There. I knew it. There is no time to be lost. You are to make sure that nothing harmful to the family gets out."

There was no mistaking the threatening note in the great man's voice. It shocked Akitada a little. He said cautiously, "Yes, Your Excellency, but I cannot change the past."

After a moment's silence, the prime minister said coldly, "So! You are very sure you'll find misdeeds. I am not. I love my brother and know he is a good man, though he may sometimes have acted thoughtlessly. I charge you with protecting his reputation."

Akitada felt cold. "I do not know if I can do that," he said, bowing humbly, "but I promise that I will not reveal my findings to anyone but you."

The prime minister regarded him silently, then nodded. "Very well. How will you proceed?"

"I'd like to see your brother."

"I told you, he is not rational."

"Nevertheless. Besides I'd like to speak to the medium. The source of the rumors is your brother and those around him. It is as well to know the worst. After that I shall make discreet inquiries into some of the events of his past."

The prime minister hesitated, then said with a peculiar emphasis, "Be very careful."

They bowed to each other and Akitada got up and left.

14

A Businesswoman

Saburo, being familiar with the workings of the capital administration, scanned the large hall of clerks bent over desks or dealing with humble applicants for this or that permit and located his most likely subject.

He was a middle-aged man, somewhat corpulent and engaged in looking deceptively busy with paper-work. The various lines of supplicants formed in front of other individuals.

"Yuki, you lazy bastard!" he shouted across the room. "Stop pretending you're working and come out for a meal with me!"

Yuki froze for a moment in outrage, then turned and laughed a little insincerely. "Better not be spreading ugly rumors, Saburo," he warned, trotting over, "or you'll get me fired and then where would you be?"

Saburo made a face. "Right you are. I was just teasing. We all know you're a hard worker. Don't you people have a sense of humor?"

"We're officials. Officials aren't allowed a sense of humor. What do you want this time?"

"Just to ask a friend out to have a bite with me. But if you're too busy . . ."

Yuki pondered for a moment and then said, "All right. I'll get one of the junior clerks to fill in for me."

Saburo, who had not expected anything else, wandered out to the entrance and waited. Yuki joined him a moment later. "Where are we going?" he asked eagerly.

"That fish place on the river?"

"Good. I love their bonito."

Bonito was one of the more expensive items, but Saburo was still in funds so early in the investigation. They walked to the river, chatting about this and that, and finally reached the River House, a popular eating place overlooking the broad Kamo River. At least the river still was broad at the moment. Later in the summer, the water from the mountains would become scarce as it was used to irrigate rice fields and there would only be a modest trickle left.

They entered, ordered, and Yuki asked again, "So what is it that you need this time?"

"Have you heard about the death of the rice dealer Sato?"

Yuki's face lit up. "Have I? Are you on that? That's a crazy story!"

Saburo had some misgivings about sharing too much information. Yuki was a gossip. On the other hand, at this point gossips could be useful. No doubt much false information would get passed around, but they would simply have to deal with all of it, sifting the good from the bad.

He said, "You heard he was poisoned in jail?"

"Yes, by his girlfriend! I tell you, women can't be trusted. He bought her for a princely sum, and she poisoned him. Cruel that. A very painful death, they say."

"Any talk about what her motive might have been?"

"Motive? Such women don't need a reason. I tell you, I would never spend my hard-earned money on one of them. No, my comfortable wife is all I need. It would never occur to her to poison my rice. She knows where her next meal comes from and doesn't expect costly presents to oblige me."

This point of view made Saburo uncomfortable. He had married late in life after struggling with disfiguring scars on his face that frightened most women away. His companions had been prostitutes who had been willing to tolerate his appearance for money. Or so he had thought. But a year ago he had taken into his home a widow with a ten-year-old daughter and gradually they had grown close. He loved Sumiko and her daughter, but he knew that he had been in a position to offer them a safe haven and support at a time when Sumiko had been desperate. Sumiko was an Ezo, descended from the despised people of the north, longtime enemies of his own people. Eventually many had become slaves to the conquering southern armies. Sumiko had been such a slave and carried the stigma in her heart. Saburo hoped she cared for him as something more the provider of their next meal.

He scowled at Yuki. "You have a very low opinion of women. And there seem to be some questions about how Sato came by the poison. In fact there are many questions about his relationship with Miyagi, the woman who was arrested. She claims she is his wife."

Yuki guffawed. "Sato didn't strike me as that stupid. Though he is said to have been enamored all right. Some men are weak with women."

Saburo asked, "Do you know a Mrs. Kuwada by any chance?"

Yuki's eyes widened. "Yes, indeed. She's the old harridan who runs his business."

Saburo shook his head. "She claims she's his widow. Very unlikely from what I've seen of her. He would have had to be bewitched to marry that one."

Yuki raised his brows. "That's interesting. Now I wonder why she told you that."

"She thought I was collecting on a bill."

"Oh. Well, she lied to get rid of you."

"I don't know. If she claims the property, she'll be a rich woman. It won't take magic to make some handsome fellow court her his time."

Yuki nodded thoughtfully. "She may make some claim, having run the business for so long."

"I noticed she didn't bother to wear mourning or close the business."

"Doesn't mean much. Business people don't take time off from making money."

Saburo felt glum. "No doubt there are all sorts of documents about that business. Can you find out?"

Yuki looked shocked. "Of course not. I'd lose my job."

Saburo sighed. "Well, I see you don't know any more than I do about her. Sato had another house where he kept Miyagi. You know where it is?"

Yuki nodded. "I heard it was near the Rokujo-dono. Small place."

Saburo asked suspiciously, "How come you know this?"

Yuki chuckled. "One of my colleagues' friends is distantly related. He always talked about his rich cousin. Shall we have another flask of *sake*?"

Saburo ignored the question. "What is your colleague's name? Perhaps he might join us next time?"

"He just left on his annual pilgrimage. Going to Ise but plans to take in a lot of temples and shrines on the way. You'd have to wait a few months."

"Pity!" Saburo reminded himself that you win some and you lose some. At least the meal had been good and he had learned a few things.

*

But on more reflection, Saburo found the information Yuki had provided confusing. Would Sato's cousin not be outraged by Mrs. Kuwada's claim to the property? Surely the cousin had an interest. And why was the hatred focused on Miyagi, a young and pretty woman, when Mrs. Kuwada was so much easier to hate?

But he put such thoughts aside and went to the Rokujo-dono. The Rokujo-dono was a noble mansion, but as with many such, especially in outlying regions, more humble neighbors had gathered in adjoining streets. A question took him to a small side street and in this side street to a pretty gate, overgrown with a flowering vine, and behind the gate to a small house tucked amongst trees and shrubs.

The house was quiet. No one answered his knocking for a while, but eventually a bent old woman opened the door and peered at him with eyes red from weeping.

"Nobody's home," she said and tried to close the door.

"Wait! I've come to help Miyagi," Saburo said quickly.

It had been a gamble. For all he knew, she, too, believed that Miyagi had killed her master. But it turned out he had guessed correctly. She opened the door wider. "How is she?" she asked, looking anxious. "Amida, the poor child! She's all alone in that terrible place. How could they suspect . . .?" She broke off to wipe her eyes. "Come in, sir."

She took him to a charming room overlooking a small garden where a cherry tree was in bud and azaleas promised to bloom. Thick *tatami* covered the floor, and the four clothes boxes—one for the clothes of every season—were painted with flowers and birds of each season. A clothes rack was lacquered and held several fine silk gowns and embroidered jackets. A silver mirror stood beside a box holding make-up. And a very pretty painted screen was partially folded up near some silk pillows. Not even Lady Sugawara's room back at the Sugawara mansion had finer or prettier furniture. Saburo stared around in amazement.

"How elegant!" he said.

The old woman nodded and brought him a plain pillow to sit on. "My master loved her. You can see how much."

Saburo nodded, then introduced himself. "I'm Saburo and I work for Lord Sugawara. He's taking an interest in your lady's case."

"May Amida bless him. And you. I've been taking her food, but those guards won't let me see her. They just take what I'm bringing. Yesterday I watched them throwing it away. Have you seen her? How is she?"

"I haven't seen her, but my master has. She was all right but very sad."

Tears rose to her eyes again. "The master's dead! She loved him so much. And he her. How such things can be in this world! There's so little happiness in life, and before you know it you're old like me and you've never had a chance. It was like a miracle with them."

She paused. "Can you get in to see her and take her some food?"

"I don't know. And they won't let anyone bring food at the moment."

She nodded. "Yes, I can see that. Oh, my poor lady."

Intrigued, Saburo asked, "You call her your lady, but people say Sato never married her."

She blustered, "They lie. Master Sato himself told me to make the dumplings for their wedding night. It's all just gossip after what happened."

Saburo regarded her doubtfully. Sometimes people carried out such customs to please a lover. And Miyagi with her background as a successful courtesan might have expected this ritual. He said, "Did he buy her out or was she just, you know, spending a bit of time with him?"

She glared. "More nasty tales. Master Sato bought her out right enough. He had the papers and everything. My lady showed them to me."

Saburo pursed his lips. "There's a woman at his place of business. She claims she's his wife. Maybe Miyagi was just his concubine."

"That one!" the old woman spat in disgust, then bent quickly to wipe the floor with the hem of her gown. "That Kuwada woman's a fox, an evil spirit. She tells lies. Master Sato wasn't married until he brought my lady here."

"Hmm. And when was that?"

"Two months ago. And they were like lovebirds ever since. Till the constables came and took him away."

Saburo counted back in his mind. "Then they hadn't been together long before he was arrested."

"Not long. One day they came. Late. My master and his wife were right over there." She pointed to the open doors to the garden. "He was relaxing after his bath, wearing only his *yutaka* and she was playing her *biwa* and singing about love. He looked at her with such eyes! I'd just decided it was time to spread out the bedding and leave, when there was the pounding at the door."

Saburo thought about that, wondering if the timing had been planned. But at the moment, it did not make much sense. If the unlikeable Mrs. Kuwada had hoped to interfere with a marriage, she had been too late.

The old woman sniffed. "I never saw the master again. My lady was calm at first, but after some days she went out to ask questions, and when she came back, she was very worried. She told me to cook the master's favorite food, and later she went and took the food to the jail." Her face crumpled. "I cooked his food myself!" she wailed. "There was nothing wrong with it, I swear it by Amida. May I be cursed to the hell of fire, if I don't tell the truth."

Saburo said dryly, "Apparently the police believed you. They arrested Miyagi instead."

She glared. "She'd never do such a thing to him. She was as gentle as a bird."

"Well, can you think of anyone else?"

"That woman that works for Sato. The Kuwada woman. She came by here to ask questions and I could see she was angry. She didn't want to believe my mistress was married to Mr. Sato."

"Anyone else?"

She thought, but then shook her head.

Saburo sighed inwardly, thanked her, and departed, hoping that Tora had come up with more helpful information.

15

Lessons from the Past

Akitada left the prime minister's office, feeling completely out of his depth. Warning signals had rung throughout the interview. The fact that he could not refuse what the prime minister asked—any more than he could have refused the crown prince—put him into a position of offending both or his own convictions. And there were grave penalties for offending men in power, penalties that affected not only himself in his life and career, but his entire family and his people. For the first time, he wished he could escape a situation that presented a challenge.

He came to the decision to postpone a decision and went to see Nakatoshi, as he had intended to do from the start.

Nakatoshi received him with pleased surprise. "I hadn't expected you so soon after our last visit," he said, "but after your long absence I shall not complain. You look upset. What brings you?"

Akitada seated himself and waited to answer as his friend poured some wine. Taking his cup and emptying it to get the bad taste of his recent interview out of his mouth, he sighed.

"Is it that bad?" Nakatoshi asked sympathetically, refilling Akitada's cup.

"You recall mentioning Tadanobu's illness when we last met?"

Nakatoshi frowned. "Yes. Don't tell me you're involved in that."

"Worse. My assistance has been requested by both His Imperial Highness and the prime minister."

"No!"

Akitada nodded bleakly. "What shall I do?"

"You cannot refuse? No. I see that you can't. It's a strange coincidence, though."

"Not so strange perhaps. I must by now have attracted the notice of the great because of my wife's new ascendancy at the imperial court." Akitada could not keep the bitterness from his voice. It seemed that the punishment for his rash marriage would continue and grow. Not only that, it would extend to others. He looked at Nakatoshi. "I should not have come," he said. "Forgive me. I have no right to involve anyone else in my . . . mistakes." He drank his wine and rose. "Say nothing.

Forget what I told you. It will be best that we don't see each other for a while."

Nakatoshi also jumped up. "No, Akitada! Sit down again. If I cannot stand by my friends, I truly have nothing to live for."

"You forget your family."

"I do not. But at the moment, my obligations are to you."

They looked at each other in silence. Tears rose to Akitada's eyes. "You grieve me. I cannot bear the thought of rewarding such friendship by putting you in danger."

Nakatoshi smiled. "Come, don't make so much of it. You would do the same."

Akitada sighed and sat down again. Nakatoshi joined him and reached for the wine flask.

"No, not for me. I shall need a clear head."

"Tell me."

And Akitada told, leaving out nothing and adding his own convictions that in this investigation he was headed for his own downfall.

"Perhaps not," said Nakatoshi. "You are a Sugawara. It seems to me you have suffered enough from your relationship to the great *tenjin.* Now perhaps that relationship will protect you."

Akitada gave a snort. "What? You think Michizane's spirit will hover above me and defeat my enemies?"

"Don't laugh. This is a case of *ikiryo.* They believe Tadanobu is possessed. They are a superstitious lot, even if you are not."

Akitada digested this. The Fujiwara ancestors had caused Michizane's horrible death in exile. Then, when a series of calamities befell the nation, they had assumed these had been sent by Michizane's vengeful spirit and decided to appease it by making him a god and erecting shrines for his veneration. He had become *tenjin.* What Nakatoshi implied was that the current Fujiwara nobles would surely not repeat their past mistake with him.

He shook his head doubtfully. "Even if you're right, that will not protect you."

"Akitada, please. We've settled the matter. Now what do you need from me? I suppose I can get you some information about Tadanobu's worst excesses. But I doubt I'll do more than scratch the surface. They have been very careful to cover up for him."

"Surely if they want me to save the man's life, they will reveal what might be troubling him?"

"Not necessarily. We cannot assume that Tadanobu's life is their foremost consideration. What Tadanobu has done may involve his brothers. And sisters."

A fine point. Several of the women were imperial consorts, and two were empresses and mothers of the emperor and crown prince respectively. For a moment, Akitada saw court intrigue as a bottomless pit and a shortcut to hell itself. He covered his face with his hands and muttered, "Dear heavens above!"

There was a moment's silence, then Nakatoshi said, "Some good may come of this. Your investigation may stop the continued cover-up, some of Tadanobu's victims may receive justice, and Tadanobu himself—if he lives—may be sent into exile."

Akitada lowered his hands and looked at his friend. "Very well. Gather what information you can, but be very careful. I'd better not come here again. Can we meet some other place?"

"My house."

"That's too dangerous for your family."

"I live outside the city now. Once or twice will not be noted. Otherwise, your house?"

"All right. If you do come, come alone and by the back gate. Thank you, my friend." Akitada made a face and rose. "I shall now go and call on Tadanobu."

*

But Akitada did not go directly to Tadanobu's mansion. Instead he walked across the capital to the *tenjin* shrine. All of the talk about his illustrious ancestor had reminded him that he had not paid a visit in many months. He did not like or believe in the godlike powers of Michizane, but his father had raised him to venerate the tragic figure of their ancestor out of respect. Frequent visits to the shrine had been part of his youth, as had been the study of Michizane's life and works.

He felt guilty to have neglected this custom when he had become distracted by the personal problems of his marriage to Yukiko. And yet he should have sought answers for his misery in the life of Michizane. Only now when his life and position were threatened by the Fujiwara once again did it occur to him that he might find strength and support from the past in what he was about to undertake.

The *tenjin* shrine was impressive with its elegant roofs spreading their wings over the compound. Like shrines everywhere, its halls and galleries were plain time-darkened wood and its roofs were covered with cypress bark. Only here and there, he saw gilding and the brilliant red lacquer so abundant in the *Daidairi*, the great government compound, the Buddhist temples, and the palaces. But the Fujiwara had not spared care in construction and maintenance and Akitada's famous ancestor enjoyed great popularity among the people.

This pleased Akitada, but it meant there was no privacy. The other worshippers distracted him and he felt awkward. Some might recognize him even though he was no longer a regular visitor and had been absent from the capital for several years. In the end, he performed the usual rituals of purification quickly before visiting the main hall.

Here he was in semi-darkness, with other visitors hidden in the murk, the sound of their footsteps muffled, and he found the solitude he needed to communicate with his ancestor.

Michizane had loomed large in his youth. Akitada's father had brought him here often and pointed out in how many ways the younger Sugawara fell short of the great man's example. He had resented Michizane then, as he had resented his father. The contrast between himself and the great statesman was shocking and still pained him in adulthood.

Michizane, scholar and poet, had risen to become chancellor of this nation. He had done so by his extraordinary merits and the fact that his emperor valued his honesty and devotion. They had still believed then that rewards and promotions should go to the best men.

Thoughts of his own difficulties shamed Akitada quickly. He would never possess the qualities of a Michizane and it was cowardly to blame his own lack of success on the ascendancy of the Fujiwara family and their tenacious hold on power.

But Michizane had suffered death in exile for opposing them and standing in their way, risking all for his emperor and nation. The lesson to his descendant was there. If Akitada wished to emulate his ancestor, he, too, must risk life and family.

He knew and had always known that he was no Michizane. He had neither that man's gifts not his devotion to his emperor and country. Akitada loved his country and revered its young emperor, but he loved his family more. He thought of Yasuko, almost a young woman now and becoming graceful and pretty like her mother. She would need him more than ever now. And his son Yoshi should not be sent out into the uncertain world of government service without his father's help either. Yoshi hoped to become a soldier, but he had made excellent progress with his studies just recently, and Akitada had hopes of sending him to the university soon. And then there were Yoshiko, his wife, and her child. For better or worse, they were his responsibility.

Worst of all would be the fate of his retainers and their families. If serious punishment awaited Akitada, they would become homeless outcasts. He would die rather than be the cause of such a fate for men who had risked their lives for him and given him their entire loyalty.

He wondered what had happened to Michizane's retainers. Family history had no accounts of them. Should he blame Michizane for their fate? No, surely not. Michizane had not known his fate. He had counted on his emperor to his last breath.

Akitada sighed. He had reached a decision of sorts. He must go forward but attempt to escape punishment at all costs, and that would require more ingenuity than he felt capable of. The trouble with famous ancestors was that they tended to make you feel inadequate.

Instead of visiting the ailing Tadanobu immediately, he decided to go home. He wanted to see his children, wanted to talk to Tora, Genba, and Saburo. They would support him, but he wanted them forewarned. The thought depressed him.

16

Lady Aoi Returns

When Akitada got home, he found that neither Tora nor Saburo had returned from their investigations. He was disappointed. The case of the unlucky Miyagi might have taken his mind off Tadanobu for a little.

But Genba had seen him and came up quickly. He said, "You have a visitor, sir."

"Oh. Who is it?"

Genba grinned. "A very pretty lady. She says she's called Lady Aoi."

Akitada frowned. "I wonder what she wants now."

Genba looked surprised by that reaction. "Sir?"

"Last time I talked to her she called me a fool."

The kind Genba's face fell. "She seemed very polite and ladylike."

This puzzled Akitada, but his mind was full with his problems and Lady Aoi was a part of them. "Never mind," he said. "You showed her to my study?"

He did not want to see her, but she could not be avoided. With a sigh, Akitada opened the door to his study. The room was empty, but the doors stood open to his private garden and out there, among the budding azaleas stood a rather changed Lady Aoi.

He almost did not recognize her. Without her usual voluminous and colorful robes and shawls, she looked almost slight. On this occasion, she had disdained bright colors and wore a plain outer robe of a deep forest green silk. As a concession to the season, layers of rose colored, paler green, and white gowns peeked from her sleeves and hem. And her wild mane of hair was brushed and smoothly tied back with a white silk bow. In the spring sun it was shiny and probably fragrant with oils. There were no ropes of beads or feathers either. She looked like any proper, rather elegant lady.

Well, not like any perhaps. Lady Aoi was still as startlingly beautiful as before. Tora had been right about that. Tora was always right about female beauty. It had been Akitada's disdain for her profession that had obscured that beauty.

She had not heard him arrive, and he watched her doubtfully for a moment as she bent over an early-flowering azalea, breathing in its scent. Just then the squirrel came down and tamely approached her, expecting Akitada's treats. When she stretched out a hand, the animal sat up to find the food, then, disappointed, shot back up a tree.

Lady Aoi laughed. Her laughter was light and musical and infectious.

Akitada smiled. She seemed like someone altogether different, someone graceful, gentle, and kind.

A desirable woman.

He shook himself mentally to recall her hardness, her rudeness, her defiance of all proprieties in their past encounters. This was no time to let her cloud his judgment with pretty clothes and feminine wiles. He cleared his throat.

She swung about, startled.

"You give me the pleasure again, Lady Aoi?" he said coldly. "What brings you this time? Perhaps you've found more to deplore in my character?"

She blushed. Making him a small bow, she quickly came to the veranda and stepped up. They stood only a few feet apart now, and he could see that, while she was beautiful, she was a mature woman. Lady Aoi must be close to his own age.

She spoke a little breathlessly. "I deserve that you mock me. I came to apologize. I should not have accused you of foolishness. I did not know that you were given no choice in this matter."

Akitada raised his brows. "And knowing this changed your mind? I recall we never were on friendly, or even courteous, terms in the past."

She turned away. "That was then. You mocked my calling. Why should I do less?"

Akitada said stiffly, "I'm aware that the people of this country seem to believe and trust in matters that cannot be seen or shown to be true, but I dislike those who take advantage of it for their own purposes."

She flung back to him, her face filled with sudden anger. "You see? You mock my gift, my power. The gods will punish you. I have no purpose except to help. My birth has given me a good life. Not all are so fortunate. Their lives are often very hard to bear. I try to ease pain of body and soul much like a physician with his powders or a monk with his prayers. But you wouldn't understand that."

Much against his will he admired the slight color in her face and the flashing eyes. She had the most remarkable eyes. And, if he were to be honest, he admired her spirit. No woman he had ever met had faced up to him in this manner. But then she was no ordinary woman. She had killed the man who had raped her. He said, "You forget that you almost got me convicted of a murder you did yourself."

"You were cleared very quickly. And I made sure no one else was blamed."

This was true, but Akitada had no interest in continuing their acquaintance. He said brusquely, "You have made your apology. Was there anything else?"

For a moment, he thought she would leave. She turned and took a few steps away from him. But she stopped. In a rather small voice, she said, "Whatever your opinion of me, I came to help you. What you mean to do is dangerous. I know the men you're dealing with; you do not. Can you afford to turn down an offer of help?"

She was right about knowing the prime minister and his brother. No doubt, she also knew the crown prince and anyone else who might be involved in the power struggle that seemed to be forming. He, on the other hand, knew nothing. Still, he hesitated.

She came back to him, standing close again, closer than an unrelated woman should be to a man, and said softly, "Akitada, please let me help. What do you have to lose?"

He could not say later what came over him—perhaps it was her scent which was subtly provocative—but he was suddenly intensely aware of her as a woman, not because of her beauty, though she was beautiful with those liquid eyes and that lovely mouth, and not because she was a great lady, but because she was strong, yet pleaded with a gentle voice. He knew she was strong enough to defy powerful men, but apparently she was also strong enough to humble herself. She was a woman unlike any he had ever met.

Blinking, he took a step back. "Why offer to help *me* of all people?"

She lowered her eyes. "I do not hate you. I know you're a good man. My quarrel has always been with evil men, men who use their power and position to take what they want. I think we are alike in that respect, Akitada."

He did not know how to respond to this. To cover his embarrassment, he gestured to the room behind them. "Allow me to offer you some hospitality, Lady Aoi. May I send for wine?"

She smiled a little. "Fruit juice, perhaps."

When he returned from giving his orders for refreshments, he found her looking at his books. "You have a much better library here than Tadanobu," she said, holding up a rare Chinese text.

Akitada made a face. "I should hope so. Most of the books have come down to me from my ancestors, and I have added to them. My profession requires study. Lord Tadanobu has different interests."

She chuckled and put the book back. Belatedly he wondered if she could read Chinese.

"Yes. I think so," she said. "But his father was a well-read man. He was the former Major Counselor Tadamichi."

He sat down behind his desk and gestured to a cushion across from him. "You know the family well?"

"I am related to most of them. Yes. I know especially those who are our age because I grew up with them." She came to sit across from him, gracefully getting to her knees first, then sitting back. Taking a dainty fan from her sleeve, she fanned herself lightly.

"Is Tadanobu one of these?"

"Yes. He is a second cousin on my father's side."

She was indeed closely linked to the ruling Fujiwara family. No wonder her pardon for killing a controller of the right had been issued so promptly. He was reminded once again that knowing this woman was dangerous, perhaps as dangerous as obeying the prime minister.

"What can you tell me about Tadanobu?"

She bit her lip. "He may die soon. He doesn't eat and only sips a little water now and then. Two servants have to support him on his way to the toilet and they aren't always in time. His voice has become weak, and he doesn't like to talk. Of course, when he is possessed by the spirit, all is different. He shouts and screams and threatens. He throws himself about so violently that the servants have to lie on top of him to keep him from rushing off wildly. He nearly strangled one of them, and once, he got away briefly and tried to kill me. But afterwards he lies there like a dead man. I think we may soon see him not emerge from that state alive."

Akitada stared at her in horror. "Is he mad?"

She raised her brows. "Possession by a vengeful spirit is not madness.. When he isn't at the mercy of the spirit, he is quite sensible."

Yes, of course. She believed, or made people believe, that there were spirits who returned after death to slip into their enemy's body to torment him or her. He said, "I really meant his prior life and career. Do you have any idea whose spirit possesses him?"

"No/ If I did, I could find out how to make him go away."

"Ah, the spirit is male?"

She hesitated. "I'm not sure. He speaks through Tadanobu. Tadanobu's voice is part of the spirit's."

"Well, I shall have to pay a visit, of course." Akitada did not mention that he had no faith in the spirit but rather thought Tadanobu, at the point of death, was rambling and perhaps mad, "Do you know whom Tadanobu may have offended?"

She balked again. "As I told you, if I knew, I would be able to help."

"You misunderstood, Lady Aoi. I didn't ask about the name of the spirit but rather for names of people who had reason to hate Tadanobu enough to make him suffer like this."

She was silent for a moment and bit her lip. "There are others who know him better, but I do know that he was spoiled as a young man. His father had to discipline him for several acts."

"Such as?"

His questions made her uncomfortable, but she answered. "He had a servant beaten. The man died. His father took away his favorite horse. He was caught in the imperial apartments. His father sent him to a cousin in a distant province. That sort of thing. I don't see how such things can be useful."

"Perhaps not. It seems too long ago. Are there more recent events? He is now of middle age. I would think there were many years since his youthful misdeeds during which he was not constrained by his father or any other authority."

"You remind me of my age," she said with a sigh, looking down at her hands. "I'm not much younger than Tadanobu."

Akitada felt himself flush. "I beg your pardon. I had not intended such a comment."

He should have known, though, since she had claimed to have grown up with Tadanobu. He tried to think of some compliment and failed. The fact was, she was for all her years a very attractive woman. Her discomfiture suited her, and he wondered if behind that forceful and hostile personality there had not been a softer side all along. He also wondered about her private life. He knew nothing about that. Was she married? Did she have a lover? Or had that past rape made her turn against all men and intimate relationships? He had heard that some women, disillusioned by marriage or a lover had then sought out the company of other females. Such things were acceptable and frequently masqueraded as friendship, especially in the women's apartments at court, where many young and curious girls found themselves practically imprisoned and shut away from normal relations with men.

A long silence had fallen while he imagined her love life and he woke up to the awkwardness of this and flushed again.

To his surprise, he saw that a smile played around her lips. She said, "I think you wonder about me just as I wonder about you. Please ask me whatever you wish. If we are to work together, it would be best to know each other."

Had she read his mind? Was he so obvious? He had better laugh it off, so he chuckled. "You are right. I wondered if your life had brought you into contact with

Tadanobu in later years. Perhaps you married one of his friends or came to know his wives?"

"I have never been married. You may recall that I was a shrine virgin."

"Oh. Yes. But even shrine virgins don't spend their lives in loneliness."

"That rape you know of, for which I murdered, was the first time I had lain with a man. It ended my service as a shrine virgin. I grieved that loss more than the loss of my virginity. My service to our gods was everything to me. I know you don't understand how I must have felt then, having both my body violated and my reputation destroyed. But the worst that happened is that it severed my life from the gods forever. I shall never forget or forgive that."

A little of her past anger had crept into her voice, but this time it did not offend Akitada. He felt a regret that the rape had happened and a sense of the loss she had suffered. Was her violation as serious as the act of revenge that took her attacker's life? In his profession such distinctions were always made. Crime and punishment should correspond. He never used to think that the forced act of intercourse was much more than an unpleasant experience for a woman that would soon fade from her memory. She had not lost anything, after all. Now he tried to understand that a woman might weigh justice differently.

Again as if she could read his mind, she nodded. "I have lived a private life since then. There have been no men in it." Her mouth quirked for a moment. "I seem to have frightened them away."

She had answered his innermost, and quite embarrassing, curiosity. He flushed again. Lady Aoi had a talent for looking into his mind and making him feel inadequate. "I wondered about your knowledge of Tadanobu's later years," he said again.

"Only gossip. I find that very unreliable."

"Ah. Then I don't see how you can help me."

She stared at him over her fan. He decided that it was her turn to feel inadequate. The thought made him smile. She lowered her fan, and he admired her lips, compressed now but still very tempting.

"You are the one chosen to find answers," she said. "I'm merely a woman who has some talent in speaking with spirits. Such as my weak talents are, I make you a gift of them. I think you'll find that I can help you."

A harmless speech, so why did he suddenly feel warm in his stiff robe? In a hoarse voice, he asked, "What do you propose?"

"A collaboration. Let us find out what we may discover together."

He took a deep breath. Everything she said seemed to have other, more intimate meanings for him. Words failed him.

Lady Aoi laughed softly. "Well, I must not rush you. Think about what I have suggested. You know where to find me when your mind is clear." She closed her fan, rose languorously, and rearranged her gowns.

Akitada also got to his feet. "Must you leave already? They haven't brought the refreshments."

"There will be other times, I think. I live in the Oimikado Palace." she said with a sideways glance, then she bowed, and he bowed also, and Lady Aoi glided toward the door with a soft rustle of silks. He hurried to open the door for her, caught another whiff of her delightful scent, and she was gone.

Akitada walked back unsteadily, sat down, and mopped his face with a tissue from his sash. The woman was a witch. By her mere presence, she had put thoughts into his mind that he had long since left behind in the marital bed.

To clear his mind, he decided to see the children. He took his flute along. They might be willing to accompany him. Sadako was quite adept on the zither. And he would not mention his troubles.

17

The Brothel Master

The unexpected meeting with Ohira had left a bad taste in Tora's mouth. He walked to Saeki's establishment in a sour mood quite different from the cheerful, tolerant attitude he used to bring to brothels in his younger years. Somehow in the past the underlying sadness of lives in the amusement quarter had never penetrated his robust sense of taking pleasure in the outward spectacle of beautiful women in gorgeous robes singing and dancing in the light of colored lanterns.

The Golden Phoenix was a substantial building. He had been told it housed fifteen permanent girls and also managed six others who had their own homes. Saeki had owned it for ten years by now. He was a successful businessman, which meant that he kept his mind on his income without becoming involved with the merchandise or any of the other amusements, like drinking and gambling, offered in the quarter.

At this time of day, the house was quiet. Most of the women had worked late hours the night before and were asleep or had gone to the baths. A sleepy youngster directed him to Saeki's office.

Tora found a clean-shaven man of about fifty years, slightly corpulent, dressed in a brown silk kimono and a black silk jacket. He was surrounded by three giggling young women and was instantly suspicious.

"Miyagi? What's it to you?"

Tora eyed the girls, who were in various stages of undress. He decided their clothes looked pretty wrinkled after their night's work and they had clearly not yet been to the bathhouse, but he smiled at them and bowed. "Ladies, my compliments on your good looks."

They giggled and smiled back as women had done all of Tora's life. He remained detached, too aware of the heavy atmosphere of scent, powder, *sake,* and sweat.

"My master is Lord Sugawara," he told Saeki. "He takes an interest in murder cases."

Saeki looked sour. "I know who you are. Well, he wastes his time. She did it all right. Stupid bitch. I warned her from the start. But she wouldn't listen. It had to be Sato or nobody."

"How was she stupid? I heard Sato was pretty generous in buying her out. Are you saying she could have done better? Did she have other admirers?"

Saeki flung out his hands in scorn. "Could she have done better? Much better! But she was in love! In love! I ask you, after three years being a whore, she had to go for youth and good looks. Sato did pay what I asked, but I could've got more. A lot more. And so could she."

Tora was beginning to grasp the reason for Saeki's resentment. Miyagi had turned down a better offer. And since the payment was going into Saeki's money box, her stubborn refusal had cost him.

"Everybody says they were in love," he said. "How come you didn't refuse Sato, if you had a better deal?"

Saeki scowled. "I did, but he kept raising his offer, and she refused to see other clients. In the end I gave in."

The young women were becoming restless. One of them said, "You might've saved her rejected suitors for us, Saeki."

He glared at her. "You don't have what it takes, Chiyo. You're from the slums and have no polish."

The girl snapped. "You always favored her. I hate her. She thought she was better'n us. Look where it got her. And you with her. I'm glad."

Saeki raised a fist. "And what do you mean by that, you ill-tempered bitch? You know what they do to dogs that snap at their owners?"

The girl suddenly looked frightened. "I meant nothing, Saeki. Sorry, Saeki." She bowed.

"Get out, all of you," the brothel master roared in sudden fury. "You're all useless to me. Time I sold your contracts."

This caused an outcry. Two of the young women prostrated themselves, tears destroying the remnants of their make-up.

"Out!" roared Saeki.

They scurried out.

Tora had watched and listened with great interest.

Saeki shot him a glance. "More trouble than they're worth," he muttered. "Miyagi, stupid girl that she was, is a big loss to me."

"Surely not all that big? You got paid."

Saeki waved a finger at him. "You know nothing. She was my biggest earner. Gave the place some class. Now what will I do? The other girls are nothing, serving girls that worked in post houses and inns and bath house girls. I had to train all of them and with all that effort, they don't do much more than bring in small shopkeepers and poor clerks. My clientele's fallen off. And what comes in nowadays doesn't want to pay more than a handful of coppers."

"You should hope then that Miyagi's cleared of the murder charge. She might come back here to work for you."

The thought clearly had not occurred to Saeki. He considered it for a moment or two, then shook his head regretfully. "Won't happen. She did it all right. Besides, if she did get free, she might get some of his money and set up for herself."

"I take it that the other girls were jealous of her success?"

Saeki snorted. "The bitches made my life miserable; that's what they did. Complained to me all the time, accusing her of this and that. All lies. I ignored it. Can't trust women's gossip. They had a little dance when she was arrested, the mean bitches!"

Tora filed this information away also. "But before this you must have done very well from her work. I'm guessing she made you a lot of money."

Saeki shot him a glance. "You don't know this business very well. Had to keep her in clothes, didn't I? To impress the fine lords. What do you think that cost me? No, what Sato paid barely covered her debts. But I have a soft heart."

Tora doubted that. "So she had admirers from among the good people, eh? I thought they had their women brought to them."

"Not always. Not when the first lady objects. No, I built a special place for them." Saeki cocked his head. "You want to see how much gold I spent on Miyagi? Come, let me show you."

"Sure." Tora jumped up eagerly.

They walked through the house and into the back garden. At the very end of the garden, hidden by trees, was another house, this one quite small. For all its smallness, it had been constructed delicately with finely carved details on the door and beams. The garden around it was exquisite and just now in flower. Camellias and azaleas bloomed in shades of white, pink, and red, and the irises at the doorway had already formed buds.

Saeki wasted no time admiring these things. Taking a large ring of assorted keys from his sleeve, he unlocked the door and threw it open. "There!" he said. "Look at it! No princess lived better."

The small house contained a single large room, and this room was filled with luxurious objects. Tora saw painted screens, lacquer clothes boxes, a clothes rack covered with exquisite gowns, and a large spread of silken bedding in the middle of the polished floor. Such a bed no lover would wish to leave, especially if in the arms of a beautiful woman.

The purpose of all this was so obvious that Tora felt little admiration and less desire. But it was true that Saeki had spared no money here. It was an investment in his business, and Miyagi had been part of the investment.

Tora remarked, "Well your expenses are safe. Another beauty will stay here now."

Saeki looked about him disconsolately and shook his head. "No! Do you think I'd let those low sluts cavort in here with their pock-marked apprentices and store clerks?"

Tora did his best to soothe Saeki's pain, though his purpose was not altogether kindhearted. "Surely you have other promising girls. And if Miyagi came to you, another young beauty may also appear."

"Never again," Saeki said dully. "Such a thing will not happen again. She was special. She came from a good family. Better than mine. Sure there'll be other beautiful girls, but none with her manners. That's how she attracted the good people."

"Really? What made her family let her come to work for you?"

Saeki glanced at him. "Who knows?" he said vaguely.

Tora thought that was probably a lie. Brothel owners ask a lot of questions before taking on a new girl. "Come on. There's a story here and one that's bound to be flattering to you," he urged.

But Saeki turned his back and headed back. "No story. Seen enough?"

Tora decided not to press him further. He followed Saeki out. "But who are these great lords Miyagi disappointed?"

"Don't ask silly questions, Tora. They don't give their real names when they come here."

"How many of these noble admirers did she have?

"Three, maybe four. One really pressed me to let him buy her out, but the others were becoming regular in their visits and might have done so, too. Now they're all gone, and my business is gone with them." Saeki heaved another deep sigh.

"Come, Saeki, don't leave me in suspense. You must know something. Who were those nobles?"

Saeki stopped walking. "You know better than to ask. I'm a reputable man. I don't reveal clients' names.

With Sato it doesn't matter. He's dead. And besides he wasn't one of the good people. Can you imagine what would happen if I told you the names of Miyagi's lovers and you went around asking questions about them?"

Tora grinned. "You've got a point. Forget I asked. I was just wondering. You think your fine customers went to the competition?"

"Probably." Saeki walked on glumly. "The stupid bitch!"

"What if we can prove Miyagi innocent and bring her back to you? With your help, we might be able to do that."

Saeki snorted his derision. "I've said more than I should've already."

With a sigh, Tora thanked him.

18

The Warning

Tora reported the morning after Lady Aoi's second visit. He looked glum.

"Any hope for Miyagi?" Akitada asked.

"There's this and that, but none of it adds up to much. Has Saburo come back?"

"I don't know. We'd better give him a bit more time."

"What did the prime minister want, sir?"

Akitada told him about his meetings with the prime minister and Nakatoshi, making a point of the dangers. Tora, as expected, did not express any fears for Akitada or for his own future but instead asked a lot of questions about Tadanobu's condition, offering examples from his own knowledge of cases of *ikiryo*. These tended to be both shocking and dire in outcome, and Tora relished every detail. Akitada managed to stem the flow of narrative only when Saburo joined them.

"Genba just told me that Lady Aoi has been back. He said she looked like a proper lady for a change." Saburo chuckled.

Tora was amazed by this information. He turned to Akitada. "What? She wasn't decked out like a witch? Did you recognize her? I wish I'd been here."

Akitada smiled at the memory of Aoi in his garden. The thought made him warm again. He said, "She looked ordinary." Not precisely ordinary perhaps. Aoi was beautiful whatever she wore. He added quickly, "And she was different in other ways, too. She offered her help with Tadanobu."

Tora clapped his hands. "Good! Being a medium, she'll know what to do. Oh, how I wish I'd been here! I bet it was hard to believe she talks to spirits and has sex with gods when she looked like anybody."

"What nonsense!" Akitada glared at him. "You cannot truly believe that women have sex with gods! You're getting worse rather than better in your old age."

Saburo chortled. "He's an old married man nowadays and has too much time on his hands, sir. Idleness promotes sexual fantasies in certain types. Especially when a man worries about his fading powers."

"Speak for yourself," Tora growled. "It's you who complained about not knowing how to get your wife into bed."

Saburo opened his mouth, but Akitada had lost his patience. "Enough! Keep your mind on your work. What do you have to report?"

They fell silent. Tora was still mulling over Saburo's insult. After a moment, Saburo said, "I checked out the dead man's business. He seems to have been very successful, but it isn't at all clear who will inherit his wealth." He described his meeting with Mrs. Kuwada, her claim to be Sato's wife, and the vagueness of her status among Sato's employees and the clerks in the city administration."

Akitada frowned. "It sounds as if she intends to take over the business. If she had such intentions all along, she is a suspect in the murder of her master. Whatever the facts are about Sato's marriage, she had reason to fear that a wife and future sons would make her plans impossible. How did he come to be arrested in the first place?"

Saburo made a face. "He didn't kneel to some captain in the imperial guard."

"Some of those young devils should have been taught manners themselves. But that should get him only a fine. What a mess!"

Saburo offered, "About this Mrs. Kuwada. Why didn't she murder Miyagi instead of Sato?"

Tora finally found his speech again. "Not so easy. Miyagi is quite famous and she was never alone. Sato was sitting in jail. Anything can happen in jail and people just blame it on the prisoners. Besides, she'd get rid of both at one stroke."

Akitada said, "It's certainly interesting that both Sato and Miyagi seem to have been targets. But Superintendent Kobe would not like to hear you say that such things happen in our jails."

"No? Then why could Sato be poisoned and die before any help was called?"

"Yes, Tora, you have a point. But it is strange. I recall Kobe was in a rage with the jailer who had allowed this to happen. I thought Kobe changed. He looked older, tired, and hopeless. But leaving that aside, it would mean someone planned this murder, and if it wasn't Miyagi, then it was someone else. Another visitor? I don't think he had any. Most likely someone bribed the jailer. Did you talk to Kobe?"

Saburo said, "We tried to, but he was out. Shall I tell you about Miyagi's house?"

When Saburo described the luxurious furnishings and clothes, Tora interrupted to mention Saeki's comment about enormous expenses for Miyagi's gowns. He added, "Knowing Saeki, he kept them all, so Sato must've bought her new ones. A man in love spends money like water. Miyagi had no reason to kill Sato."

Akitada shook his head. "Even a beloved woman may turn murderous if she has a strong enough reason. What did you learn from the people she worked with?"

Tora told them about Saeki and his girls. Saburo commented on the fact that Miyagi had made enemies in her former life. "Perhaps Sato was killed to punish Miyagi."

Akitada consider this. Then he said, "Both her clients and the women she worked with had much better opportunities to rid themselves of her while she still lived in the same house, but we might as well keep it in mind. Too bad Saeki didn't divulge the names of her admirers, though they seem unlikely." He sighed. "Saburo, you and I will work on the accounts today. Tora, you'd better go back and talk to Kobe. Whatever happened, happened in his jail."

*

As he worked over the family accounts, Akitada's mind shifted from time to time to the Tadanobu problem and to Lady Aoi. He was mildly ashamed that he had found her so attractive. Perhaps his lonely life was making him susceptible to strange sexual fantasies and desires.

They were interrupted by a distant noise of a domestic kind. Saburo raised his head and asked, "Should I go see what's wrong, sir?"

Akitada listened. Several people were talking in the corridor. Their voices were raised. Women's voices. "Yes, perhaps you'd better. I hope nobody has upset your mother again." The last was unkind, for while Saburo's mother frequently argued with servants and they as frequently complained about her, Akitada knew that Saburo tried his best and worried that Akitada would dismiss them both.

Saburo flushed and shot up. "Yes, sir."

Akitada could hear him running down the corridor. The noise stopped after a moment. He shook his head at the thought of Mrs. Kuruda having started another war among the servants. Then footsteps returned, several of them. The door flew open and Saburo entered followed by his mother, Sadako, and a weeping maid.

The weeping maid looked bruised about the face and was rubbing her wrists. Sadako's eyes were wide with shock. But it was Mrs. Kuruda who burst into outraged speech and was interrupted by her son.

Saburo told Akitada, "Miss Sadako just found their maid tied up in the garden. She had a letter addressed to you, sir."

Akitada's eyes went back to the maid, who was sobbing more violently now that everyone's attention was on her. He would get nothing out of her for a while. Turning his attention to Sadako, he said, "Please explain what happened, Sadako."

She bowed and said in a voice that trembled slightly, "I had missed Maeko and wondered what had become of her. When I asked, I was told that she had been sent on an errand last evening and had not returned. I wondered if she might have fallen on the way and checked the path to the small back gate. I found her before I reached it. There was a rustling in the shrubbery, and when I looked, I saw her. She was tied up and had her sash stuffed into her mouth so she wouldn't cry out. Between her tied hands was the letter." Sadako paused to glance at the sobbing maid. "I'm afraid she is still very upset, poor girl. I only gathered that someone was lying in wait for her when she went on her errand."

It was a shocking tale – not only because it had happened inside the Sugawara compound, but also because evidently nobody had cared enough to worry about the maid until the following morning.

Akitada looked sharply at Mrs. Kuruda. "Who sent Maeko out yesterday?"

"I'm not sure, sir. There was some talk that we needed sewing supplies, but maids frequently leave on their own, using errands as an excuse. I shall, of course, investigate."

The aggravating woman always had an excuse and the maid was probably in for more misery. Akitada looked at the girl, who seemed to have missed Mrs. Kuruda's glaring at her. He said, "Well, Maeko. You've had a very unpleasant night. When you've calmed down enough, I'd like to ask you about it." He turned to Saburo. "Let's see that letter now."

Saburo handed over the much crumpled paper and Akitada unfolded it and smoothed out the wrinkles. It was short. "Stop what you're doing or you will be very sorry!"

Akitada showed Saburo the letter and then said to the others, "It is a warning to me. Someone I don't know – there is no signature – plans to do some damage here. We must make certain that we have no more intruders. Since Maeko was found inside my property, it is clear that the villain entered it surreptitiously. Saburo will speak to Genba and Tora and I want you,

Mrs. Kuruda, to be certain that the ladies and the female servants are safe. Nobody is to leave on errands without a companion until I've found out what is going on."

Saburo and his mother both bowed and Maeko, having finally been distracted by his words from her personal grief, stared back at him, wide-eyed and open-mouthed.

"Now then, Maeko," he said to her, "do you think you could tell us about it now?"

Her mouth closed and she shook her head. Tears started welling over again. Sadako went to put her arm around the girl's shoulders. "Don't be afraid," she said softly. "You're safe. His lordship will make sure that you and all his people are safe. But you must help him. You do want to help, don't you?"

Maeko looked at her, nodded, and murmured, "Yes."

"You had already bought the sewing things when it happened?"

Maeko shook her head. "I was going to get them. Mrs. Kuruda said we needed blue thread and two more needles, and to ask about the green silk for Lady Yasuko's new dress."

Mrs. Kuruda snapped, "I did no such thing. The silly girl is lying."

"Hush, Mrs., Kuruda," Akitada said quickly. "It doesn't matter. What matters is what happened next. Go on, Sadako. You seem to know how to get Maeko to talk."

Sadako nodded. "Maeko," she said, "if you had not stepped outside the little gate yet, how did the man who attacked you get in?"

The memory of the attack upset Maeko again. "I don't know," she wailed. "He jumped from a bush and hit me." Her hand went to her face where a red mark on her right cheek bone was darkening already.

"Then he was inside already," Akitada said. "How did he get in? Saburo, please check all the gates and speak to the servants. Someone may have left the gate unlatched, or – heaven forbid – was paid to admit Maeko's attacker."

Saburo looked upset. "Someone in this house? But that would mean we have no defense against whatever is happening." His eyes went to the letter in Akitada's hands. "Do you know who is behind this, sir?"

Akitada shook his head. "Not yet," he said. His mind went to Lady Aoi. She had been right. He needed her help. "Well, Maeko," he said to the maid, "I'm very sorry this happened to you. Mrs. Kuruda will make sure you get some rest and light duties for the next day or so."

Mrs. Kuruda bit her lip and bowed.

"Sadako," Akitada said next, looking at his daughter's companion, "thank you for your help and for remembering Maeko. You have never disappointed me."

Sadako's eyes became moist and she smiled tremulously. "Thank you, sir. I've been very happy here."

"I'm glad to hear it. How are you and my daughter getting along these days?"

Sadako hesitated. After a moment, she said, "Thank you, my lord. All is well."

The women left then. Saburo returned to the account books, while Akitada stood, thinking.

"Sir? Do you really believe we have a traitor among us?"

"What?" Akitada looked confused. "Oh, you mean my comment that someone may have let the visitor into the compound?"

Saburo nodded.

"No. I don't think so. It seems like a lot of trouble to deliver the note. But by all means leave the accounts for the time being and see what you can find out from the servants."

Saburo closed the ledger, rose, bowed, and left.

Akitada stood another moment to look again at the warning, then he put on a good robe, and went to see Lady Aoi.

19

Kobe's Grief

Tora was shocked by Kobe's appearance. The superintendent looked old beyond his years and sick. His skin was pale and drawn and his eyes lusterless. But he managed a smile for Tora.

"I'm told you missed me earlier," he said. "I'm sorry Tora. Things have been a little difficult lately."

Never one to beat around the bush, Tora said, "What's wrong, sir? You look like you should be in bed."

Kobe chuckled weakly. "No, no. I'm quite well. It's just . . . well, I'll have no secrets from my friends. My wife is very ill. And the maid is unable to deal with it."

Tora blinked. Kobe had famously walked out on his family of three wives to live in a tiny house with the blind shampoo girl Sachi. He had chosen to spend his life with her and this had brought him to profound poverty because he had left all of his property and most of his income to his former family. So did "wife" refer to one of the vicious females who had forced him to choose? Surely not.

"Lady Sachi is ill?"

Kobe nodded. "Very ill. The doctor says she has no will to get better. What am I to do, Tora?"

"What is wrong?"

"The doctor says it could be a number of things. Maybe dropsy or maybe some kind of natural weakness. She's been this way for weeks, so I don't think it could be a weakness. When I say this to the doctor, he shakes his head and says, 'That means she has no will to live.' And that I should prepare myself." Kobe tightened his lips.

Tora scratched his head. "I'll tell the master. He'll think of something. Is there no medicine that will help?"

Kobe put his head in his hands. "I don't know, Tora. I suppose we all must bear loss sometimes, but this is my Sachi. I've never known anyone to be so good to me."

"Is someone with her?"

Kobe lowered his hands. His cheeks were wet. "Just that incompetent maid. I should be with her. What am I doing here?" He started to rise.

"Wait," Tora said quickly, "Let me send home for someone better suited. Hanae and Genba's wife are both good at nursing."

Kobe sank back down. "Thank you. Maybe they will be able to tell what is wrong. You know, if it's women's troubles? Sachi might not have told me everything."

Kobe sent for a boy to carry the message and handed Tora a sheet of paper and brush and ink. Tora frowned at them, then labored over a simple line, "Kobe's wife is ill. Go there with Ohiro." He gave the paper to Kobe. "You'd better tell them where," he said.

Kobe looked at Tora's scrawl with raised brows. Then he added the address and the words, "Thank you," signed, and impressed the seal. On the outside, he wrote, "To Hanae from Tora."

The boy appeared, Tora gave instructions and a few coppers, telling him that his wife would give him more.

Alone again, they both breathed a little easier. After a moment, Kobe asked, "Er, what brought you here?"

"Oh. The master asked me to see you about Miyagi. He's not satisfied she's guilty."

Kobe nodded. "Neither am I, but I'll be damned if I can find out who did it. And now the judge has moved up her trial date. He'll find her guilty and send her to some labor camp where they'll beat her and rape her every day. She'll be dead in a month."

"How long till the trial?"

"Three days!"

"Dear gods! Why did he do that?"

"He says that cases are piling up and there are complaints about efficiency."

"Complaints?"

"Yes, Tora. Complaints. I get them, too. They mean you can start looking for other work." He ran a distracted hand through his hair, disordering it some more. "I wish I could find out what really happened. It has to be one of the jailers. I've interrogated all of them, and nothing. I'm afraid I can't threaten them, or I'll be called in to explain my methods. And that would lead to dismissal. There have been too many complaints already."

Tora digested that. "But you don't even mistreat prisoners. What complaints?"

"Mostly about attendance to duty. I've spent too much time with Sachi lately."

"Oh." Tora saw the problem. Miyagi's misfortune had happened at a very bad time. Her karma must be terrible. He felt the first doubts that she could be saved. If the gods were against you to this extent, human intervention was useless.

Kobe heaved a deep sigh. "But never mind my problems. What makes you and your master think something can be done?" He paused. "Other than my incompetence in investigating."

There was nothing to say to this, so Tora instead reported about what he and Saburo had learned.

Kobe was silent when he was done. After a while, he said glumly, "No help there. I should have fired that jailer months ago. It was well known that he was a lazy bastard who was rough with the prisoners. Mind you, prisoners do complain, especially the ones that are used to the soft life. Sato was the type. Thank God we don't get many. You'd think a wealthy man like that could send out for food."

Tora nodded. "Yes. That way Miyagi wouldn't have had to bring him his meals."

"It wasn't the jail food. The jailers all said he'd been complaining before when there was nothing wrong with him. But that night he died. After eating Miyagi's food."

Tora said sharply, "We don't know if there was anything in the food. You didn't give some of it to a cat or dog, did you?"

Kobe looked bleak. "I wasn't here. By the time I found out, the food had been thrown away and the cell cleaned."

"Isn't there anything you learned that might help clear Miyagi."

"I wish I could help you. I have questioned all the jailers. They checked all his visitors before allowing them to talk to him. There were a number at the start, but by the time of the poisoning, his only regular visitor was Miyagi."

"What about a Mrs. Kuwada? She runs his business and claims to be his wife."

Kobe raised his brows. "She didn't claim she was his wife when she came, right after he was arrested. She came for instructions on how to deal with his customers and the day to day business. She's his wife?"

"Probably not, but if she had such hopes, she may have had a motive."

"An unattractive female in her forties?" Kobe said. "The prisoner was twenty-six and handsome. It isn't likely . . . though if he made her promises and she found out about Miyagi, she would have been angry."

"Exactly."

"Strange she didn't think to bring him food."

"Yes. If he complained about your fare."

"That was later. Do you want to talk to the prisoner?"

"Yes. Thank you."

Tora felt more discouraged than ever in his life. He had hoped to learn more from Kobe who had once been a very good policeman. But a man with Kobe's burden could not be blamed. That cursed karma.

20

The Tigress

Akitada recalled perfectly that Lady Aoi had told him she lived in the Oimikado Palace, which was, as its name suggested, on Oimikado Avenue. It belonged to one of the empresses, he was not sure which, and was frequently used to house Fujiwara women who, for one reason or another, needed accommodations. It occupied an entire city block with its gardens and outbuildings.

The sun had set, but it was still light enough to reveal elegant blue-tiled roofs and gilded trim. At the gate, a guard in the imperial uniform took his name and called a servant to take him to Lady Aoi. After traversing a confusing network of roofed galleries giving occasional glimpses of small elegant courtyards and rooms with women in rich gowns behind partially open blinds, the servant reached an end pavilion and gestured to the door before disappearing.

Akitada tapped softly. Nothing happened and he tapped a little louder, calling out, "Lady Aoi?"

After a moment, the door opened and Lady Aoi looked at him. Her face lit up with a smile."Welcome, Akitada," she said, inclining her head.

She again wore ordinary clothes, though Akitada did not take note of them on this occasion. His eyes were on her face. He was trying to convince himself that this was a mature woman he had come to see on business, and not at all a seductive female who made his heart beat faster. He said awkwardly, "You are alone?" realized how that must have sounded, and flushed. "I mean . . . I expected a servant to open the door."

Her lips twitched. "No servant. I actually have two maids but they have gone to assist with a child birth in another part of the palace. Come in."

"Oh," he said and came in. Like many pavilions assigned to female members of a family, this one was a single large room. Eating, sleeping, conversation, amusements all were carried out in this one room. Food was prepared elsewhere in the kitchens and brought by servants. Akitada had been in many luxurious women's quarters, notably those belonging to his wife. This one was modest, almost austere, but it possessed something unusual in most women's rooms: it contained a library, and it was not a library of current romantic tales and poetry books beloved by women.

Before he could investigate further, she touched his sleeve, led him to a cushion, and seated herself beside him. "I cannot offer you any food or wine," she said, "but it means we will be uninterrupted and you can speak freely about the Tadanobu matter."

Akitada breathed in her scent. It made him slightly dizzy. Her closeness was disconcerting. He could reach out his hand and touch hers.

He looked and thought he could touch her arm, even her breast under the silk of her gown—which was a strange, deep red color, as warm as he imagined the skin underneath—he could touch her face and caress it the way he used to caress Tamako's, brushing her hair aside to admire her ear, wondering how soon he might get her to let him make love to her.

He drew a ragged breath and looked away, shaken.

"Akitada?" She leaned toward him. "What is wrong? Has something happened? You can speak. We are alone."

He tried to pull himself together. He should jump up and run, run away quickly before it was too late, before he made a fool of himself with his cursed lust for her.

With a great effort, he steadied his breathing. "There has been a warning," he said, taking the letter from his sleeve.

She searched his face. "What sort of warning?"

Akitada moved away a little and handed her the letter, hiding his shaking hand in his sleeve. "I shouldn't have come. It's late. And it's nothing."

She read the note and said, "This is outrageous. How was it delivered?"

He told her and felt incredibly foolish. No doubt she wondered why he could not manage his household without her advice.

But she took it seriously. "Yes," she said, "there is clearly someone who wants Tadanobu to die. He is afraid that you'll find out who he is and stop him. We must hurry."

He had trouble following her logic. "Well, I thought you should know," he said. "But I'd better be on my way. It is late and you are alone. This is quite unsuitable."

She laughed at him. It was a warm, soft laugh. "Unsuitable? In what way? I have no reputation to lose and you are surely not worrying about offending your wife."

He did not look at her and said nothing.

"Akitada, I know about Yukiko. She, too, is a cousin. It grieves me that you should have been treated like that and made to suffer."

Appalled that his shame was apparently common knowledge at court and among the large Fujiwara family, he said harshly, "Never mind my wife. We were discussing Tadanobu. Do you have any information that might help me?"

"Very little, but I have jotted down what I recall of his offenses. Mind you. There are probably more." She rose and went to a set of writing boxes on a bamboo stand. From one of the boxes she took a sheet of paper which she brought to him. "I have added at the end the names that Tadanobu uttered when asleep."

Akitada glanced at the notes, again much too aware of her as she sat down beside him. "What about his words when he is possessed?"

Aoi looked at him with raised brows. "For that you must speak to others. I am a medium. The spirit speaks through me, but I lose myself when he or she possesses me. All I know about it is that it is very unpleasant, like being very ill. When I return to my body, I feel as though I had been near death. Which, of course, I have been."

Akitada bit his lip. Was she lying to him, or was she slightly mad? He decided on the latter. "A pity," he said lightly. "I can hardly trust what the people in Tadanobu's house will tell me."

"No. Not really."

He raised the notes she had made. "Do you recognize any of these names he uttered? I mean in his own voice?"

"One or two. He calls out to his brother, the prime minister, quite often. It means nothing. His brother sits with him frequently. They are close."

Akitada thought that such closeness between a brother with Tadanobu's reputation and the prime minister surely did not promise well for Akitada or the country. He sighed. "Well, I'll do my best to find out who these people are and what happened. And now I'd better leave. He started to his feet.

She held him back. "Please don't go," she said. "I get very lonely here. They only tolerate me because they are afraid of my powers." She gave a toneless laugh. "Little do they know I have no power to hurt them. But I let them think so because I need shelter and clothes and food. It is shameful, but I have no choices left."

Shocked he sat back down. "Surely your family would always stand by you. As they did."

She turned her head away. "Yes, the emperor pardoned me, Akitada. And you have not forgiven that."

"That isn't true," he protested. But she was right. He had not forgiven that she had killed and had not been punished. But he remembered what she had told him about the rape and was ashamed of his stubborn righteousness. He searched for words to apologize.

She saw his face, perhaps read his thoughts. After a moment, she said, "I am very fond of you, Akitada. I've wondered what it would be like making love to you. If you have truly forgiven me, stay and spend the night with me."

Shocked, he asked, "How could you possibly imagine that we'd be good lovers? We fought like cat and dog."

She laughed softly. "You know very little about women, Akitada. Even though you are past middle age and have been married to two beautiful women, you have no notion how passion may make a woman feel like a ferocious tigress. Few men are up to making love to tigers. I think perhaps you may be."

He had trouble breathing. His eyes were on her face, searching for answers, and then he lost himself in her eyes, in their deep, fathomless darkness. It was so simple, he thought. She will lead me to her bed and make love to me, and all I have to do is to let her.

And why shouldn't I? Yukiko betrayed me and is probably still betraying me. Tamako is gone. I'm alone, more alone than I have ever been. Just once I want to lie in a woman's arms again. Just this once.

But he rejected passivity and said with a voice shaking with passion, "Then let us find out together about cats and dogs, or men and tigresses." Rising to his feet, he pulled her up with him, embracing her roughly, burying his face in her scented hair. "Aoi," he said hoarsely in her ear, "you have bewitched me."

She turned her head and kissed him. It had been long since he had tasted a woman's lips—Yukiko's in a forgotten, happier time—and he found himself seized by a lust that made him groan. His tongue invaded her soft mouth and he pulled her close until his hips crushed hers. She responded with a soft sound, a small moan in her throat, then she detached herself.

"My poor Akitada," she said, her eyes shining softly, "has it been so long?"

"Don't ask stupid questions," he snapped, and reached for her again, pulling her against him, his hands busy with her clothes, his mouth seeking hers again. She chuckled in her throat and loosened his sash.

Akitada had been fumbling in vain for her breasts beneath the many layers of silk that were slippery as eels under his questing fingers, and he now remembered that simple, single obstacle, her sash. Undo the sash, and all the outer layers of clothes fall aside.

All but their trouser skirts.

The brief meeting of bare breasts and hands merely set their breaths to racing and made them more impatient. With some tugging at the ties, they stepped out of the final garments. Letting trousers, shirts, and robes slide off their naked bodies, they met again and stood together naked, hungrily searching, touching. He could not remember ever seeing one of his wives naked or offending their eyes with his own bare body. But now he felt invincible and gloried in the moment when the tigress in his arms trembled and sank to the ground. He followed her down into that welcoming embrace of soft arms and thighs and was lost.

When it was over, they were both spent and covered with a thin film of sweat. Akitada could not recall a time when he had felt such deep pleasure, such liberating relief.

"Aoi?" he asked softly after his breathing had steadied. What about the maids?"

"They won't be back for hours."

"I didn't hurt you, did I?"

"No. Oh, no." She leaned on an elbow and bent over him. In the dim light, her face looked like that of a young girl. Her lips were moist and a little bruised, and her eyes shone. "You are gentle. I love you, Akitada," she said. "I think I always have. I'm finally content. Thank you."

This second declaration shook him a little. Did he love her? He desired her, but love was something else. He had loved Tamako. He had not loved Yukiko, even though for a while he had convinced himself of it. But no, he did not love Aoi. He needed her. Even now, drained by their recent encounter, he wanted her again. Instead of speaking, he pulled her close. His lips sought her breasts. She tasted salty and that increased his desire. Her breasts were full, but softer than Yukiko's because Aoi was older, old enough almost to have been Yukiko's mother. Somehow that was good. His body did not care about her age. It only cared about the heat and passion in that body and about the way it drew him in.

And so, after a short and deeply pleasurable time, he took her again, triumphantly, and this time he delighted in her outcry, in her fingernails digging painfully into his back, in her strong and violent movement against his own until she relaxed abruptly under him, and lay trembling.

The tigress overcome.

He left her long before dawn, walking home in a warm daze, still lost in her arms, unwilling to return to the real world, to his family obligations, the world of dangerous men and cruel plots.

Someone had spread his bedding in his study. He lay down, staring up at the dark ceiling, knowing that he had been caught in an entanglement that might well be more dangerous than the case of Tadanobu's *ikiryo.*

21

Tales of Sorrow

The next day brought doubts and a deep sense of guilt.

The doubts had to do with the night he spent in Aoi's arms. The experience had shaken him badly. He was frightened by his own passion for this enigmatic woman.

The guilt had to do with Tora's report about Kobe and Sachi. Akitada recalled his shock at how much Kobe had changed, but he had ascribed it to aging rather than the sort of grief and agony his friend must be feeling when faced with the death of the only woman he had ever fully loved. Kobe had not told him, and that pained Akitada when Tora seemed to have gained Kobe's confidence so easily. He decided perhaps his own manner had been such that it had discouraged Kobe from telling him his bad news.

He thought about this. Kobe had been convinced that Miyagi was innocent. Perhaps too easily convinced. But the troubling thing was that he had not started an investigation into what had happened in his jail. That was, to Akitada's mind, a dereliction of duty. The old Kobe would neither have accepted Miyagi's innocence so easily, nor have neglected a thorough review of the events preceding Sato's death.

Now, however, these troubling matters were explained. Sachi was dying and Kobe had no time for anything else. That was why he had asked for Akitada's help. And Sachi's own case, the case of a blind shampoo girl accused of murdering her client, had reminded him that young women were frequently helpless victims of the evil that played out all around them in the amusement quarter.

Akitada had refused to help, claiming prior commitments. And so Kobe had not confided his real tragedy.

Akitada approved of Tora's offer to send Hanae and Ohira to look after Sachi, and gave him a message to the Sugawara physician to visit the ailing woman and confirm or correct the verdict of Kobe's doctor, who was also the coroner. The coroner was a good man, but Akitada hoped against hope that another, better, outcome might be found, or at least some soothing medicine to make Sachi more comfortable. He had become fond of the young blind woman for her devotion to Kobe.

Then he put on his outdoor robe and went to see Kobe.

He found a distracted Kobe questioning the dismissed jailer again and, being invited to listen, sat down quietly. The jailer, who knelt on the floor, his head bent, looked frightened and babbled. The two guards with whips stood on either side again but apparently had not used them yet.

"Listen, Otsuga," Kobe growled, "you know who else was with him that day. Tell me, or the blame falls on you."

The jailer moaned, "I don't know. I'm innocent, sir. I did nothing. I watched. I worked. I swear by the Buddha." He pulled his head in, expecting to be struck.

"If nobody came from the outside except his wife, then it must have been someone in the jail. Who among your colleagues have had any dealings with Sato?"

"I don't know. I'm mostly on night duty. I didn't watch Sato that day. The others wouldn't have gone to him either. He'd given us enough trouble and kept us from our work."

Kobe growled, "And so you let him die?"

"I swear I didn't know he was dying. She'd brought him food before. He liked it better than our food. You can't blame him."

"Did you watch them together?"

The jailer hesitated. "She came just when I came on duty. I unlocked the cell for her, but someone was calling me away. There was trouble with some rowdy visitors. When I went back, she was ready to leave. And Sato was all right."

Kobe sighed. He looked at the guards. "Take him away."

When they were alone, Kobe said, "You see? I cannot shake him and I think he may be telling the truth. And her trial has been moved up."

"Yes. But I came about something else. I talked to Tora. Why didn't you tell me?"

Kobe looked away. "I couldn't. It would have sounded like making excuses."

"I was afraid of that. It is my fault. I told you I was too busy to look into the Miyagi case and you decided not to burden me with your troubles. But, Kobe, we are friends. You stood by me when I lost Tamako."

Kobe looked at him. "You think Sachi will die?"

"That's not what I meant. I hope and trust she'll get better. Meanwhile, I'll make sure she is looked after properly."

Kobe flushed. "I can look after her."

"Kobe, don't deny me this small thing when I'm so deeply in your debt. At least it will free some time for you and keep your enemies from using this as an excuse to get rid of you."

Kobe was silent for a long time. He sat with a bowed head and Akitada saw that his hair was beginning to turn white and he feared for his friend.

Finally, Kobe spoke. "I no longer want this work. I'm too old and too tired. I have already submitted my resignation and am waiting to have it accepted. I have a small farm that hasn't done much but supply my wives and children with vegetables. Sachi and I will go there. Or I'll go there alone."

So it was already too late. Akitada felt the loss like a painful stab to his stomach. Kobe would be gone soon, just as if he had died. Someone else would be here, some court functionary. And Akitada would have lost another friend. Soon there would only be Nakatoshi, for Kosehira had become more distant since the birth of the child who was not Akitada's. Akitada knew that shame was the reason for Kosehira's distance, but in the end it was a breach of the old closeness.

"You understand, don't you, Akitada?" Kobe asked anxiously.

And Akitada nodded. "I understand, my friend. But it makes me sad."

Kobe nodded, then straightened his back. "Well, in whatever little time is left, I'll try to help this poor young woman. Do you have any ideas?"

"I think we must find out who hated them both enough to do this."

"Yes. Of course. What did Tora and Saburo think?"

"They reported that the woman who runs Sato's shop has a motive. They also wondered about disappointed suitors, but they couldn't get any names out of Miyagi's former master. I'll send them out again. The willow quarter should give us some answers."

Kobe managed a grin. "Tora's good at that."

They parted after this with an embrace. Akitada held Kobe close. "Don't ever forget your friends."

*

When Akitada reached home, he sent Tora out to get some answers about Miyagi's suitors. Saburo he kept with him while he discussed Lady Aoi's list.

"It's probably woefully incomplete," Akitada told him, but there may be something in this. I'll start from the beginning. Tadanobu was still a child when he killed an elderly servant in his father's house. He was ten and it seems he went into a rage because the man, who was his tutor, reprimanded him. The boy picked up one of the heavy carved candle sticks and hit the man on the head."

Saburo raised his brows. "He had a temper even then. I suppose he never outgrew that?"

"I doubt it. Tadanobu's father paid off the family."

"I suppose that makes the father better than the son."

"At least he cared more for appearances," Akitada said with a grimace. "But young Tadanobu acted a good deal more deliberately as an adult. The next incident happened when he was twenty. He had inherited an estate west of the capital and wished for more land. His neighbor, a free farmer called Heishiro, would not sell. For a while, he carried on a series of intimidations perpetrated by people almost certainly in his pay. When that didn't work, he brought charges of having been attacked by the farmer. Before Heishiro could stand trial, he was found murdered. No one was ever arrested for the crime. Tadanobu demanded the land as penalty for the wounds he claimed to have suffered at the farmer's hands."

"Any witnesses?"

"I don't know. The farmer's family may have left the area. We could find out about them. Or about the judge who dealt with all of this."

"This was thirty years ago. Even if we find them, they won't risk raking up the old troubles while Tadanobu is still alive."

Akitada sighed. "Yes, I think that may be our problem with all of these. In any case, at twenty-three, Tadanobu served in the imperial guard and concentrated on love affairs. One of these involved a young noblewoman who trusted that he would marry her. Her name was Ikeda Hatsuko. The Ikedas are an old, respected family descended from emperors, but this branch has fallen on hard times. Nevertheless, she was a court lady and served in the women's quarters of the crown prince. When Tadanobu deserted her quickly for another, she drowned herself in the Imperial Garden, leaving a letter begging her family's forgiveness. The Ikeda family still resides in Heian-Kyo."

"Well, such things happen, sir."

"Yes, but she was young, only sixteen and without friends at court. Young nobles like Tadanobu are forever slipping into women's quarters at night. Tadanobu may well have resorted to rape initially, and later convinced her of his affection. In this case, I would think the family would bear a grudge."

"Ah. Perhaps. The good people, especially their women, can hold on to their anger and grief for a long time."

Akitada thought about this comment. Did the poor forgive and forget more readily? Perhaps. The necessity of surviving in a harsh world left little time to dwell on past wounds. "Yes, I think you are right," he said. "Tadanobu's offenses become more serious after this. Appointed governor of the Northern Province Rikuchu at age twenty-nine, Tadanobu had a quarrel with a local landowner. This man belonged to a northern branch of the Tanaka family and was a nobleman in his own right. The quarrel originated in Tanaka Juntaro's protesting against Tadanobu's systematic draining of the province's rice taxes for himself. Tadanobu did not take such opposition lightly. He retaliated by accusing Tanaka of treason by associating with an Ezo chieftain. Tanaka protested to the court but was killed in the provincial jail. The blame fell on an Ezo jailer who supposedly acted on enemy instructions to keep Tanaka from talking. The jailer was executed, The Tanaka family was driven away or enslaved, and Tadanobu confiscated their lands for himself. The latter was an outrageous land grab, but the court in the capital seems to have overlooked it since treason was involved and an active war with the Ezo was going on."

Saburo nodded. "Terrible story. They have no idea of the situation in distant Northern provinces. They believe whatever their emissaries tell them."

Akitada gave him a curious glance. "Have you visited those territories in your very checkered career as a spy?"

Saburo merely grinned and nodded.

When nothing further was forthcoming, Akitada said, "Right. The next incident was considered too minor to have raised many brows. Tadanobu rode down the child of one of his own retainers in his own compound. He claimed it was an accident."

"But you don't think so?"

"Tadanobu is not a nice man, but I'm not certain. I think the fact that the matter was remembered at all suggests that there was more to it. The father's name was Harada"

"Riding down a child on purpose is a horrible thing."

"Yes. You may be able to find out little more by talking to Tadanobu's servants.

Saburo shook his head. "Frankly, it boggles the mind sometimes what the good people get up to."

"The last case is recent. Three years ago, Tadanobu punished a servant called Isaburo by leaving him tied up outside on a freezing night. The old man died. His wife still works in Tadanobu's kitchen."

"Ah, something else for me."

Akitada nodded. "Yes. That's it. And we'd better get busy, because Tadanobu seems to be close to death. If he dies, I'll be blamed."

22

Miyagi's Suitors

Tora decided to begin his search by talking to Miyagi's maid. Saburo had already seen her, but he had not asked about Miyagi's past, and Tora had a notion that the maid might have been with Miyagi before her marriage to Sato. And if she had not, then the women might have talked together later.

He passed the Rokujo-dono and turned down the small side street. Miyagi's house struck him as typical of many such places that had been purchased by noblemen to keep their mistresses in. He was not sure that this proved anything, though. Sato was a commoner. For a moment he considered Sato. He had been arrested for not bowing low to a ranking official. Good for him. Tora himself had frequently been guilty of the same thing. But Sato was arrested. That was strange, especially since Sato was a man of some standing in the community. A man of wealth. Had that arrest been due to mere irritation on the part of the official, or had there been another motive, something to do with money? Perhaps the official had owed Sato money. Many rich rice dealers lent sums of gold to well-paying clients. He must get the name of the accuser.

His knock on the door was answered by a small elderly woman. Her first words told him that she was from the country, a plain-spoken small female with work-worn hands and the rough clothing of peasants.

"I'm Tora," he said, smiling at her. "My friend Saburo talked to you a few days ago. About Miyagi, your mistress."

She opened the door wider. "Is there news?" she asked anxiously. "How is my sweet lady? They wouldn't let me see her."

"She's well enough for where she is," Tora said. "What's your name?"

"I'm Nihoko. I've been with my little lady since she was a girl. Her family had bad karma and so we came here. I stayed with her and I'll wait here for her until they throw me out in the street. Then I'll wait outside the jail."

Tora frowned. "Who are the people who may throw you out?"

She looked down and wrung her hands. "There's a woman. She says the house belongs to her and I have no business here. She said I had to leave. She will send men to throw me out and beat me if I don't get out."

Tora had a notion that this must be Mrs. Kuwada, the manageress at Sato's business who claimed to be his wife and heir. He said, "Don't worry. If anything happens, you can come to the Sugawara house. We'll look after you."

She cheered up a little. "Please come in. I have only water, but it's cool and fresh. I walk to a spring in the foothills every morning to get it."

Tora accepted and sipped the water gratefully. It was indeed very good water. "Tell me, Nihoko," he asked; "didn't your lady have another admirer before she married Sato?"

She smiled. "Oh, my lady had many, many admirers."

"Yes, of course. But I meant someone special. Someone who also offered to buy her out."

"Maybe. She was afraid of what Master Saeki might do. That's why she begged Sato-san to offer him more money."

"Then she didn't like this man?"

Nihoko shook her head. "No, not at all. She always made excuses not to see him."

"What's his name?"

But here Tora ran out of luck. "No idea, "said the old woman. "He didn't give his name. Very high and mighty. The good people never do in a house of assignment."

Tora nodded. "They're afraid someone will tell the emperor they visit the girls in the willow quarter. Why didn't he just send for her to come to his place like most do?"

"My lady said she thought he was afraid of his wives." She giggled.

Tora laughed, too. "Cowards," he said. Their women run their lives."

She nodded, grinning.

"But how did she address him?"

Nihoko thought. "She called him 'His Honor of the Cedar Grove," once or maybe it was a pine grove. Something with trees."

This was not helpful. The capital had many groves of trees, and those in private gardens could not be seen behind the tall walls and roofs. Tora thought. "You saw this man?"

"I opened the door for him, but it was always dark. You couldn't see much."

"Still, surely you could tell if he was tall or short.

She looked up at Tora. "He was tall, but shorter than you."

"Good. About how old was he?"

"A handsome, well-fed person In the middle of his life," she said, smiling, enjoying the game.

"They can afford to become fat," Tora said dismissively. She giggled. "What about his face?"

"Just a face. I only caught a glimpse once or twice."

"And his voice? What did that sound like?"

She wrinkled her brow in concentration. "A bit like a woman's."

"Excellent. You're learning fast. Anything else about him that you noticed?"

"He has a mustache. Smaller than yours."

But in the end, all of this described the majority of court officials. Tora shifted the topic. "What about Miyagi's other admirers? Anyone who was getting serious?"

"I think so. She was very popular. But none from the good people."

It was a lost cause. Tora had a notion that only a man with power could have arranged Sato's death. Silence fell as he considered his other options. To be thorough, he would go speak to Miyagi's hairdresser again. She might have picked up something about the disappointed suitor.

That was when Nihoko said, "My lady called him the middle counselor."

"Did she? Was that his title?"

"Well, maybe. She said he was the middle counselor of that cypress grove, or whatever."

"What?" That could not be true. There were middle counselors—very powerful officials indeed—but none served in cypress groves. He thanked the maid, tried to reassure her again, and left.

*

He had to return to the willow quarter and the Lotus Pod to find out where the hairdresser might be found.

Kozuke received him with great cheer in hopes of selling some wine and enjoying a lengthy chat, But Tora for once came right to the point.

"Kozuke," he said, "Miyagi's not well. We must hurry. I need to ask the hairdresser some questions. If she has an answer, we may be able to solve this murder."

Kozuke regretfully shelved his hopes and gave Tora directions, but he demanded a promise that he would return as soon as he had some news.

Mrs. Matano lived in one of the large one-storied buildings on the outskirts of the quarter. For a modest fee they housed single people who worked in the quarter. Mrs. Matano's place was at the end of one building and had a tiny garden where a few vegetables shared space with some berry bushes. Tora was lucky: she was home.

When she opened the door, she recognized him immediately. "Oh, Tora-san, right?"

"You have a good memory. Yes, Mrs. Matano. I came to ask you a question."

"It's still about Miyagi?"

"Yes."

"Then come in. I have to leave soon for the Golden Palace. Several ladies are waiting to have their hair washed and oiled."

Her room was as modest as the building and crammed with possessions, ranging from clothes to dishes and boxes holding perhaps her tools of trade. In the center lay two simple straw mats, and there they sat down.

"A cup of wine?" she offered hospitably.

Tora, seeing that she had few luxuries, declined. "It's about Miyagi's customers," he said.

"Oh, I wouldn't know much about them. She was popular, but a person like myself only comes in the day-time before the gentlemen arrive."

Tora's heart sank a little. "I'm only interested in one, the one who wanted to buy her out."

"Two," she corrected. "One was a very noble person; the other owns the bathhouse here in the quarter."

"Really? The bathhouse? Does he make enough money to buy out someone like Miyagi?"

"They say he has land from his mother's side of the family. He was very angry when Saeki sold her to Sato. I know this because I have friends who work for him."

"Interesting. Did he do anything about it?"

"Miyagi told me that he has been a nuisance, bothering Sato at his business. He also threatened Saeki, but Saeki doesn't care about anything except who pays the most."

"What about the noble person. Do you know anything about him?"

"Nothing. Only that he was very eager to have Miyagi."

Tora thanked her and decided on another visit to Saeki.

Saeki was outside his establishment, chatting with a neighbor. He looked cheerful enough, and Tora approached hopefully.

"Saeki," he cried, "I have a bit of time. Let me buy you a meal."

It was midday, and Saeki grinned. "Why not?" Turning to his neighbor, he said, "You must excuse me. A grateful customer."

Tora chuckled at Saeki's quick praise for his business, and the neighbor faded away. Saeki took Tora's sleeve. "Come, the shrimp place around the corner just got a fresh delivery. I don't have much time."

The shrimp place served quickly and the shrimp were fresh and sweet. Tora, who had been unaware of his empty stomach, decided to treat Saeki and himself to a second helping. Before this generous gesture, the conversation limped along.

"So you're still trying to free Miyagi?" Saeki asked. "Doesn't your wife object to your spending so much time on her? Better you should come spend an evening with some of my pretties."

Hanae would indeed object if Tora strayed, but he had become monogamous in his middle age. He loved his wife, and upsets in his marriage were a good deal more troublesome than the fleeting pleasures of a few flirtations. Tora laughed. "This is work. And a good deed, Saeki. You should feel some pity for this young woman who made you so much money."

Saeki pursed his lips, greasy from the fried shrimp he was gobbling. "As to that, I cannot afford to offend customers by taking sides. Most people think she's guilty."

Tora switched to the topic of the suitors. "I hear the bathhouse owner wanted Miyagi. Bet he still wants her. If you help me get the charge dropped, she'll come back to you. She has no place to go."

Saeki cocked his head. "How'd you find out about Yasuie? I don't recall mentioning names."

"Never mind that. Other people know what you try to hide. And why bother? When it's to your interest to help Miyagi."

The shrimp bowl was empty. Saeki eyed it regretfully. "I must get back to work," he said, wiping his fingers on a crumpled tissue from his sash and making moves to get up.

Tora said quickly, "I could eat some more. They are very sweet and fresh." He smacked his lips. "How about it, Saeki?"

Saeki subsided and put the tissue away. "Well, if you insist."

The second order of shrimp arrived, and Saeki dug in. Tora was no longer hungry and watched. After a while Saeki looked up. "You're not eating?"

Tora took a shrimp and chewed it slowly, his eyes never leaving Saeki. After a moment, Saeki said, "Look, I can't tell you. I promised."

Tora said nothing.

Saeki looked at the shrimp and back at Tora. "I don't know his name."

"I don't believe you. You have to put names on contracts. It's the law."

Saeki sighed. "He used someone else's name."

Tora raised his brows. “That’s illegal. And how do you know that?”

“He brought the other man with him to sign.”

“Did he now? How interesting. And who is that other man?”

“He signed the name Kagehira.”

“And his personal name?”

“Akushiro. Kagehira Akushiro.” Saeki looked at Tora anxiously. Are you going to make trouble?”

Tora grinned. “Of course.” He slapped Saeki’s shoulder, popped another shrimp into his mouth, and got up. He paid for the meal on his way out.

23

The Dance of the Moon

Akitada had gone over the list of Tadanobu's crimes and eliminated those cases where proof was impossible or no charge could be brought. That included the murder he committed as a child, since his age excused him, and the case of the young Ikeda woman who committed suicide, because what had been done to her had been acceptable behavior by young noblemen, A third case that he decided to ignore for the time being was the trouble in Rikuchu Province. While Tadanobu's crimes were repulsive and shocking, the place was simply too far away to talk to people. Anything that might have reached the court archives would surely have been cleaned up carefully.

But that left, apart from any investigation Saburo could undertake, several cases where Akitada needed help from his friend Nakatoshi.

He was kept late by Tora, who had returned to report on his latest researches into Miyagi's suitors.

Akitada listened attentively and commented, "You got all but the man's name."

"Yes. I'm sorry, sir. I really think Saeki doesn't know. That man has been very careful. He must worry about his reputation."

"Which suggests that he holds a high rank. Or else he is married and afraid of offending his wife and her family. Either way, he must be well known among the courtiers. Hmm." Akitada frowned. "You know, that name he used–'Middle Counselor of the Cypress Grove'–must mean he writes poetry, or at least dabbles in it."

Tora nodded. "I guess he's a middle counselor, but which cypress grove?"

"It's just a phrase to hide behind. He may not be a middle counselor at all. And there is probably no cypress grove."

Tora threw up his hands in frustration. "That makes no sense. Why not just give a false name?"

"Yes. Good point. It makes me think that he really does write poems and signs them that way."

"Why would he do that?"

"It's an elegant way of being modest."

Tora snorted. "I'll never understand how you good people think."

Akitada chuckled. "Well, I'm seeing Nakatoshi later. I'll ask him if he has heard of this poet."

*

It was after the evening meal that Akitada finally went to Nakatoshi's house. It was a long way, though an easy one on horseback. His friend had risen in the world and purchased one of the charming villas in the eastern foothills. There he resided among pine woods and cherry trees and gazed down at the capital from the clean air of his mountain. He rode to work every morning and returned that way at night.

Akitada welcomed a chance to ride, even though it would soon be too dark to see much. It was, in any case, safer since he was not as likely to be seen visiting Nakatoshi. The investigation into Tadanobu's possession had just taken a dangerous turn with the warning that was delivered to the Sugawara house, and Akitada did not want Nakatoshi involved. He thought with some anxiety of his children and of Sadako who had joined his family. He had grown fond of her quiet ways and grateful for her help with his daughter, who had become willful since she had fallen under the influence of Yukiko. Sadako had had a very hard life, and he hoped to make things easier for her now.

It was a pleasant evening. The air was still cool after sunset, but there was already a moist earthy smell in the air that signaled new spring growth. The sky was clear, and the moon sailed majestically among twinkling stars like an emperor among his courtiers. As his horse took him into the hills, Akitada looked back. Far below some other horsemen were headed for the hills. He caught glimpses of the city below with many lights flickering across the hazy plain. Cooking fires had left that haze behind. When there was a wind, this haze dispersed quickly and the smell of burning wood and grease with it, but this was a still night. Nakatoshi was a lucky man to breathe nothing but this fragrant pine scent.

Alas, the quiet, lonely ride also made him think of Aoi again. The very thought of her, lying alone this night under her silken blankets, heated his blood. The troubles of the present faded when he thought about embracing her again.

Oh, to hold her in his arms again!

So powerful were these memories and images that he found himself outside Nakatoshi's villa before he knew it.

He was received joyfully, greeted Nakatoshi's small children, and refused politely the offer of a meal extended by Nakatoshi's wife. Like Akitada, Nakatoshi had only the one wife, an amiable and cheerful young woman who was the daughter of a provincial nobleman. Nakatoshi, though from a very good old family, had risen due to his own talents.

They withdrew to the study, where they admired the view of the capital below from the veranda before going back inside and closing the shutters against the night air. Then they sat down beside a brazier with some warm wine.

"That feels good." Akitada, put down his cup. "It's still quite cold coming up into the mountains." Though in fact, he had not felt the cold at all while thinking of Aoi.

Nakatoshi smiled. "I'm sorry you had to come so far. Has anything happened?"

Akitada told him about the warning.

This caused concern. "You mean they got inside your compound? How was that possible?"

"I don't know. It could have been carelessness of a servant who left the little gate ajar or someone in my family admitted the man who tied up the maid and left the warning."

"Oh, I hope not the latter. That would be very disturbing."

Akitada nodded. "I went to see Lady Aoi," he said somewhat diffidently. "She had offered to help and I thought I could use all the help I could get."

Nakatoshi frowned. "Lady Aoi?"

"You remember her surely? The medium who committed that murder and got me into some trouble before I could clear matters up?"

"Oh, yes. A Fujiwara cousin of His Majesty. She offered to help? And you accepted after all the trouble she caused you?"

Akitada blushed. "She had been treated abominably by her victim. And she was very apologetic about having got me involved."

Nakatoshi shook his head. "Yes, hers is a sad story, but can you truly trust her?"

"I don't know, my friend. Do you know anything against it?"

Nakatoshi shook his head again after a moment's consideration. "It's just that she is a medium. You hate that sort of thing."

"Yes. But she has access to Tadanobu and she knows the whole family."

"Both of those facts also make her potentially dangerous."

Akitada was becoming frustrated. "I have to trust someone for information. At any rate, she has given me details for a number of cases that may well have led someone to take revenge."

Nakatoshi raised his brows. "And do you now believe that Tadanobu is possessed by an evil spirit?"

Akitada glared at his friend. "Certainly not. He is sick and will probably die. But I must come up with some answers for the prime minister and the crown prince."

"Ah, yes. You had me worried there for a moment. What do you expect to happen when you tell them who plagues Tadanobu?"

"Why, that they try to make some amends for Tadanobu's deeds. Justice, in other words. I'd like to take them the names of all these families, but I want to make sure first that their stories are true."

"And you have come to me to get some confirmation?"

Akitada was still irritated. "If you have any information."

"I'm sorry. I have made you angry. Forgive me. I see that this is a complicated assignment and I should compliment you on having gained the support of Lady Aoi. That's no small matter. She lives like a hermit in the midst of all the court intrigue. A remarkable woman."

Mollified, Akitada nodded. He took Lady Aoi's list from his sleeve and handed it to Nakatoshi. "The first case is useless," he said, "but there may well be something to the rest. Saburo is looking into the matter of servants and retainers harmed by Tadanobu. I thought you might know something about the others."

Nakatoshi pondered the paper a long time, nodding from time to time and frowning occasionally.

Then he lowered the list and looked at Akitada. "The matter of the ten-year old killing his tutor is well known. It seems to foreshadow other instances where Tadanobu lashed out at someone who stood in his way. He has always had a quick temper. But let's look at the land dispute in Fujimi. There was considerable gossip about this. Fujimi is not too far from the capital for the story to have reached the court. In the end, I think, they reassigned Tadanobu and people forgot. I can get you some details, if you like."

"Yes, if you would. If I have to, I could make the trip."

"The matter of the Ikeda daughter is also well known. It was court gossip for a while, I think. It may be that Tadanobu really wanted to marry her. Her father held an influential post as advisor to the crown prince. But the crown prince was forced to resign. It was then that Tadanobu turned his back on her. She was dismissed from court service, and shortly after committed suicide. That caused more talk, since she chose to do so in the imperial gardens. Her family is still in town."

Akitada nodded. "I don't know them, but perhaps I'll pay them a visit." He made a face. "Though it will be embarrassing and cruel to stir all this up again."

His friend smiled. "I doubt that ever stopped you if you really thought it worthwhile."

"True, but in this case . . . well, let's say I have more hope for some of the other stories, the ones where actual crimes were committed. Besides, I don't think there is enough gold in the country to help the Ikeda family."

"Well, then let's move on to Rikuchu. There will be documents in the archives. I can get access without causing too much curiosity. Do you want me to pursue this?"

"Only if it's perfectly safe. I had eliminated this tale as too remote to pursue. It's a shocking instance of the misuse of power and should have had repercussions, especially since this Tanaka had complained to the court about Tadanobu's malfeasance as governor. As a rule, such cases involving theft from tax revenue are carefully investigated. Aoi does not mention any emissary from the capital being dispatched to look into the charges. I wondered about that."

Nakatoshi said dryly, "By that time, Tadanobu's father had become minister of the left, and an uncle was the chancellor. I expect they suppressed it."

"I see. Can you find out anything about the treason charge? Was there really a problem with the Ezo at the time in Rikuchu Province? I recall a fairly peaceful period when I served in Echigo at the time, and our troubles had to do with territory to the north of us."

"I'll see what I can do. Now, the story of Tadanobu riding over a child is new to me. I never heard anything about it."

"The father, Harada, is Tadanobu's retainer. Saburo will look into it."

"Good. That brings us to the last item, the death of the servant tied up in the snow."

"That is also Saburo's investigation. I had really hoped that you might have heard of something else. Something that Lady Aoi isn't aware of."

Nakatoshi raised his brows. "There is one thing. And I think she was very much aware of this matter. I asked you if you could trust her. The fact that she did not mention it in her list troubles me."

Akitada's heart sank. "What? Go, on. Tell me."

Nakatoshi gave his friend a thoughtful glance that made Akitada uncomfortable. He ran a finger around his collar. The brazier was getting unpleasantly warm.

"Well?" Akitada said, irritably.

Nakatoshi refilled their wine cups. "Yes," he said. "Some ten years ago, when Tadanobu was about forty-two or forty-three and had gained promotion to the third rank, he got involved in Fujiwara family politics. He seems to have plotted with his older brother Tadafusa to block the daughter of Fujiwara Motosuke from becoming an imperial concubine. This Nabuko was fifteen at the time, served in Her Majesty's court, and had already attracted His Majesty's attention. But Tadanobu's brother hoped to get the position for his own daughter, twenty-seven-year-old Hiroko, and had hinted so to His Majesty. The emperor was cold to the offer. The brothers seem to have decided that it was young Nabuko who stood in their way. Apparently Tadanobu, who had access to the imperial palace since his promotion, managed to enter the young girl's room under cover of darkness. She claimed he raped her. The visit was discovered by a maid and reported. When he was informed, His Majesty sent Nabuko home. Tadanobu, claiming to have been overcome by his love for Nabuko, promptly proposed, and the family, hoping to put a good face on the scandal, accepted. Tadanobu gained a rich dowry with this wife, whom he elevated to first lady, but Nabuko was apparently desperately unhappy and became a nun the following year."

Akitada was struck dumb by this tale. It was not that he found it unbelievable–indeed with his own wife now active in the imperial quarters, he believed it instantly–rather it was the ingenuity of the plot that ended up benefitting Tadanobu so richly. Tadanobu's methods had been mostly rather crude and obvious in the past. This one had been thought out and managed most carefully.

"What happened to the rejected woman?" he asked.

Nakatoshi smiled. "Nothing. His Majesty looked elsewhere."

"So only Tadanobu benefitted?"

"Yes."

"Do you think that this memory is what is driving him mad?"

"Why not? He was apparently really obsessed with Nobuko. This is something close to him and to someone in his own family. And that probably explains why Lady Aoi did not include the story in her list. It is a Fujiwara family issue. Close family in this case. Her cousins are involved."

Akitada sighed. Nakatoshi was right. Tadanobu's condition might well be due to something that touched him personally. All the other crimes he inflicted on others would hardly leave much of an impression on this man. It made things more difficult. The prime minister would not accept the fact that one member of his family was killing another.

And Aoi? Why had she kept this from him? He found his sudden doubts painful.

"Well," he said after a moment, "thank you. I shall think about Tadanobu's wife, but will you do what you can about getting more information about the others?"

"Yes, of course. But why not spend the night? The road is not safe in the dark, and going down the mountain is worse than coming up."

Akitada smiled. "Thank you, but no. I enjoyed the outing and have faith in my horse. Besides, I want to start my day early tomorrow. There is another matter that needs looking to. And that reminds me. Have you ever heard of someone who goes by the poetic name 'Middle Counselor of the Cypress Grove'?"

"No. I can ask around."

"Thanks. It may be something other than a cypress grove, but I have a suspicion this man dabbles in poetry."

Nakatoshi walked Akitada outside where a servant brought the horse, and Akitada got in the saddle. "Be careful. That downhill stretch is treacherous in the dark," he warned again.

The moon was still out and seemed very bright. Akitada had no concerns about the journey back and set out at a lively canter. His mind was full of what Nakatoshi had told him and his concerns about Aoi's honesty. He did not want to doubt her. He longed for her and toyed with the idea of seeing her tonight. It was not too late and if he hurried . . .

But when the trees closed in, his horse began to slide on loose rocks and he woke from pleasurable thoughts to rein it in. The road now took his whole attention. At one point, they almost fell. After that he slowed to a walk. It was pitch dark under the trees and the moon appeared only fitfully between the branches above. Once or twice he thought he heard another traveler, but it turned out to be nothing. Nobody caught up with him, and he was going so slowly that a more experienced traveler on this road must have done so by now.

He looked out hopefully for the place where another, lesser road split off, because soon after that junction the trees would recede, the light improve and the road get better. And he would once again see the capital spread below in the moonlight.

Then it happened.

A sharp whistle.

He heard the hoof fall behind him, quite clearly this time, and turned in the saddle to look back. The road was dark but he saw a horseman approaching in the murk. At that moment, his horse shied and reared. Taken by surprise, Akitada tumbled from the saddle and fell.

He fell hard on his right shoulder and hip and lay stunned for a moment. He was aware of the sound of other horses on the rocky road. It occurred to him belatedly that his sword was tied to the back of his saddle when he heard his horse whinny in fright and take off. Then they were around him, the one who had come from behind and at least two more. He wondered where they had come from. In the darkness he could only make out looming, moving forms near him and feared being trampled. He called out to warn them.

They did not answer but jumped off their horses and approached.

Painfully he struggled to stand, and that was when they fell upon him with kicks and fists and crushing blows from some object. They took turns, breathing hard, stepping in to hit him and then away.

He stumbled after each attack but tried to fight back, hitting one in the face, and kicking out at another. But the cudgel caught him viciously across the back and sent him to the ground again, where he lay with his face in the dirt and gravel of the road, while his attackers belabored him with cudgel and kicks. He decided they intended to kill him and felt a pang of panic. He tried to plead for his life but was ignored.

Covering his head with his arms, he curled up his body protectively and wondered how long it would take to be beaten to death. He felt increasingly dizzy and unable to breathe, or concentrate, or act.

After what seemed an eternity, the blows that had been raining down on him ceased. Someone pulled his head up by his topknot, bent close, and snarled, "You've been warned. Next time you die." Then he was dropped again.

He was alone.

Akitada lay still, barely breathing. Breathing hurt. Once or twice he gagged on vomit, but managed to suppress it. There was an agony like fire in his chest and back if he moved too much.

After a long time, he tried to shift a foot, then a hand, and an arm. When he tried to roll on his side, he cried out with the pain. When the agony subsided, he tried again, more cautiously.

Eventually, he was kneeling in the road, his head swimming, and his breathing shallow to avoid the stabbing spasms. He sat like this for a long time, swaying a little, resting, only half conscious.

It was the middle of the night by now, and he was not likely to be found. The possibility of his attackers returning to check on him and finding him like this shamed him enough to open his eyes and look around. His horse had wandered back and stood on the side of the road, grazing.

He straightened his back slowly. Each quick movement brought instant agony. Then he attempted to stand and cried out again with distress. He swayed for a moment, doubled over, then collapsed.

When this bout of pain had receded a little, he straightened his back again and raised his head, looking up at the moon while he gathered strength to get to his feet.

The moon danced among the branches of the trees.

He stared at it, afraid that his head had suffered some dreadful injury. Willing the moon to stop, he concentrated, and when its dance slowed a little, he stood up again.

He swayed as before, moaning a little, but this time he did not double over. This time he swallowed the pain and took a step. And then another.

The horse raised his head and watched his approach.

Akitada was grateful. At least the animal did not move away. Step by aching step, he crept closer, murmuring its name, and when he put his hand on its neck, he was bathed in sweat in spite of the chill night air.

Then his hand was on the saddle, and the other reached for the bridle, but the act of getting on the animal's back seemed impossible. He tried, and gasped. He tried again and persisted, groaning with the pain, dizzy with the effort, and this time he got a leg partially over, before falling forward across the horse's neck.

Unperturbed by this unusual style of horsemanship, the horse started off down the mountain, walking slowly and easily as if aware of his master's condition.

24

Household Matters

Akitada's arrival at his home caused consternation and shock. Genba, who had been waiting up for him, opened the gate, and lifted his half-conscious master from his horse. His shouts brought others: the stable boy, who stared, then took the horse away when reminded; Tora, who put his arm around Akitada and with Genba supported him inside and to his room; Mrs. Kuruda, in startling undress, who shouted for maids; and Sadako.

Surrounded by his gathering household, Akitada was placed gently on the bedding that had been laid out for him.

With the awareness of home and his people, Akitada had tried to keep his groans to a very minimum, but the transfer to his bed was excruciatingly painful since the others were unaware of his injuries.

They asked questions. What happened? Who did this? Shall we send for the doctor? Where are you hurt? Are you bleeding?

Between gasps, he tried to answer them.

Tora cursed, then said, "But you had your sword, sir."

Akitada gave him a dirty look. "Don't be stupid. Never got a chance to use it."

"Oh. Sorry, sir."

Akitada decided his response needed more explanation. "It was a trap. Two waited for me and another followed. They startled my horse. It reared and threw me. That's when they fell upon me."

"Bastards!"

A brief silence fell, and then a soft voice asked, "Hadn't you better send for the doctor right away?"

Akitada turned his head and saw Sadako. She was pale and her eyes were wide with worry. She had thrown her everyday gown over the white undergown she slept in, and her hair was loose. He thought her very beautiful at that moment and tried a reassuring smile.

"You are hurt," she said. "I can see it in your face. You are hurt badly." She came closer and knelt by his side.

He saw fear in her eyes and said reassuringly, "Don't worry. I've had worse." He tried to chuckle and regretted it instantly.

Her hand went to his shoulder. "Don't talk. Be still. The doctor will be coming. Are you thirsty?"

He shook his head and winced.

"Oh," she whispered, and now there were tears in her eyes.

Akitada lay still, looking at her. He was breathing shallowly, trying not to move even to rub his nose which itched. Alas, the itch turned into a sneeze he could not suppress, and the convulsion caused his chest, back, and belly to explode in red hot agony. The sneezing bout continued, as they will, and it was Sadako who cried out in sympathy and produced a tissue. He reached for it and managed to stop the painful paroxysms. Then he lay exhausted, ashamed that she had seen him in this condition, with tears running down his face and his nose still running.

Sadako produced another tissue and gently dabbed at his face. "I'm sorry," she murmured. Their eyes met, and something stirred in Akitada's mind, a feeling of gladness, some vague euphoria completely at odds with the situation.

Things settled down then as they waited for the physician. Akitada saw that Saburo had come in and sat quietly by the door, watching.

He smiled and Saburo raised a hand and waved a finger at him. "Sorry about the attack, sir. We didn't know what happened to you. Her ladyship came to see you and said to tell you she'd come back another time."

"I don't want to see her," Akitada said.

Saburo nodded. "We'll say you're asleep"

They all cared for him, really cared for him. The thought brought tears to his eyes again. He was most astonished by Sadako. She had joined his household so recently that he had no reason to expect more than the most basic loyalty from her. It was puzzling. He looked at her anxious face and gave her the best smile he could manage.

She smiled back, a little tremulously, and again he felt that jolt of joy.

He closed his eyes then and tried to rest.

The physician came eventually, asked questions, and had Akitada's clothes removed. The latter was painful as well as embarrassing with so many of his people watching, two women included. Well, he thought, both Mrs. Kuruda and Sadako had been married and must have seen a naked man before.

The doctor probed his chest, tsked, and probed some more. Akitada gritted his teeth.

When the examination was over, the doctor sent for lengths of thin silk and fed Akitada some potion that made him go to sleep.

*

When he woke again, it was broad daylight, the room was empty, and he felt stiff. At least his torso was unable to move. He could move his arms and legs. They were not much help though, when the rest of him was immovable. He could not sit up or get to his feet. And he could not roll over. It reminded him of a beetle on its back, struggling in vain. He wondered what his attackers had done to him to produce this state and was afraid. That cudgel. Yes, they had used it on his back when he lay curled up and helpless in the road. Had they broken his back?

The pain was much better, even the breathing, but what was he to do about the rest? It would be better to be dead. Even feeling the pain was better, because then he had still been able to move a little.

He lay, staring up at the ceiling, wishing he had listened to the warning.

That brought to mind that his attackers had waylaid him on the return from Nakatoshi's house. It meant that they knew where he had gone and that now Nakatoshi was in great danger also, and with him his family.

Akitada closed his eyes and groaned.

A silken rustle and a hand touched his. "Are you in pain, sir?"

Startled, he opened his eyes. Sadako was bending over him, her eyes wide with concern. He croaked, "Not really. I just remembered something I forgot." His mind rebelled against telling her that he was unable to move his body.

She smiled. "Shall I call Tora? You will need help getting up and walking."

Walking? He could walk?

The relief was enormous. He almost laughed, but a weak chuckle hurt. He would be able to stand up? But why was he so stiff? His entire chest felt tight and hard.

Never mind.

"Yes, please call Tora. And there is no need for you to stay." She rose, and he regretted the curt dismissal. "Thank you for looking after me."

And there was the smile again. She bowed and was gone.

Tora came quickly, cheerfully. "Got to have a pee?" he asked.

"Yes. What is wrong with me? I can't move."

"The doctor wrapped your chest while the medicine made you sleep. He says it will keep your ribs from poking into your organs. The bastards broke a couple."

"Oh." More relief, followed by an ungrateful sense of frustration. He had things to do.

He allowed Tora to pull him up and help him to the privy. He found that he felt passable, was able to walk, a little unsteadily, without support, and felt a ravenous hunger.

But first!

"Tora, I need someone to carry a message to Nakatoshi." He glanced up at the sky. "He'll be in his office by now. I'm concerned that the three men who attacked me may be told to do the same to him and his family. I blame myself. I hope we're not too late."

"Not your fault," said Tora. "But I'll take care of it."

Tora helped him to sit at his desk, put paper and writing implements within easy reach, and waited while

Akitada wrote to his friend about the attack and where it had happened, and warned him to take precautions.

*

The day brought visitors. The story of the attack had spread quickly.

Akitada's sister was the first. She rushed in while Akitada was eating his morning gruel, which seemed unusually delicious and laced with fruit and nuts. Sadako had brought it, and he thought she was responsible for the improvement on the usual bland version. His heart warmed whenever he saw her, and he felt glad that he had offered her a place in his home all those months ago.

Akiko looked at him, sat down, and said, "There! I told you to take the children and visit our sister. You will be death of me."

Akitada thought the last funny under the circumstances and chuckled weakly. "It's all the fault of the prime minister and the crown prince."

"What do you mean?"

Akiko did not know apparently. Perhaps Tadanobu's condition was kept a greater secret than he had expected. He explained and saw her eyes widen with surprise and interest.

"But that's wonderful," she said, forgetting all about the attack. "That will surely bring you a promotion and a fat assignment. I shall help you."

Akitada made a face. "I'm not at all sure I want them at this cost . . . not to mention the threat to my family. And no, this is too dangerous for you to meddle in."

Akiko sat up. "What do you mean, 'meddle'? I recall a number of occasions where you were grateful for my help."

"Yes, but Akiko, this is different. I'll not draw your family into this as well."

She regarded him with raised brows. "What threat to your family?"

Akitada explained about the warning.

"Oh," she said. "I see. I thought . . . well, you must take precautions, of course. How did this happen?" She gestured at him.

"I was attacked on my way home from a visit to Nakatoshi's place in the mountains."

"Nakatoshi? Can he be trusted?"

"Absolutely. In fact, I'm afraid I have put him and his family in danger."

Akiko frowned. "All this because Tadanobu is dying? It seems farfetched."

"They believe it's *ikiryo*."

Akiko stared at him. "That doesn't make sense." Her eyes widened. "Is that why you are visiting Lady Aoi?"

"Precisely." Akitada's voice was firm enough, but he avoided his sister's eyes.

After a brief silence, she asked in a deceptively pleasant voice, "What does she look like these days? She used to be a beauty before she started going about in all that fantastical garb, pretending to talk to the gods."

Akitada stole a look at his sister. Her eyes were bright and inquisitive. "Normally she dresses like women of her station," he said repressively, "and yes, she is still beautiful." It was seldom a good idea to give his sister too much information.

"Ah! I am surprised. You used to mock mediums when we were young, and there was that appalling affair a decade or more ago when she turned out to have murdered someone."

Akitada snapped, "She had good reason. And don't be ridiculous."

Akiko merely said, "Hmm," and changed the subject to the children. She left soon after, warning him to be more careful. Akitada was somewhat relieved that she had forgone her passion for investigating his cases, but he was not at all certain that she would be so easily detracted from his relationship with Aoi.

Kobe was the next to arrive. He expressed his concern and listened to the details of the attack. When Akitada finished, he shook his head regretfully. "Not much to go on. It sounds like hoodlums. They often roam the roads just outside the capital. Either they were hoping to find money on you, or they were paid by someone else."

"The latter, I suspect," Akitada said.

"Oh? Who and why? I'll get my people to investigate immediately."

"No, Kobe. This is connected with the prime minister and I'm not at all sure yet how. But it isn't a matter for you and probably will never be. How's Sachi?"

Kobe's face brightened a little. "Thank you for all your help. Your doctor has given her something to make her more comfortable, and Hanae and Ohiro have been wonderful."

It was obvious that the doctor had not had good news about Sachi's illness, or Kobe would have said so. Akitada refrained from asking and merely nodded. Kobe asked a few more questions about the attack and the prime minister, but when Akitada steadfastly kept his silence, he left.

To Akitada's embarrassment, Lady Aoi arrived next. She walked in while Sadako knelt beside him, serving him his midday meal on small trays. Aoi eyed her with surprise and asked, "Who is this?"

"Sadako is my daughter's companion. Sadako, this is Lady Aoi, a friend of mine."

Sadako bowed. Aoi ignored her and came to sit on his other side in a proprietorial manner, pouring out questions.

"My poor Akitada. Should you be up?" she asked, putting her hand on his arm. "Are you in pain? What exactly happened? Oh, Akitada, I'm so sorry. I wish I could have spared you this."

Sadako had frozen in mid gesture of handing him a cup of wine she had poured. She rose. "Perhaps Lady Aoi wishes for privacy. I can return later," she said with a catch in her voice.

Aoi nodded to her. "Yes. I can easily look after him, my dear. You will have other work, no doubt."

Akitada regretted this encounter and thought Aoi rather high-handed. On the other hand, he had introduced Sadako as one of his servants, and Aoi was his lover. Though unacknowledged still, the fact gave her the right to speak to him privately. He eyed her a little nervously. In daylight, she looked older, more self-assured than Sadako. She was, perhaps, the more beautiful. He let his eyes trace her features, saw her smile a little, and relaxed.

"You are beautiful and desirable," he said, "but I'm in no shape to prove it to you. The doctor says I have broken ribs. They make moving painful."

She chuckled. "As long as it isn't worse. I was frightened. Oh, Akitada!" She caressed his cheek and added softly. "I'm afraid you're going to be my ruin. I think of nothing but you. I even wrote a poem after our night together."

He had forgotten the convention of exchanging poems after a night of lovemaking. Taking her hand, he kissed her palm. "Forgive me. I'm no poet, Aoi. Did you bring the poem?"

"No. I was ashamed to have you see it."

Such shyness was not like her, but he found it very attractive. "A pity. It would have pleased me." He wished to go on with this conversation, but in his present state it was inadvisable. Even holding her hand was too tempting. He kissed it again and released it.

But there was the matter of the attack, the danger to Nakatoshi, and the whole sick business of Tadanobu's possession. He asked, "Do you have any idea who might be behind this?"

She looked horrified. "Oh, no, Akitada. I would have warned you. Oh, you still don't trust me." She turned away.

"Don't be silly. I have to find out who is behind this and you are the only one who might have some information. I fear for Nakatoshi and my family."

"Nakatoshi?"

"He's my friend. I asked for his help also, since he works in the Ministry of Ceremonial and knows most of the influential people. I was on my way back from his house when I was attacked."

"I know of him. Can you trust him?"

That was what Nakatoshi had asked about Aoi. This amused Akitada and reassured him somewhat.

Once or twice he had worried that Aoi might be playing some cruel game with him. But she could not have known about Nakatoshi. And then there had been their night of love. Surely no woman could pretend such passionate desire unless she was in love. He reached for her hand again. "Yes, my dear, I can trust him. But your presence here beside me is an agony when I cannot make love to you."

Her face glowed with pleasure. She bent toward him and kissed him. The touch of her lips was like a jolt and he responded eagerly. With a small chuckle she sat back. "I shall leave you now, but mind you come to me as soon as you can. I shall make love to you and promise you you'll not feel any pain."

There was a loud hissing sound, and both looked toward the door. In it stood Yukiko, gorgeously gowned in pink, red, and white with palest green layers for the spring season.

She glared at both of them. "So, Aoi! Have you finally managed to take my place beside my husband?" Yukiko's voice was as icy as her expression.

Aoi rose, pale and shocked.

Akitada, beyond furious at Yukiko's behavior, snapped, "You have no place beside me, Yukiko. You lost that a long time ago."

Aoi found her voice. "Cousin," she said, inclining her head, "You look well. How is Lord Okura these days?"

Yukiko flushed and shot a glance at Akitada. She opened her mouth to reply, but Aoi had already swept past her and out the door.

She left Akitada behind, aroused by her kiss and her promise, to try to deal with his wife. He did not think he could hate Yukiko any more than he did at this moment when Aoi had revealed the name of Yukiko's lover who was most likely the father of the child she had pawned off on Akitada.

Yukiko said, "Have you no shame? She's a whore!"

"Get out!" he snarled.

Yukiko flushed with anger. Her chin came up. "Unlike your lover, I have a right to be here. I am your wife."

"You have no right. You lost that quite a while ago. I don't want to see you."

The red in her face receded, leaving her pale. "We have a child. In the eyes of the world we are married."

"Your world isn't my world. And your child isn't my child."

Her eyes widened. "Are you breaking your word?"

"I am divorcing you." He had not planned this moment, but once he said the words, he knew it had been inevitable.

She stared at him. "You can't. Think of the scandal. You would kill my father."

He had agreed to maintain their sham marriage because of his affection for his old friend, but it no longer seemed possible to bear. He said, "Things have gone too far to let them continue like this."

She came closer, suddenly intent. "Don't be a fool, Akitada. I can help you with your career. I have been working to have your rank raised twice this year. I have Her Majesty's ear and frequently attend His Majesty also. As a matter of fact, I came today to warn you about meddling any further in the Tadanobu matter. Apparently I was too late. You must stop this nonsense. You've gone far enough. Leave it be or things will turn out worse than a couple of thugs in the forest."

"I don't want your help. And I want you to stay away from my daughter."

She was silent for a moment. Then she bowed her head. "I'm sorry. I see you're in pain. I won't plague you now. But Akitada, you must reconsider this. For the sake of the love we once had for each other."

He did not honor this with a response and, after a moment, she turned and left.

A period of calm intervened. Akitada thought about the exchanges between the three women. He acknowledged for the first time that Aoi was now very much a part of his life and that Yukiko no longer belonged. Divorce was unavoidable. Even if he did not take Aoi for his wife, he wanted to be free to love her. Years of restraining his desires in order to be a good husband or because he feared another entanglement had brought him to this place where he no longer cared. He was getting old and he was alone. He hated both facts of his life. Aoi offered love and companionship.

Briefly his thoughts turned to Yukiko's lover. Okura? Had he met the man? There were so many handsome young nobles hanging about the court, it was unlikely. It was not his world and would never be. Strangely, knowing his name no longer mattered.

25

Saburo and the Strange Character

Having completed his work of keeping the Sugawara accounts straight, Saburo put on his blue robe with the black sash, the one that suggested he was a minor official, tied on his black hat, and set out on his investigations.

It had been easy enough to discover the name of the retainer whose child Tadanobu had ridden down. The Harada family still lived in a house belonging to Fujiwara Tadanobu, though the child's father had since died. The mother and the rest of the family made a living supplying Tadanobu's kitchens with produce from his farms, utensils from the markets, plain fabrics for servants' clothing from the shops in the capital, as well as reed shades, woven mats, and all other basic household needs.

Harada had three sons who variously managed transportation, and two daughters who helped their mother run their household and served when needed in the great house.

Saburo was received politely by Mrs. Harada, a middle-aged woman in a neat black dress who wore her long hair in a knot at the back of her head. The house was substantial and made Saburo wonder if they had been given it to live in as pay-off for the child's death.

He introduced himself as a city clerk who was verifying the entries in the tax accounts.

"But we serve Lord Tadanobu," she said quickly. "We don't pay taxes."

Saburo frowned. "Is that so? Allow me to make some notes. I expect you'd like to have this matter cleared up?"

She nodded eagerly. "Oh, yes. You see, we are retainers of the family. And we still serve them." She led the way to the main room of the family dwelling, where they seated themselves on cushions and Saburo took a small box from his sleeve. This he opened, removing a sheet of writing paper, a brush, a small ink stone with a cake of ink, and a small, stoppered water bottle. Dripping a bit of water on the stone, he rubbed some ink while continuing his interrogation.

"A very pleasant and large house," he said, glancing around.

"It belongs to the master."

"Ah. I see. He treats his loyal retainers well, does he?"

"He does." She nodded firmly.

"You are fortunate." Saburo had some ink now and took up his brush, making notes.

"And how many in your family?"

She answered, giving their ages and genders.

Saburo looked up from his notes. "We seem to have another child, a boy, in our records."

Her face became sad. "That was Yuki. He had an accident and died."

"Really? What sort of accident?"

"He fell under a horse. It was terrible." Tears filled her eyes. "He lived for a while, but in such pain. The master was good. He sent us food and a monk to pray. But it was no good."

"Ah. Your master must be a very good man who walks in the Buddha's footsteps."

"Oh, he is, but now they say he's dying himself. I worry about what will become of us."

"Have you served him long?"

"All my life. My mother was Lord Tadanobu's nurse."

Saburo was pleased with this information. Perhaps his visit was not pointless after all. "They tell a story that he was violent as a child. Is that true?"

She became angry. "People tell lies. It's that old tale about him killing his tutor, isn't it?"

Saburo nodded.

"Well, he was a little boy and that man, an old man, was very harsh with him. A little child like that cannot kill a grown man. My mother told me that the tutor was too old and sick to live. And the tutor's widow and children were taken care of by his lordship's father, who was as kind as his son."

"Ah, I see. Well, thank you for clearing all that up." Saburo cleaned his brush, folded his papers and packed everything away, then took his departure.

He next walked to Tadanobu's palatial residence. There he found signs of worry about their master's condition. An abundance of monks sat about praying, and the sounds of ringing bells and chanting came from inside the main house.

Taking off his hat, he tucked it into his sleeve, then identified himself as a merchant who wished to verify an order with the cook. He was passed on into the walled service yard where he entered the kitchen building. There were a lot of servants at work, most of them women. Saburo asked for the cook and was taken to a fat middle-aged woman who glared at the interruption.

"Mrs. Isaburo?" Saburo asked pleasantly.

"Nah," she answered with a disdainful nod toward a corner where a frail elderly woman knelt, cleaning radishes and cutting them up. "She used to be the cook but she's getting too old."

Saburo thanked her and walked over to the old woman. She raised a small round face, heavily wrinkled, and looked at him from dull eyes. Saburo squatted beside her and said, "Good morning, grandmother. I see you're busy getting the evening rice ready."

She shook her head without stopping her work. "The evening rice is cooking over there." She nodded toward three large rice ovens. These are for pickles for the monks' meal."

"I bet your pickles are famous."

She nodded. "The master always loved my pickles." She paused in her work to cough, then looked at him. "They say he's dying."

"Yes." Saburo arranged his face into a solemn expression. "Ah. It comes to all of us."

"My husband died. It was too soon. If he'd been careful he might've lived." She was matter-of-fact about her loss.

"He was careless?" Saburo asked quickly.

"Yes. He spilled wine on one of the master's guests."

"How did he die from that?"

She summed up the story efficiently. "The master punished him by making him stand watch all night. It was cold and he got sick and died."

Again there was no sign of any resentment. The old man was justly punished and happened to catch his death because it happened to be cold. Saburo asked, "You don't blame your master?"

She stopped working again to blink at him. "Blame the master? It was his *karma.* Being old, he'd gotten very shaky. That's how he spilled the wine."

Saburo shook his head and departed.

So far he had nothing to report. Not that his own master believed an angry spirit could travel from one person's body into another. But he had hoped for a good story anyway; something that the master could use in his report.

Outside Tadanobu's mansion, Saburo paused in thought. He was not too far from the amusement quarter. While Tora was occupied looking after his injured master, he thought he might as well pay a visit to that bath house owner who had hoped to purchase Miyagi. She was running out of time; the trial was the next day. He shook his head again. Too much was happening too fast.

He set out, walking rapidly, feeling foolish. As if his hurrying might help Miyagi's case.

He found the owner of the Transcendent Pleasures Bath House in an argument with an odd-looking man. The man was elderly, thin as a stick, and draped in multi-colored women's robes that had clearly been tossed out by some fastidious courtesan. The effect, with his long, straggly hair tied lopsidedly on top of his head and his bare feet and legs, was that of a fancy scare crow.

The argument apparently dealt with the scarecrow asking to be paid to move away from the entrance to the bath house. The owner seemed to think the dirty creature discouraged trade.

Fascinated, Saburo joined the little crowd that had gathered. They had smiles on their faces. The bath house owner scowled. The scarecrow enjoyed the attention, pausing now and then to make elegant bows to his audience and getting applause.

"Who's that?" Saburo asked the housewife standing next to him, clutching her towel to her breast.

"It's old Ohiya," she said. "He's a drunk."

"I'm not paying you, you thief!" the bath house owner roared. "Get away or I'll call the warden."

"You can't make me leave. I'm a free citizen of the capital. I have a right. If you want me gone, make it worth my while, you skinflint." Ohiya countered.

Saburo recalled Tora talking about his recent meeting with this scarecrow. Ohiya was someone who knew the quarter well and he was not yet drunk, though clearly getting desperate for his favorite refreshment.

"Come, gentlemen," Saburo said, smiling benevolently at both, "it's too nice a day for altercations. What say, we'll have a warm cup of wine next door and contemplate the future in a relaxed fashion? I'll pay."

They both stared at him in surprise. Ohiya was the first to wake from his consternation. "Ah, good morning, friend!" he cried, embracing Saburo with a smell of unwashed clothes and bodies. "You are wise and generous to a magnificent measure. The Buddha smiles upon you."

The bathhouse owner frowned. "What do you want and who are you?"

Saburo made him a bow. "Name's Saburo. I manage Lord Sugawara's household and take an interest in my master's work."

Ohiya clapped his hands. "A friend of the handsome Tora, I think?"

Saburo nodded. "He mentioned you and how you met."

"Ah, those were the days1" Ohiya turned to the bathhouse master. "You should have seen me then, Morikage. Come along. What can you do here? Business doesn't start for an hour yet."

Morikage glanced back at the bathhouse, its doors open but only his attendants peering out, and nodded reluctantly.

The wine shop was modest and also empty at this hour. They sat outside on benches so Morikage could keep an eye on his business. Saburo ordered and said, "As I mentioned earlier, I take an interest in my master's work, and he's taken an interest in the case of the beautiful Miyagi. I believe you both know her?"

Morikage scowled. "Beautiful but stupid," he said darkly.

"Brains are not required in her business." Ohiya was watching for the waitress with their wine.

"True, but she did well for herself," Saburo commented.

Morikage gave a snort. "Look where it got her. What a waste!"

"I understand you courted her yourself?" Saburo said with a grin.

Morikage scowled. "I didn't have enough money for that greedy bastard Saeki, and she didn't think I was good enough." He added in an injured tone, "Though I would have ruined myself for that woman. I was mad about her."

The wine arrived, Saburo paid, and Ohiya was pouring his second cup before the waitress had disappeared. He raised his cup. "That's what you get for loving women. Drink, my friends."

"You loved boys and ended in the gutter," snapped Morikage.

Ohiya looked offended. He considered an answer, but then drank down his wine instead.

To keep the conversation on the topic, Saburo said, "I understand she almost went to a high-ranking nobleman. I wonder she preferred Sato to becoming a great lady."

Morikage nodded. "Can't blame her for that. Sato was young and handsome. And besides that counselor liked hurting his women."

"Really? How do you know?"

"I have a bathhouse. I see the girls coming in with the bruises and cuts, calling for lotions and ointments. Miyagi looked like that a couple of times." He became reminiscent. "What a body that girl has."

"But how do you know he did that?"

"The women talk. They talk to each other and to my attendants. I hear all about it."

"And he hurt Miyagi?"

"That's what made me go and make that greedy bastard Saeki an offer I could ill afford. Terrible way to treat a sweet and beautiful girl!"

Saburo raised a brow. "I thought you were mad at her."

Morikage shook his head. "I'm mad at what happened to her."

"Good. So am I. So's my master. We think she's innocent. We think that counselor may be behind Sato's murder. Unlike you, he did get angry that Sato got her."

Morikage put down his wine cup and stared at Saburo. "You think so? The dirty bastard!"

Ohiya had emptied the flask. Waving it, he interrupted, "Hey, Saburo, how about another? I need just a bit more inspiration to remember that counselor's name."

Now the other two stared at him in surprise.

"You know his name?" Saburo asked in disbelief. "How come?"

Ohiya grinned toothlessly and waved the empty flask in front of Saburo again.

Saburo muttered a curse and shouted to the waitress for more wine. "Now give!" he snapped.

"Not until I've had my wine."

Morikage laughed. "You can't believe anything he says. Most of the time he's too drunk to see, let alone find out things."

Ohiya gave him a look and raised a shoulder disdainfully. "I'll have you know there was a time when I visited the houses of the great. Believe me, they served me better wine than this." He waved a dirty hand toward the waitress, who was filling their cups. Ohiya emptied his, snatching the flask and holding on to it.

Saburo paid and then they sat and watched as Ohiya emptied another cup and refilled it.

Saburo said through clenched teeth, "I swear I'll beat you if you lied to me."

Ohiya's eyes were becoming glassy. He belched. "What was the question again?"

Saburo made a fist and held it up before the scarecrow's face. "I want the name of the man who tried to buy Miyagi."

"Oh, why didn't you say so? Ishikawa. Yes. He has a fine big house and garden. I took my best five dancers there to perform at his coming of age party. You should have seen us." He belched again and held up the flask. Saburo snatched it away.

"What's his full name and where is this house?" he demanded.

Ohiya wrinkled his brow. "I can't think," he whimpered. "Some more wine?"

"No." Saburo leaned toward him. "Out with it, you wine-sodden useless piece of dung!"

"I . . . think maybe Ietada. Or maybe Nagatada. It was a long time ago."

"How do you know he's the same man then?"

"He limps. Saeki says he has a clubfoot."

"Saeki knew him?"

"Of course? How else could he sell him Miyagi?"

Saburo suppressed a curse for the lying Saeki. "Where is this Ishikawa's house?"

"On Ogimachi. A big house. Cypresses at the gate. You can't miss it."

Saburo handed him the flask. “Well done, old fellow.” Rising to leave, he added, “It’s been a pleasure, gentlemen.”

26

The Exorcism

There was another visitor late that day. Kosehira came.

His friend looked as bad as Akitada felt. The flesh seemed to hang on him more loosely and his normally round cheerful face was drawn and old.

He came in slowly and on soft feet and said, "Akitada?" so tentatively that Akitada had not noticed his presence as he lay dozing.

"Kosehira?" Akitada tried to rise and subsided instantly with a groan.

"Don't move! I'm so sorry. I had to come."

"I'm glad. It's been too long. Are you well?" The latter question was due to the shocking change in

Kosehira. It reminded him of Kobe. Both men were shockingly altered, but there was a difference. Kobe suffered from the sickness of grief. Kosehira's appearance was more puzzling.

Kosehira sat down beside Akitada. "Yes, yes. But how about you? I heard of the attack. Is it very bad?"

"They hurt something in my side. It was very painful to move at first, but the doctor has wrapped me tightly in silk and there is little pain now. The trouble is, I cannot bend enough to get to my feet at the moment. Tora has to give me a hand. I expect it's temporary."

"Sounds nasty, but it will get better. I couldn't get any information out of Yukiko."

So Yukiko had gone straight to her father after their quarrel. Akitada made a face. "My wife was preoccupied with other matters."

Kosehira sighed and looked down at his hands. "Yes. I blame her. I really do, Akitada. She says you found someone else and that you wanted to divorce her. Can that be true?"

Akitada felt a great urge to spare him and lie, but in the end he just said, "Yes."

Kosehira's face contorted painfully. "It's my fault. And hers. I told her so."

"Let's not apportion guilt, Kosehira. I don't feel up to claiming my own share at the moment."

Kosehira said nothing, but he wiped away a tear. They remained in silence until Tora walked in, saying cheerfully, "Time to pee yet, sir?"

Akitada flushed and snapped, "No. Get out!"

Tora saw Kosehira belatedly, muttered "Sorry," and left, closing the door behind him.

The friends looked at each other warily. Akitada's lips twitched, and Kosehira chuckled.

"Poor fellow," he said. "He meant well."

"Yes. I'll have to apologize."

"I trust you'd accept my assistance if needed?"

"Yes, of course, my friend."

Kosehira's eyes watered again, but he still smiled. "I shall always love you, you know. I hope you haven't given up on me?"

"No, Kosehira, but I was afraid of coming between you and Yukiko."

"No. I'll also always love my daughter. And my grandchild." He shook his head. "Will you wish to renounce her?"

"No. Of course not." Akitada was aware that his debt to his friend and to Yukiko still saddled him with a daughter he had not fathered. There was nothing to be done about that. He could not shame either of them and ruin the child's future."

"I wish to adopt her," Kosehira announced.

"Oh?"

"Yes. I've become very fond of the little sweetheart and look forward to raising her. All my children are too old to have much time for their father these days."

Akitada smiled. He recalled vividly Kosehira's delight in playing with his children and the cheerful gatherings of the whole family at mealtimes. These had been in such contrast to his own loveless upbringing that

Akitada had been envious. It had been a large factor in his marriage to Yukiko. Alas, for him such a family life was apparently not to be. But for the first time it occurred to him to feel sorry for the fatherless child his wife had forced him to accept. He had been unable to feel anything apart from resentment for the girl. How unfair this was to the child! Of course, his innate sense of justice would have made him treat the growing child as gently and with as much care as he had shown his own children, but was it enough? He said, "She is lucky then. I know of no better father than you."

Kosehira suddenly looked happy. "Then you will permit it?"

"Yes, Kosehira. I'm afraid I could not have forgotten, and that would have been very hard on her."

"My dear Akitada, that's not true. I know you. You would have been just. But my daughter has hurt you badly, may the Buddha forgive her."

Kosehira hurried home to start the process of adoption, and Akitada called for Tora. The message from the prime minister arrived while he was eating his evening rice. Tadanobu's illness had worsened and he was to attend a formal exorcism at his house the next day. Apparently Tadanobu's condition had reached a crisis stage and a last effort was being made. This last effort included Akitada.

*

Tadanobu's crisis had also become Akitada's. He could not excuse himself from the summons under the circumstances. Thus, with Tora's help and some ill-tasting powders left by the doctor to subdue the pain of movement, Akitada dressed in court attire, though he opted for the most comfortable clothes he could find. He sent a message ahead that he had suffered injuries and would need some assistance when he got there. That should at least excuse him from kneeling and touching the floor with his forehead, a complete impossibility under present circumstances. Actually, he felt less pain than he had expected.

He traveled by carriage, accompanied by Tora. They were readily admitted by the gate guards and found themselves in a great courtyard filled with carriages and milling people. All around them rose the curving roofs of many great halls and gates. Among the people outside were court officials and a large number of monks. Elegant carriages were drawn up along a gallery, their oxen removed. Akitada's carriage backed up to the gallery surrounding the main house, and Tora extricated Akitada from it. Standing on his feet again, Akitada felt strangely buoyant as he followed the servant who met them to Tadanobu's private quarters. Akitada walked slowly, paying attention to his surroundings, noting the obvious wealth of Tadanobu and the beauty of flowering cherry trees in tubs. It was quite enjoyable.

Tadanobu's room was large and full of people. Smoke of many censers being swung by chanting monks filled the air with a silver haze and a scent that was pervasive but pleasant. All the shutters had been closed so that all but the center of the room was murky from lack of light and the dense atmosphere. Akitada was dimly aware that many people stood and sat around.

The center of the space, by contrast, was brightly lit and contained only four people. The light came from a number of tall candelabra whose wax candles burned brightly, flickering in the air currents from the many swinging censers. The dying man lay on his silken bedding, covered with rich court robes. He was breathing heavily. Beside him sat a high-ranking monk in a gray robe covered with an ornate purple and gold silk stole and Aoi. Aoi wore a simple white silk gown and her long hair lay spread out across her shoulders. Her eyes, large and mysterious in the pale oval of her face, met Akitada's but she gave no sign of recognition.

The only other person close to the dying man sat on his other side with his back to Akitada. A servant now approached this man and whispered something, and he turned to look at Akitada. It was the prime minister, his face wet with tears. He waved a peremptory hand, and Akitada approached stiffly, inclining his head.

The prime minister asked in a low voice, "Can you sit?"

"With help."

Another gesture and a servant brought a pillow and lowered Akitada gently on it next to the prime minister.

"We are just beginning," said the prime minister, wiping away tears with his sleeve and turning back to his brother.

The dying man, his eyes closed, took another stertorous breath, as if preparing himself for an ordeal.

It occurred to Akitada that the doors and shutters of the room were closed to keep evil spirits out, but the close air, the many people, the guttering candles, and the incense made it hot and even more unhealthy for the dying Tadanobu. Akitada was soon sweating, and the abbot or bishop fanned himself as he began to recite the magic formula of the thousand hands. Aoi's skin wore a sheen of perspiration, though her light silk gown must have been a lot cooler than Akitada's court robe or the abbot's heavy stole. Aoi had no fan, but she held a thin wand with white papers attached.

Akitada wished himself elsewhere, but he was also fascinated. The priest had begun to read mystic incantations in the usual mellifluent recitation style. The rhythms lulled Akitada into a relaxed, dreamlike state from which he woke abruptly when the voice suddenly became louder and harsher. The priest gestured at the sick man with his fan, making stabbing and slashing motions. The air above Tadanobu seemed alive. It shimmered and danced. Akitada gave himself a mental shake. The priest turned to Aoi. He seemed to be asking questions. Akitada saw that she was trembling violently. Her eyes were closed and her face had sunk to her breast. She twitched and moaned as the priest shouted his demands pointing his fan at her. He was addressing the vengeful spirit that had resided in Tadanobu and now occupied the body of Aoi. Each demand was emphasized with a violent slash of his fan. Aoi cried out and collapsed, falling forward. She rolled and kicked as if in agony, ending up on her back. Her gown was disordered, revealing bare legs and leaving one breast exposed. She moaned, twisting her hips upward and beating the floor with her hands. Akitada thought of the night they had lain together. The whole performance resembled the climax of the sex act. He could not take his eyes off her, off that white breast, off her hips and spread thighs, and he shivered with desire and shame.

Suddenly nauseated, he wanted to get up and shout at all of them to stop. He wanted to go to her to cover her and straighten her skirts. But he could do none of those things. He sat paralyzed, not just by the tight silk bindings around his own chest, but by the strange lassitude that had seized him.

Aoi screamed and arched her back, then screamed again. Then her struggle stopped suddenly. She began to talk in a strangely high voice. The priest asked for the spirit's name and why it tormented the patient, and a high voice answered from Aoi's lips. The priest spoke again, angrily, telling the spirit it must go away and leave Tadanobu in peace. Aoi wept, tossing her head back and forth; she wailed and argued. After a long time of these exchanges, she finally became quiet and lay still.

A stirring went through the room as people woke from the spell of the event.

The priest looked across at the prime minister. "How is your brother?" he asked.

The prime minister started, bent over Tadanobu, and said, "He is breathing better. I do believe the crisis is over. May the great Buddha be eternally praised." And he burst into tears again.

The audience moved and voiced expressions of gratitude to the Buddha, the gods, the spirit world, the priest and other, more obscure, influences.

Akitada felt strangely detached from all of it. It must be the incense, he thought. It was making him lightheaded. He knew he should get outside and breathe some clean air but did not have the will power to rise.

The priest and some young women bent over Aoi who seemed to be coming round after her trance.

Could her possession have been real? The idea was distasteful. He wanted the woman he loved to be in control as she had been with him, not subject to fits of delirium. But if she had pretended, then it was shocking behavior to roll about on the floor half naked before an audience of strangers. He felt sickened, literally nauseated, by what he had witnessed.

The women, all high-ranking members of the Fujiwara family to judge by their elegant and expensive clothing, surrounded Aoi as she got to her feet and escorted her out of the room.

The prime minister now turned to Akitada. He was smiling with happiness. "A miracle! And you, Sugawara?" he asked. "You have nothing to say?"

"I am overcome, sir," Akitada said truthfully.

"Ah, yes. A powerful exorcism. It took the work of the very best to exorcise this evil. The abbot normally only serves the imperial family, and Lady Aoi is my own cousin, a former shrine virgin."

"I don't think I caught the name of your brother's tormentor."

"It meant nothing to me. Some peasant no doubt who objected to paying his rice taxes. Let's be glad it's over."

Akitada said dryly, "An official's work entails some unexpected dangers."

The prime minister nodded. "As you have discovered also. We serve the emperor and the people and bear such burdens gladly and eagerly."

"Is you brother truly well now?"

They both peered at the sick man. He lay quietly and appeared to be asleep. The prime minister nodded. "The Buddha willing, he will soon be his old self again." He turned back to Akitada. "This means your services are no longer needed, Sugawara."

Akitada, dazed and at a loss for an answer, struggled to rise. Another servant came to pull him upright. Swaying a little, Akitada bowed as best he could, murmuring, "Thank you, Your Excellency," and started to walk away. But the floor seemed to rise and fall under his feet and his surroundings became blurred. He nearly fell once, but someone caught him. He managed to get outside by supporting himself against walls, door frames, and the gallery railings.

27

The Cypress Grove

Tora looked at him with concern. "Is everything all right? Are you feeling ill?"

Akitada paused and breathed the clean air. It was refreshingly cold but he still felt disoriented and had trouble with his balance. "I think it's the incense," he muttered, letting Tora help him into the palm leaf carriage, specially hired for the official court visit.

As the vehicle made its slow way homeward, he tried to account for what he had witnessed and could not. The thought of Aoi in the throes of her trance sickened him again, as did the swaying of the carriage. It was all he could do not to vomit.

Mercifully the distance was not great. He emerged from the carriage on his own veranda and leaned on the railing for a while.

"What's wrong, sir?" Tora hovered at his side. "Did the bastards give you anything to drink or eat?"

Akitada shook his head, and the courtyard below spun.

"I'm sending for the doctor."

Akitada didn't care. He staggered to his study, bracing himself against the wall of the corridor and sat down hard behind his desk. The room seemed to move around him and nausea rose again. Tora returned with water and Akitada drank thirstily. It seemed to make matters worse.

"I think," he said, looking blearily at Tora, "that cudgel must have struck my head. I can't see straight. Help me to lie down."

"The doctor will be here any moment."

The door opened and Sadako entered, bringing a tray with bowls. Akitada tried to smile at her. How kind she was, and how pretty, as she walked toward him, balancing the tray carefully, her eyes downcast, her glossy hair tied neatly at her neck.

The tray held his gruel. His stomach lurched again.

"You left without your morning rice, sir," she said, placing it beside him and looking at him. "Are you still in much pain?"

"I can't eat," Akitada said though clenched teeth, pushing the tray away and nearly upsetting the gruel.

She caught it in time. "Oh!" Her eyes went to Tora. "What is wrong?"

Tora said, "I don't know. I've sent for the doctor. He's acting like he's drunk, but he says he's had nothing to eat or drink. He thinks a cudgel hit his head."

Acting like a drunk? Akitada wanted to protest, but it was a fair description of his dizziness, nausea, and staggering. What must the prime minister and his guests have thought!

"Thank you, Tora. Go and get some rest. I'm in good hands." He smiled at Sadako.

She knelt beside him and reached for his head. He leaned away. She said, "Hold still, sir!" in a rather motherly fashion, and Akitada submitted meekly to her feeling his skull for injuries. He found the experience pleasurable and when she was done, he caught her hand and held it for a moment. "I didn't mean to push away the food, but it nauseated me. I'm sorry, Sadako."

They looked at each other as he held her small, warm hand in his and smiled. After a moment, she blushed and smiled back, and Akitada's heart gave a small leap in his chest. Then she withdrew her hand and reached for the tray.

"I didn't find anything wrong with your head, sir," she said. "I'll take this away. Could you drink some fruit juice?" Her voice trembled a little, and Akitada wanted to reach for her hand again to thank her for her solicitude, but at that moment the doctor walked in.

Like everyone, he asked what was wrong. Akitada explained that he felt dizzy and nauseated.

"Do you have much pain?" the doctor asked.

"Very little."

"That is because of the powders I gave you. They numb the pain, but they tend to make you a little dazed."

"What?" Akitada glared at him. "Why didn't you say so?"

The doctor threw up his hands. "Sir, you did complain about pain. I did what I could for that. You have a choice: either suffer the pain or have your head spin a little. You were resting in bed, weren't you?"

"Not precisely. The prime minister summoned me."

"Oh." The doctor's face fell. "You could have made an excuse."

Akitada bit his lip. "How long will this last?"

"Only today."

"Very well. You may go."

When the man had left, Akitada glowered, but his eyes fell on Sadako, who still stood there with the tray in her hands. His spirits lifted. Suddenly the incident struck him as funny. He chuckled. "Oh, well," he said. "Being thought a drunk has never hurt any of the Fujiwaras. Let's be glad I'm not suffering from some new ailment."

She also laughed a little and Akitada smiled. Then she was gone, and when he was alone again, he remembered the more unpleasant developments.

He was relieved of the dangerous assignment but burdened with the tales of Tadanobu's crimes and no way of bringing justice to the victims or their families.

The prime minister would now consider him useless and too risky for important assignments, and this most likely would bring his career to an end.

The healing of Tadanobu offended not only his sense of justice, but also his faith in facts. Could he have been so wrong about *ikiryo*? Or about Aoi's spiritual abilities?

And what about the alternative? What if he had been right all along, and the strange atmosphere in Tadanobu's room had been the effect of those cursed powders the doctor had given him?

He was convinced now that it must have been so. And Tadanobu had either passed the crisis in his illness to begin to recover or he would soon be on the point of death again.

And Aoi? Had Aoi played an elaborate and disgusting role in a performance master-minded by someone else?

He had been a fool! In more ways than one. He had been seduced by a woman who had no doubt relished her sexual power over him—just as Yukiko had done in the past.

As for the rest of the players: it might well be that the prime minister and his people had been equally fooled. But if so, what had been the purpose? Who was playing this dangerous game?

Tadanobu himself?

It was possible. The man had shown himself a master plotter when he had interfered with the appointment of an imperial consort. Then the objective had been very clear, but was it now?

Akitada's head hurt. Even lying down, he felt dizzy. He decided to stop thinking about the day and wait until the doctor's medicine had worn off.

Saburo's arrival aided in this plan. He put his head in the door and asked softly, "Sir? Are you awake?"

Akitada said gratefully, "Yes, Saburo. Come in."

Saburo came and sat, searching Akitada's face. "They told me, sir. Stupid doctor!"

"Well, he couldn't have known."

"So the exorcism worked and Tadanobu has been healed?"

"So it seems."

Saburo frowned.

Akitada had no wish to discuss his troubling thoughts again and asked, "What news do you have?"

Saburo's face brightened. "We've got him, sir. His name's Ishikawa and he lives on Ogimachi Road. Oh, and he seems to have a club foot."

Akitada gaped at him."Really? How did you get this astonishing information?"

"Ohiya knew. You may recall the former dancing master, who is presently a drunk and beggar?"

"Vividly. But Tora had already talked to him."

"He must not have asked the right questions."

Akitada sighed. "Yes. It happens to all of us."

Saburo rubbed his hands. "Well then, let's go get him arrested. Just in time for Miyagi's trial."

Akitada said bleakly, "Saburo, there is no proof he poisoned Sato. You surely don't believe they can beat a confession out of a high-ranking official."

Saburo's jaw sagged. He scratched his head. "Looks like I got ahead of myself. Tora and I, we've been trying for days to get his name and now . . ." He broke off. "What can we do? There's no time left?"

"Help me up!"

"Are you sure, sir?"

Akitada said irritably, "Yes, I'm sure or I wouldn't have asked for help."

Saburo pulled him up, and Akitada regretted his ill temper. "Sorry, Saburo. I'm still angry with the doctor. The fact is the pain isn't bad at all, but these wrappings make it hard to get up or down.' He walked to his desk and managed to sit by holding on to his book shelf.

"Now," he said, "Let's consider Ishikawa. What's his full name?"

"Ishikawa Ietada."

"I don't know him, but there is a counselor by that name. Hmm! Difficult. The man has powerful friends. I think I'll go see Nakatoshi. He knows everybody."

"I'm coming along, sir."

Akitada suppressed a smile at the peremptory tone. Saburo worried about him. "Of course," he said mildly.

*

Nakatoshi was still in his office. He looked concerned when he saw Akitada. "Should you be up?"

"Yes. I don't like lying flat on my back, and there's work to be done. Saburo is with me to lend a hand."

Nakatoshi greeted Saburo who helped lower Akitada onto a cushion and they all sat. Nakatoshi offered wine.

"Not for me." Akitada explained about the effects of the doctor's medicine and his fear of stirring up more trouble by adding wine.

Saburo also declined.

"I heard about the exorcism," Nakatoshi said.

Akitada made a face. "I bet." He had no doubt that the court now gossiped about his drinking problems. "They all think I was drunk. Not that it matters. I have far more serious flaws as far as they are concerned. In any case, I have been officially dismissed from the case. I hope this means that we are safe again."

Nakatoshi raised his brows. "I agree. If Tadanobu is well and you are off the case, why continue to plague you? Besides, I'm now convinced your warning had nothing to do with the attack. These days there are desperate characters on all the roads outside the capital. I'm afraid I sent you into danger that night."

"No. Those men were on horseback and they repeated the warning." Akitada frowned. "Something is going on and this cure by exorcism may not have changed things. The trouble is, I see no way to continue the investigation."

"Good. You need time to heal."

Akitada nodded. "There is another matter, though." He told his friend about Miyagi. "We now have the name of her other suitor. He's a second counselor called Ishikawa. Saburo says he resides on Ogimachi Road. Do you know anything about him?"

"Ishikawa Ietada. Wealthy. He has a limp. Ishikawa's father had large estates in Mino Province but moved to the capital some twenty years ago to gain influence at court. This Ietada is his oldest son. He isn't well liked though he spends lavishly on parties, as did his father. The old families detest such behavior. Do you suspect him?"

Akitada glanced at Saburo, who nodded, and said, "We have no proof, but time is running out and Ishikawa is the only one with a motive. He is said to have been very angry that Miyagi chose Sato, a mere merchant, over him. Her former master is clearly afraid and won't talk, but others who knew about it say that Ishikawa beat the women he hired and he did so also with Miyagi. Given his reputation for violence, I think we should look more closely at him."

Nakatoshi nodded. "I'm afraid I have very little information about his love life. He has three or four wives, all but one live elsewhere. The senior wife is here. She is a daughter of Fujiwara Kaneie and some fifteen years older than he, I believe. Ishikawa is rumored to have married her to gain his court position."

Akitada thought about this. "I see. The problem is that someone of Ishikawa's status is hardly going to visit the jail in order to poison his rival for the favors of a prostitute."

Nakatoshi smiled. "He would send someone."

It struck Akitada that Ishikawa had done that very thing when it came to signing a contract with Saeki. He said, "I gather you don't like him."

"No. I've met him here and there. Nobody likes him much, though some may find him useful."

"I agree he would send someone to poison Sato, but Kobe found nothing." Akitada sighed. Kobe had worries of his own. "I suppose I must look elsewhere for the rest of the story. Thank you, Nakatoshi."

As they left, Akitada felt suddenly very tired. The dizziness and nausea were gone, but the sun was down, and he only wished for his bed.

Saburo said, "It all goes back to the jail, sir. That's where it happened. We must start with the jail."

Akitada, who had been thinking about Ishikawa and the fact that only his senior wife lived with him in the capital, adjusted his thoughts. "Well, I think it must have been someone close to Ishikawa. I thought you and Tora both checked into what happened at the jail. So did I, for that matter. I don't want to trouble Superintendant Kobe at the moment. He is with his dying wife."

"Oh." Saburo looked shocked. "Is she dying? I didn't know it was so bad. I know he's very fond of her."

"Yes, he found the one woman who filled his life completely and gave up his family for her, and now he is losing her. Did you know that he has handed in his resignation?"

"No!" Saburo stopped walking. "But that's terrible. What will happen to the capital police without him?"

"I'm trying not to think about that. He'll move away and I'll lose one of my best friends." Akitada thought with some gratitude of the fact that Kosehira, at least, wanted to remain close to him even after Akitada divorced his daughter.

A silence fell until they reached the Sugawara residence.

There, Tora greeted them. "What's happened?" he asked, searching their faces.

Akitada told him, "Very little. I'm going to bed. Saburo will tell you. We'll talk about it tomorrow morning."

28

The Doctor and the Wrestler

The next morning, Akitada found that he was moving much better. He managed to get up by himself and put on his clothes without too much discomfort. Outside, a soft rain fell.

Tora and Saburo joined him as he was eating his morning gruel.

Tora said immediately, "So the bastard is Ishikawa Ietada, second counselor to His Majesty, and we can't touch him? Even if he killed a man?"

Akitada was glum. "Probably not, but the real impossibility lies in the fact that Ishikawa cannot have done it himself."

Silence fell as Tora thought this over, then nodded. "He sent someone else. But who?"

"I think the answer will be in the jail. We will need to know exactly who visited there during the crucial period. What did they tell you when you asked?"

Tora and Saburo looked at each other.

Tora offered, "I don't think we pushed very hard. Kobe wasn't in the first time, and after that his wife was dying. Sato's jailer was adamant that Sato was fine until he ate the food Miyagi brought. If that's true, how can anyone else be involved?"

"Poison does not always act immediately. If we assume it was not Miyagi, then it must have been someone else. Could Sato have been poisoned by one of the jailers or a guard? Or anyone who routinely visits the jail?"

Saburo said, "It's possible. But the jailer who was on duty when Sato got sick said Sato had stopped eating the food they gave him. He claimed it made him sick. If someone there offered him something, he surely would have refused it or mentioned it. They said he complained a lot and objected to the drunks that crowded in that day to visit their wrestler friend. Apparently a fight broke out."

Akitada pulled his earlobe. "Curious, that! Explain."

"They had a wrestler in one of the cells. His friends came to celebrate his birthday. But according to the jailer, Sato was a spoiled rich guy who complained about everything and sent for his doctor when the food didn't agree with him. The doctor said there was nothing wrong with Sato or the jail food."

Akitada sat up. "Doctor? What doctor? Did Sato have a doctor?"

Tora gave a snort. "He could afford one. Saburo's right. The jailers didn't like it that he complained so much. That's why the man who let him die didn't look in on him."

Akitada ignored that. "The doctor wasn't the prison's doctor, Doctor Mori?"

"No, sir."

"I don't like it. Where is this doctor? Why didn't he come forward after Sato died? Why have Sato's people not mentioned him? Why didn't Miyagi mention him?"

Saburo said after a moment, "Yes. We should have seen that, sir. It was very strange. Maybe we need to find this doctor."

"There's not enough time," Tora objected. "The trial's this afternoon."

Akitada sighed. "We must try. Let's go to the jail. Kobe won't be there, but maybe I can get some answers."

*

Kobe's sergeant was in charge at police headquarters. This was a somewhat shocking situation to Akitada who liked to think that administrators actually carried out their duties. In this case, Kobe's second in command, the Assistant Superintendant, was a young nobleman from a good family who spent all his time at court and practically never showed his face at headquarters. He drew his salary and would in time also be promoted because he was well-connected. The great worry was that he would take over from Kobe officially.

The sergeant preened himself a little as he sat behind Kobe's desk, but Akitada knew that he was a capable man. He explained that their errand was a last ditch effort to clear Miyagi.

"The Superintendant has tried and failed, sir," the sergeant pointed out.

"I know," Akitada said, "but we have come across some information that may help. There is another person who has a much better motive for killing Sato than Miyagi. Saburo, tell the sergeant what you have discovered."

Saburo, who did not have much regard for the sergeant, complied reluctantly. The sergeant, however, seemed pleased with this show of respect. He said, "They keep a record of who comes and goes. At least they're supposed to. But I'm afraid all of the visitors on the day of Sato's death or the previous one have been cleared."

Akitada nodded. "I felt sure this was checked, but could we have a look at those records?"

The sergeant hesitated. "I'm not sure they are allowed to show them to people."

Akitada raised his brows, and Tora snapped, "Remember who you're talking to, Sergeant."

"I am, I am," the sergeant protested. "You don't know how stubborn those jailers are. Oh, well, maybe I can try."

Akitada said, "We'll go together, if you don't mind. That way you won't get into trouble."

The sergeant looked doubtful about that, but he took them across to the prison without more objections. There an awkward conversation ensued with the gatekeeper who sent for the head jailer. The head jailer recognized both Tora and Akitada from previous visits and brought out the record book as soon as they explained their intention.

"She's prepared to die," he said. "It's pitiful. In the time she's been here, the men have become fond of her and have tried to make her more comfortable, but she doesn't seem to care what happens to her."

Akitada said, "Could I have a word with her later?"

The head jailer nodded. "Just you, sir. But she probably won't talk to you."

Akitada thanked him and bent over the heavy book. The head jailer located the pertinent pages, and he started reading. Saburo and Tora looked over his shoulders.

Unfortunately, the list for those two days was surprisingly long because it contained all deliveries to the jail in addition to visitors. More aggravating was the fact that only names and dates were listed. The sergeant recognized a few names, but these were regulars who delivered food, straw, and other supplies. It was, of course, possible, even likely, that the killer might lurk among them, but Akitada took a greater interest in one long list of people, all of whom had visited the day of Sato's death.

When asked about them, the sergeant looked puzzled at first, but then his face cleared. "That must be the crowd that came to see Kuranojo, the wrestler. He had won a big bout, and they decided to have the party in jail. He'd been arrested the night before for drunken brawling. Presumably the guards checked his visitors for liquor, but something was smuggled through. The fight started again, egged on by Kuranojo from inside his cell. Mind you, his supporters were all men, all drunk, and mostly wrestlers themselves. They broke most of the furniture and we had to send constables over to throw them out. Kuranojo got another week added to his sentence."

Akitada muttered, "It could have been easy to slip something to Sato while there was this disturbance in the jail."

The sergeant shook his head. "They'd need the keys to unlock Sato's cell and then they'd have to get Sato to eat or drink what they brought with them. Impossible!"

Disappointed, Akitada said, "But one of the jailers could have taken him some doctored prison food."

"He wasn't eating the prison food," Saburo reminded him.

"Yes, I suppose you're right." Akitada bent to the list again. He read, then pointed his finger at a name. "Who is that? He doesn't look like a supporter of the wrestler."

The sergeant looked and shook his head. "No idea. I'll have to ask whoever was in charge at the door that day." He checked the bottom of the page. "Oh, it was Yasui. Just a moment." He dashed out of the room.

Tora and Saburo also took a look.

"Kage something?" Tora looked puzzled. "Can't make it out. You recognize it, Saburo?"

Saburo just shook his head.

The sergeant returned out of breath. "He says that must have been Sato's doctor."

Akitada stared at him, "That doctor again! But that must be it! A doctor! Of course. Let's go speak to Miyagi."

The sergeant made no objection, and they walked across to the jail building. The rain had eased a little, but the low gray clouds made their errand doubly depressing. The jailers looked anxious, but one got the keys and unlocked Miyagi's cell. Only Akitada entered. He was relieved to see that it had been kept cleaner than such places usually were. She sat on a bundle of straw, her head bowed over her folded hands. She had heard them, but did not bother to look up. "Is it time?" she asked listlessly.

"No. It's Lord Sugawara, Miyagi."

She inclined her head a fraction but did not raise it to look at him. It seemed as if she had been preparing herself for death, even if that was still long away.

"Miyagi," Akitada said gently, "I have come to help you. There has been some new information and I need to speak to you."

She finally looked up at him. The beautiful face was now pale and drawn, and her eyes had lost their luster.

"You are kind, my Lord," she said tonelessly. "It doesn't matter any longer. I just want to be left alone."

"Justice always matters," Akitada said firmly. "I believe you have been accused unjustly and Sato's killer must be punished."

She bowed her head again and sighed.

"Miyagi, just tell me this, who was Sato's physician?"

"His physician? I don't know. He was never sick until he came here."

"The jailers say his physician came to see him the day he died."

"When I saw him, he wasn't sick. Why would a doctor come before Sato got sick?"

Good question.

"The jailer says Sato complained that the jail's food was making him ill."

She looked up again. "It did at first. He wasn't used to it. But I had been bringing him food for several days. I don't think he ate their food."

"Yes, I thought so. Did Sato say anything about the doctor visiting?"

"No. That last day . . . there were a lot of drunken men outside, making noise. Sato was afraid for me and told me to leave quickly." The memory clearly hurt.

"Ah! Yes, it hangs together. We must find this doctor. Don't give up. We know you're innocent."

She gave him a hopeless look. "Thank you, sir."

After he left the cell, Akitada paused to confirm that on his last day "Sato's doctor" had come before Miyagi and the wrestling crowd.

Yasui confirmed it. "Yes, sir. I knew him. But as I've been saying, Sato was fine until after she brought him food that day."

"What about the wrestler's party. When was that?"

"Oh, they came after the doctor. Now that you remind me, sir, they had just started getting noisy when she arrived. By the time we got rid of them, they had made a terrible mess, broken furniture, and got blood all over the walls. We worked for hours to clean the place after we got rid of them."

"This might account for the fact that you didn't realize Sato was ill until late that night?"

"Yes, sir. That's why. Plus by then, Otsuga was alone for the night shift."

"And so this doctor came to see Sato before the wrestler's friends arrived?"

"Yes. A nice quiet gentleman. Said he'd been called to take a look at the prisoner. I let him in the cell. He wasn't there long. Came back out and said the prisoner was fine and not to worry anymore."

Akitada suddenly fixed on something in the jailer's earlier words. "Did you say you knew him?"

"Yes, sir. Doctor Kagehira. He treated my father when he broke his leg."

"What does he look like and where does he live?"

"About your age, my Lord. Getting a bit bald. He lives on Ogimachi".

"Thank you. That's very helpful."

They left after that.

29

Ishikawa's Plot

The rain still fell as they were walking south along the Omiya Canal where the cherry trees were budding but no court officials in their spring robes were leaning on bridge railings as they discussed government business or court gossip. Only a solitary figure in the uniform of some noble house trudged along behind them.

Tora broke the silence first. "So that scrawl was Kagehira?"

Akitada said, "Yes, Kagehira.. The man tried to disguise his name when he signed in."

Saburo chuckled. "Proof of his guilt. He must worry about that jailer."

"Yes. It's fortunate the man remembered him and was there today."

Tora glanced at the sky. "It's getting late. Are we going to talk to that judge?"

"Later. I want to know exactly who that Doctor Kagehira is. I have a suspicion he is somehow connected with Ishikawa."

Tora stopped abruptly. "Holy Buddha! Kagehira! No wonder the name sounds familiar. I'd forgotten. He's the man who signed the contract with Saeki. Remember, Ishikawa sent someone else to make the purchase?"

Akitada and Saburo had also stopped. Akitada said, "You didn't mention that this Saeki actually sold Miyagi to Ishikawa."

Tora said, "He didn't, sir. She refused to go to him, so it came to nothing. I'm sorry, sir. I meant to follow up on that, but then other things happened."

"Yes, I know. You told me and I forgot also. No sense in wasting time blaming ourselves. It's just another piece that proves we are finally on the right track. Let's find out about this man."

Doctor Kagehira had a house in the eastern city within walking distance. They walked along Sanjo Avenue, crossing two canals, and then turned into one of the quarters where they found a well kept house in a lush fenced garden. A plaque at the gate advertised

Doctor Kagehira's great skills with all sorts of herbal treatments.

"There's your poisoner," Saburo said, pointing at the abundance of green, glistening leaves. "Who knows more about killing potions than a doctor?"

Tora peered over the low wall. "Bet he grows his own. Probably has poisonous snakes too for milking their fangs. Clearly it's the place to come to if you want someone dead."

"It's a perfect business. You arrange for your enemy to feel a bit under the weather and then send for the good doctor." Saburo shook his head at such depravity. "Mind you, I once knew a monk who practiced healing and killed one of the temple's enemies that way. But that was once. This man may have been practicing for a long time. What do you think, sir?"

Akitada remembered only too well the powders his own doctor had given him and their effects, but he felt a little more hesitant to assume Doctor Kagehira had been a hired killer for years. He said, "Well, he doesn't seem to have a motive for killing Sato while Ishikawa did."

Tora asked, "What shall we do?"

"The police will need to make the arrest. Kobe is unavailable, but the sergeant was very cooperative. Tora, you'd better go back and ask him to send us some constables. Saburo and I will pay the good doctor a visit in the meantime."

Tora looked disappointed. "Can't we all talk to him and then get the constables?"

"No. Tora. He could escape before we got back with the police."

Tora left reluctantly, and Saburo set the bamboo clappers beside the gate in motion.

A servant ran out almost immediately. He was bowing and welcoming them as he flung open the gate. "Come in, gentlemen, the doctor is in. Is it an emergency?" He looked at Akitada, who wore a slightly moist silk robe.

Akitada said, "It may be. Please lead the way."

"And what names shall I give?"

"Sugawara."

They followed on the servant's heels rather than waiting patiently to be called. In the entry, they removed their shoes quickly and stepped up on the glossy floor. The house, though modest in size compared to noble residences, was well kept and clean. The servant led them along a corridor to a door. There he stopped and said, "Allow me to see if my master is busy."

Akitada frowned. "Make it quick."

It was quick. The door opened again, the servant stood aside, and they walked into a large room with the usual furnishings of a book case, a low desk with writing utensils, assorted cushions and trunks, and a collection of lamps, candleholders, and braziers. A heavy-set, middle aged man who was balding, awaited them, small black eyes scrutinizing Akitada carefully.

"My lord? Is it really Lord Sugawara? A man famed for his brilliant mind who was most recently one of the nation's governors? A very great honor!"

Akitada nodded, gestured to Saburo, and said, "My clerk. Since you know me, you may also be aware that I have on occasion investigated crimes."

Doctor Kagehira, rising from a deep bow, swallowed. "Er, yes. I have heard it mentioned. Very clever. Most admirable." He gave a nervous laugh. "But surely that isn't what brings you to me in this terrible weather?"

"Don't worry. Honest men have nothing to fear. You may be helpful in a case I'm interested in."

Kagehira relaxed. "Indeed. What an honor! I'll shall do my best. Shall we sit? Some refreshments?"

"No, nothing. This shouldn't take long." Akitada seated himself on one of the cushions and glanced about him. "You're quite comfortable here. Is business good?"

The doctor looked modest. "I depend on my skills, such as they are, and the gratitude of my patients."

"Ah! You have had many successful healings then? And now you have many patients?" Kagehira gave another small laugh. "I have been fortunate. The gods be praised."

Akitada turned to Saburo. "We should consult the doctor about Genba's painful back. What do you think?"

Saburo nodded. "Yes, sir. Nothing has helped the poor fellow so far. He walks like a cripple."

Akitada asked the doctor, "Is there someone who can vouch for you?"

Kagehira cited some names with successful treatments, ending after a small hesitation with, "And then there is Lord Ishikawa. I'm by way of becoming his family physician. He has done me the honor of consulting me."

Akitada smiled. "I'm impressed. Would that be the Second Counselor Ishikawa, by any chance?"

"Yes, indeed. A very fine man." Kagehira smiled broadly and bowed a couple of times as if the great man were present in the room.

Akitada was hoping that Tora and the police were on their way. "Well," he said, "This is very convenient. Since you come so highly recommended by him and know Lord Ishikawa well, I'd like to ask you about this case I've been working on. You see, there has been a recent mysterious poisoning in our jail." He paused.

Kagehira turned pale and goggled at him. His right hand twitched, and he seemed speechless.

"What's the matter? Are you feeling all right, Doctor?"

Kagehira pulled himself together and said calmly enough, "Shocking! You mean the case of the prostitute poisoning her client?"

"Her 'client,' as you call him, was a wealthy rice merchant by the name of Sato."

Kagehira's hands clenched and unclenched inside his full sleeves. "Yes, I believe that is so."

Akitada fixed him with an intent stare. "I have been told that Lord Ishikawa is acquainted with her?"

The doctor had clearly expected another question, one about his visit to the jail. He was eager to talk about Ishikawa. "It may be so, sir. I think she is a well-known beauty. No doubt, she was known to many fine gentlemen." He chuckled a little. "His lordship certainly is a connoisseur of beauty and has celebrated many a great courtesan in his fine poetry."

"Ah, yes. The poems are collected under the title, "Poems of the Second Counselor of the Cypress Grove," aren't they?

Kagehira nodded eagerly. "Exactly! I'd forgotten the name. Poets, it seems, choose some fanciful title to hide behind. Out of modesty, I think. Lord Ishikawa chose his because of the cypress trees at his gate."

"You don't say." Where was Tora with the constables? "I notice that you treat patients in all walks of life."

"I am fortunate that many have found my services beneficial. Of course, I do not treat the poor. They lead such unhealthy lives and have so many contagious diseases and I must take great care not to infect my ordinary patients. You may be quite certain, sir, that I shall not allow your family and household to be endangered because I have just treated someone with smallpox."

Akitada felt a surge of hatred for the man and decided not to wait any longer. "Really? You surprise me. I've just come from the jail," he said. "They remember your visit there."

The doctor gasped. "It must be some mistake. I do not treat prisoners."

"According to the jailer, you saw Sato the day he died. Given your dislike of jails, I wonder if this was one of the services you performed for Lord Ishikawa."

Kagehira's mouth fell open. He turned red, then white, and jumped up. "I don't know what you mean," he cried, looking around the room as if he sought to escape.

"Of course, you know what I mean. Your actions prove it."

The doctor cried, "What actions? You have no proof. You cannot go around making accusations like that. I'm a respected physician. I have friends who will testify to my good character."

"You were recognized by one of the jailers. And don't count on friends like Ishikawa. He has his own skin to save. He'll put the blame firmly on you." Akitada paused. "Let's see. Ishikawa will say you were so eager to get his business that you poisoned Sato because Ishikawa hated the merchant. No doubt, we'll find examples of other reprehensible actions you performed for your client, such as serving as his stand-in on the contract to purchase Miyagi."

Kagehira gulped, but words failed him.

At that moment, the servant stuck his head in at the door to announce, "Master, there are police officers here. With constables."

He was pushed aside unceremoniously by Tora who threw the door wide admitting Superintendent Kobe, looking grim, his sergeant, and five uniformed police constables.

Kagehira fell to his knees, babbling, "It wasn't me. I didn't want to do it. I was forced. It's all Ishikawa's fault."

Kobe turned to Akitada. "Has he admitted it?"

Akitada was struck by how worn and tired Kobe looked. Even so, there seemed to be a new determination about him. He said, "I think he was about to confess when you arrived. I didn't expect you to come in person. I'm very sorry, Kobe."

Kobe compressed his lips. "I know. She died last night. No point in not going back to work." He turned to his sergeant. "Take notes!"

The sergeant knelt and prepared to record Kagehira's confession.

Kagehira had watched these preparations with horror. "It wasn't my fault. It was Ishikawa," he said again, pleading.

Kobe growled, "Stop denying it. It will make things much worse for you. If you're the man who visited the rice merchant Sato in jail on the fourteenth day of the month, you've been recognized. We brought the jailer along, just in case you try to weasel out of it."

The sergeant waved a man in the jail's uniform forward. He looked at Kagehira and nodded. "That's him, Sergeant."

Akitada was sick at the news of Sachi's death and barely heard what Kobe said to the doctor. If Sachi had just died, how could he be here now, working as if nothing had happened? He saw the pain in Kobe's face, he saw the many hours without sleep, he saw a mere shadow of the man Kobe had been, and he understood. When the bubble of happiness bursts and there is nothing left to live for, you reach for whatever there is to fill the void. Kobe had fretted over neglecting his job. He had now returned to it with a vengeance.

It was Akitada who had tears in his eyes when he woke again to the proceedings.

Tora cried, "Well done, Superintendent!"

Kagehira had evidently confessed while Akitada's mind had been on Kobe's pain. The doctor was explaining what had happened.

"When I first started treating Lord Ishikawa, he would ask me if there were things one could give someone to make him sick without having people know about it. I said there were many such things. He laughed and said he'd have to be careful to keep me as his friend. I didn't pay much attention. Many people suspect their physicians will cause them to die or make them worse. Once, Lord Ishikawa consulted me about a prostitute he'd been with. He blamed her for a loss of his male vigor and wondered if she could have given him something to cause this. I thought it unlikely, as prostitutes don't often discourage customers, so I said I didn't think so and examined him. There was nothing wrong with him except his age, but I didn't tell him this. Patients don't like to hear it." He paused and took a deep breath.

Kobe said impatiently, "Get to the point."

"Well, he blamed this woman for all his troubles and yet he evidently wanted to buy her out. I couldn't understand his obsession. He seemed to think once she was his, he would regain his powers, but he decided he didn't want it known that he had bought her. That's when he sent me with the gold—a shockingly great deal of gold for a mere prostitute, even if she was one of the top women in the quarter—and I paid and signed the papers with my name. Only, the woman refused and threatened to kill herself rather than accept the offer. It seems she had fallen in love with a young merchant. Her owner tried everything to change her mind, but in the end he returned the gold and tore up the papers."

The story made a perverted sort of sense, Akitada thought. He could see what would happen next. Ishikawa would be outraged and seek vengeance.

Kagehira spread his hands to show that none of this was his fault and said, "Lord Ishikawa went nearly mad when he heard. He was humiliated that she'd preferred a commoner, a mere merchant, over him. He saw it as an unbearable insult. I tried to calm him down, but he strode around the room ranting and raving about how he would teach them. There was nothing I could do. In the end, he remembered me, and said, 'You can go now.' So I went." Kagehira stopped.

"Come," said Akitada, "That's not the whole story. What happened next? Did Ishikawa send for you again?"

Kagehira hung his head. "Not right away, but I'd become curious and asked some questions. I found out that the merchant who bought Miyagi had been arrested. That seemed like a strange coincidence to me, and so I asked more questions. I thought that it had been Lord Ishikawa who had brought the charge against him, but it turned out to be someone else, a captain in the imperial guard. So I tried to put Lord Ishikawa from my mind and went about my business. Only, he sent for me again."

It was all coming together with a sort of dreadful inevitability. Ishikawa's revenge. Akitada thought about the captain in the imperial guard who had brought the charge against Sato. One of the Fujiwaras, a large and overbearing family. But in this case, he suspected that Ishikawa was behind the arrest and the charge was trumped up. That explained why Sato had been so adamant that he was innocent. He had been sure that the matter would be cleared up quickly and that he would go home again.

Only it wasn't cleared up. And the reason for this also must be investigated. What was the relationship between the Fujiwara captain and Counselor Ishikawa? Who handled the charges and who prolonged Sato's jailing? And who had managed to get the judge to move up Miyagi's trial date. Money and power can buy all sorts of things.

Even if they had not been able to buy Miyagi.

Kagehira had now come to the crucial part. "Lord Ishikawa wanted me to visit the merchant in jail. He wanted me to give him something that would make him very ill. I refused, of course. Lord Ishikawa said it was only a small matter, just something to teach the man a lesson and to save some face for Ishikawa. He pleaded with me. I refused. Then he threatened me. He was very angry. I knew he could ruin me. A man like that becomes obsessed and won't rest. So I said I would try, but some of the things that cause sickness can also kill. He said, I was the doctor and if something went wrong, he would protect me." I went home and looked over my herbal preparations. I was angry to be put in this position, I was a man who had never hurt a patient. I decided I couldn't do it."

Kagehira paused to let this sink in. He met with hard stares from his audience, sighed, and continued.

"When a day passed and nothing happened, Lord Ishikawa called me back. This time he handed me a couple of small pills. 'Here,' he said, 'Take these. Dissolve them in wine. He's complained about the food. Tell him Miyagi sent you with medicine."

Kagehira stopped again. He looked exhausted and hung his head.

Kobe asked in a cold voice, "Are you trying to make us believe that you, a physician, took those pills without question and gave them to Sato?"

The doctor looked from Kobe to Akitada and back again. Seeing their implacable faces, he fell to his knees. "Please, you must believe me. When a man like Counselor Ishikawa makes a demand, a simple man like myself cannot refuse a small favor."

"A small favor!" Akitada snapped.

"Yes. He said nothing was going to happen to Sato except maybe some vomiting and the flux."

"You believed that after this man told you how he hated Sato and Miyagi?"

The doctor wailed and beat his forehead against the floor. "I wanted to believe it. You don't know what he could have done to me if I made him angry."

They were all silent at this. Kagehira was probably right about Ishikawa. The man was not altogether sane. Akitada's thoughts went to Tadanobu who had also shown signs of persecuting anyone who stood in his way. And he would go on living because no one could stop him. He said harshly, "Then you must know that your testimony will send the constables to Ishikawa's door. He will know you turned him in. Then what will happen to you?

Kagehira wept and pleaded. He offered to join the northern army. He would agree to go to any place they wanted to send him, as long as it was far away. "I'll leave tonight," he promised.

"You will do no such thing," Kobe said. "You will go to jail and stand trial. If you can make a judge believe that you didn't know those pills were a deadly poison and testify against Ishikawa, perhaps you may join the army or become a monk." He shook his head. "Take him away, sergeant!"

In the end, Akitada and Kobe were left alone. Even Tora and Saburo, though clearly full of questions and comments, departed, leaving the two old friends to walk back together.

The rain had finally stopped, but the clouds were still heavy and dark. They paused outside the doctor's house to look at each other for a moment, then Akitada embraced his friend. "You will come home with me? Share my evening rice? Perhaps be my guest overnight?"

Kobe returned the hug, then stepped away. "Thank you, but there is work to be done. I have to stop Miyagi's trial. For a short while longer I am on duty."

"You shouldn't be alone. Will you come later? You must eat. I don't imagine you bothered with that."

Kobe started to shake his head, then changed his mind. "Very well. Perhaps it will do me good to talk. Later!"

They parted then, and Akitada walked home. The streets were busier now. Women with baskets headed to the market. Messenger boys darted along. A food seller was setting up his stand. And the liveried servant he had noticed during the rain was also still about. Or perhaps it was another man belonging to the same house.

30

The Nighttime Visit

Kobe arrived after dark, looking pale and tired. He announced that Miyagi had been released.

Akitada had sent out for a sea bream and urged cook to make a special effort. Kobe took no notice, but he ate, almost absent-mindedly while they discussed Kagehira's arrest and what to do about Ishikawa.

"It's dangerous to tangle with Ishikawa," said Akitada, "and that goes double for the Fujiwara captain who trumped up the charges against Sato."

"He is Fujiwara Uchimaro," said Kobe. "A very unpleasant youngster. Son of a cousin of the prime minister. That accounts for the fact that he has this reputation while still free to abuse people."

"Ah. You traced him already? What can be done?"

Kobe pushed away an empty bowl and wiped his mouth with the moist towel. "I have given orders to arrest both tomorrow."

Akitada set down his rice bowl abruptly. "That will bring you no end of trouble, Kobe. Let's try to think of something less direct."

Kobe looked at him with tired eyes. "You forget. I have resigned. And Sachi has died. There is nothing anyone can do to me."

Akitada's appetite vanished and he put back the juicy bit of fish he had meant to put in his mouth next. " Surely . . ." he said weakly and stopped. He saw no way out of the problem with Ishikawa and the captain and had no hope to give to a man who had already resigned his position and his future.

And that, of course, shamed him. He had not had the strength to make a similar decision in the name of justice. He had done nothing about Tadanobu. At this moment, that monster was recovering and would soon be well enough to inflict his cruelty on others. He was more dangerous than Ishikawa and the Fujiwara captain and they, in turn, could well become like him if not stopped.

Kobe put a hand on his. "Don't look so distraught, my friend," he said. "I have nothing left to lose but my life, and that surely is in no danger." He paused and muttered, "More's the pity."

"Kobe," said Akitada, seizing the other man's hand, "I need you. I shall always need you to show me where I must do better. I cannot bear parting with you. I don't mean that I need a superintendent of police to help me out of my assorted missteps and disasters. I mean, I need you, my friend, to be near me to give me strength. I very nearly failed to make the right choice, and you have just reminded me."

Kobe withdrew his hand and frowned. "Oh, no, Akitada. You always taught *me*. I'm not sure I want that responsibility. I have been doing away with responsibilities. And you still have many."

It was true. Choosing between duty and family was painful.

"Nevertheless," Akitada said, "I, too, must do what is right," and then he told Kobe about Tadanobu.

*

Sleep did not come easily that night. Even the long soak in the bath, possible with Tora's help, who unwound and later rewound the bandages around Akitada's chest, did not relax him enough to close his eyes and let go of his troubles. In his mind, he turned over and over again how to approach the Tadanobu matter. Saburo had eliminated some of the man's victims as unlikely to be vengeful because they had been paid off in one way or another. Their grief had been soothed by the application of favors and perhaps their own sense of loyalty. The loyalty of retainers was a marvelous thing. Akitada often felt that burden.

This left the noble families Tadanobu had hurt or destroyed, and several of these were too far away for him to investigate. And what was there to investigate anyway? There was no doubt in his mind that Tadanobu was guilty. He had never intended to identify a vengeful spirit in the first place. No, he must work without the prime minister, and that was both a problem and a danger.

He was about to revise his good intentions, when there was the sound of soft footsteps in the gravel outside his room.

With spring in the air and the scent of flowers and fresh leaves strong after the rain, Akitada was sleeping with the doors to the garden wide open. He sat up, too quickly and with a groan, to stare into the blackness outside. Inside, there was just a small oil lamp flickering.

"Who's there?" he called out, remembering the cudgels in the forest.

"Hush! Do you want to wake the house?"

Aoi.

She stepped up onto the veranda and became visible, a dim figure wrapped in a cloak of some sort. When she walked into his room he saw she was barefoot. And when she dropped the cloak, she was naked.

And beautiful.

Akitada smiled and opened his arms.

It was a strange lovemaking, as strange in its way as the first one. Neither spoke. She came into his arms, straddling him, kissing him, peeling away his bedclothes and his undergown until their bodies met and joined. He tried to rise to assume his normal position, but she pushed him back down. As their bodies found each other, he submitted, allowing this astonishing woman to take him as he had meant to take her.

For him it was an amazing and strangely exciting experience, this submission. Why not, he thought. It was not all that uncommon to change roles in sex play. Skilled prostitutes did it all time. But still, it felt strange to yield when one wished to master. And there was the niggling curiosity about where she had learned her astonishing moves and her ways of touching and caressing that kept a man vigorous without his volition.

Repeatedly.

At his age!

Eventually, he murmured, “Enough, my love. Leave me some self respect.” She chuckled softly and lay down by his side. They fell asleep in each other’s arms, with Aoi’s long hair draped over both of them.

He woke to daylight and the sound of the door. Then he heard a soft gasp, and the door closed again. He pushed Aoi’s hair from his face. The sun was shining through the open doors and fell across their naked bodies in the tangle of bed clothes. Whoever had come in could have been in no doubt about his night of lovemaking. It had not been Tora, who would not have crept away so quietly. Or Mrs. Kuruda, who would certainly not make that small sound of shock and pain.

Sadako, then.

Akitada was ashamed that she, of all people, had found them together. And then his shame made him angry. Why was he not allowed privacy in his own home? And what was the meaning of that small sound of pain? Surely he had not been mistaken in that. Since when did the women in his employ take such a personal interest in his love life?

He moved then, struggling to sit up, and Aoi woke. Either it was the bright sun, or her exertions during the night had not been kind to her. Her face seemed flushed and puffy and her body too fleshy. He averted his eyes and said, "Good morning, my love."

She pulled the cover around her, and brushed back her tangled hair. "The cruel sun," she murmured. "How will I get home?"

Certainly not naked and barefoot, he thought. "Never mind. We'll find you some clothes and send for a chair."

She chuckled. "Oh, Akitada. Always practical. Most men would have demanded another demonstration of my skills in bed. Were you not pleased? You were eager enough last night."

"Of course, my love. You know I cannot get enough of you. But duty calls."

She pouted a little, then said, "That reminds me. Tadanobu has had a relapse. This time they didn't bother to call me. It seems they've lost their faith in my powers. No doubt, you'll get another chance."

Akitada was stunned by this news and said nothing for a moment. He had just wished for a chance to prove himself useful again, and now that it was here, it felt as if death had walked into the room.

Aoi gave him a curious look. "Come, don't look like that. You should feel vindicated. You never believed in my powers, did you?"

This was dangerous territory between a man and the woman he loved. Akitada said rather lamely, "What makes you think so?"

She narrowed her eyes, then got up, wrapping her cloak firmly around herself. "If you don't mind, I'll be on my way."

"You can't go like that," Akitada cried scandalized.

"I've done worse," she countered, making for the door.

He got up, caught her, held her, and kissed her. He felt the tension leave her body and she sighed, putting her head against his shoulder. "Oh, Akitada! I swore I'd never let another man hurt me, but I'm helpless when it comes to you."

Ashamed, he said, "Let's have a bath together. I'll have a maid bring some clothes for you, and then I'll take you home in a chair."

She murmured, "Thank you."

Of course, this meant that his entire household would now be aware of the fact that he had found a lover and perhaps a wife. So be it. Two people who had been alone and lonely would try to be happy together. He would be solicitous of her, accompanying the bath with caresses and loving words. He thought it would all work out. They had much in common, not least the maturity and intelligence needful for companionship and conversation.

And she was a wonderful lover.

When they were about to bathe together, it almost came to that again. She dropped her cloak and helped him unwind his silken bandages. His chest felt much better. He could breathe and move a little without pain, and her proximity and the touch of her hands aroused him. He slid quickly into the tub, hoping Tora had the good sense not to barge in.

They looked at each other with the smiles lovers smile. I should ask her to be my wife, Akitada thought. But in the end, he did not.

*

The summons came in the afternoon. By then,Akitada had prepared an account of Tadanobu's crimes. He had not spared him. At this point, his decision was made and he was interested in nothing but getting justice for the victims, dead or alive. Even if the prime minister turned out to be a fair man–something that was most unlikely when it came to attacks on the Fujiwara name–he would not like Akitada for reporting the truth and would remember him as a troublemaker in the future. The situation was aggravated by the fact that Akitada was between assignments and without pay. True, he was much better off than he had been years ago, having managed his property well by adding to it and by restraining expenditures, but his household had grown and marriage to Yukiko had been expensive, even though she had brought him a rich dowry. That would have to be returned now.

The thought of his wifeless status reminded him of Aoi again. There, too, he had come to a decision. He would ask her to be his wife and stepmother to Yasuko and Yoshi. He reflected wryly that life would at least be entertaining with another Fujiwara female in his household, one who was also opinionated and a practicing medium.

The prime minister's emissary arrived in due course, and Akitada changed into the court robe he had held ready on the clothes stand. They walked together to the *Daidairi*, past curious glances from clerks and courtiers who recognized the prime minister's emissary and wondered what sort of fate awaited the man who was being taken to him. The feeling was not unlike that of a criminal being escorted to his trial.

His Excellency had been waiting, and this time he was alone. Dismissing the emissary, he waved Akitada to a cushion near his desk. He looked drawn and unhappy.

"You've heard the news?" he asked. "My brother had a relapse."

"I heard," Akitada said, without revealing the source. "I regret it extremely." There was some truth in that, though his reasons were personal rather than charitable.

"Can you help?"

"I have brought the results of my earlier investigations with me, Your Excellency." Akitada produced the neat paper scroll he had written earlier in the day from his sleeve, rose to bow, and proffered it with both hands. "I believe somewhere in these accounts there must be the answer to your brother's problem. Appease the victim and the victim's family and you may bring him relief."

"Ah!" The prime minister unrolled the scroll and started reading.

Akitada stood, watching his face nervously. The stories of Tadanobu's crimes made for unpleasant reading by his brother. He saw anger and revulsion pass over the prime minister's features and wondered how he would be punished for his attack on the Fujiwara name. Nothing happened for a long time. The prime minister went back to reread some passages. His face was grim when he rolled up the scroll and laid it down.

"You have been busy," he said, staring up at Akitada. "Sit down."

Akitada bit his lip and sat. "The information was not too difficult to obtain. Much of it is common knowledge."

"Based on gossip by our enemies. You have been less than discreet, I take it."

"Only I and two of my retainers have been involved. I thought that speed was of the essence." He could not very well mention Nakatoshi or Aoi.

The prime minister said sourly, "I suppose you did your best."

Relieved, Akitada offered, "I have not been able to confirm all accounts. There has not been time. But what I did confirm suggests that these things happened. In the case of family retainers, it appears that the victims do not bear any malice, so they can probably be eliminated. Allow me to explain." He went carefully over the families Saburo had visited, stressing the fact that they bore Tadanobu no resentment.

The prime minister nodded impatiently. "Naturally. Our branch of the family has always looked after its people. I'm glad to hear Tadanobu is doing likewise."

"It is indeed an admirable characteristic. However, that leaves a number of cases where your brother was either unable to make reparations or decided not to. Those are the ones that I think should be of concern." Akitada paused, praying that the prime minister would accept his advice and do so quickly, because if Tadanobu died before justice had been served, it would be too late for his victims.

The prime minister glanced through the scroll again. "I'm aware of some of these, though my brother's explanations showed him to be justified."

"That would not matter to the person bent on vengeance."

"No. You're right. So your advice is to offer reparations, appeasement, apology? What?"

"All of those. We must be quick."

The prime minister ran a hand over his face. "Yes, yes. We must be quick. This Tanaka business. I think Tadanobu acted in good faith. Tanaka was very close to the Ezo leader. Surely we can eliminate that?"

"As I said, we cannot be certain how the people affected felt. I was told that Tanaka and the Ezo chieftain were childhood friends. Their relationship may have been natural rather than political." Akitada offered this a little anxiously. It seemed to him that, even if Tanaka had never filed an official protest with the government against Tadanobu's scandalous draining of public and private property for his own benefit, someone else would surely have informed the central administration. And some official, no doubt, had then suppressed the fact.

"There was discontent in the province." The prime minister sighed. "A difficult post, and so close to the enemy. But I see that we must do something. What do you suggest?"

Heart beating, Akitada offered, "Tanaka's family must be reinstated. And some prayer services for Tanaka's soul might be in order."

The prime minister's lip twitched. "You don't recommend deification then?"

Akitada said quickly, "No."

It had been a reminder that he was a descendant of Michizane who had in fact been deified to stop what the Fujiwara clan considered his ghostly persecution of them in revenge for what they had done to him.

"As it happens, I had already directed an investigation into the Tanaka matter. There has been a great outcry on their behalf by people here and in their domain. Most of the property has been restored to Tanaka's heirs recently. But we could, of course, order Buddhist and Shinto priests to conduct services."

Akitada, greatly relieved, nodded. "Perhaps then your Excellency has already taken similar steps in the other cases?"

The prime minister sighed and bent to the scroll again. "No, I don't think so." He pursed his lips. I see you list the Fujimi affair. For a moment Akitada did not know what he referred to, then he recalled that Fujimi was one of the estates owned by Tadanobu.

"You know, of course," said his Excellency, "that the farmer who caused so much trouble over a small border issue was killed by another man." He gave Akitada a questioning look.

Gathering his courage, Akitada said, "There are those who say that your brother ordered that murder and then drove the farmer's family from their land with threats."

The prime minister sat up stiffly. "What? Are you accusing my brother of murder?"

"The stories about your brother mention several murders and two suicides. They seemed to me serious enough charges to account for a case of *ikiryo.* Grief over the loss of a family member will often drive people to do strange things."

The prime minister's anger receded. "You know, Sugawara," he said wearily, "all of us manage to anger people sufficiently if we just live long enough and have some responsibilities."

He meant power, thought Akitada. And it was power that tempted men into such actions. He did not say so, but nodded.

"What would you have me do about Fujimi?"

"Restore the land."

The prime minister waved a hand. "The land is insignificant. My brother's life is worth a good deal more."

"I agree, Excellency."

"I refuse to countenance blood money. My brother did not kill the man."

"I quite understand."

"Now the Ikeda matter. That was embarrassing. I recall meeting the young woman's father who came to discuss her dowry. I was astonished that Tadanobu had not mentioned his plans to me. Tadanobu acted badly there. Many young men behave this way, I fear. Tadanobu's problem was that he seduced one of the ladies-in-waiting who was also an Ikeda. Lord Ikeda is a very proud man. I have tried many times to make peace with him, but he's a stubborn old man. I really don't know what else can be done."

"Perhaps there may be a brother or sister of the unfortunate young woman who may benefit from an appointment?"

The prime minister snorted. "Well, old Ikeda will certainly not send any more daughters to serve at court."

Akitada recalled what had happened to his own marriage. "That hardly seems to be something that is always desirable."

His Excellency raised a brow at this. "I hear moral outrage, Sugawara. I didn't know you were a dry old stick. Boys will be boys, and they seek out pretty girls."

"Such behavior is reprehensible and an insult to the emperor," Akitada snapped, becoming angry.

A short silence fell. Then the prime minister returned to the scroll. "I see I am coming to the last offense on your list. It's clear now why you attached so much effort to this one. How did you learn about Nabuko? I know it was not Aoi who told you."

Akitada's anger fled like fog before the wind. Yes, they were on very dangerous ground now. Not only did this story accuse Tadanobu of raping another young noblewoman, in this case a senior Fujiwara's daughter, but it accused her family, and by implication the prime minister, of collusion in the imperial succession. He said, "I think this story may have involved a romance. The young woman became your brother's wife. I included it because she seems to have left him to become a nun."

The prime minister threw up his hands. "Nabuko is profoundly religious. The rest is nonsense. Insulting nonsense. You should be ashamed. Now is that all?"

"Yes, your Excellency." Akitada was tempted to add, "So far as I know," but wisely bit his tongue. Things were bad enough. He would be lucky if there were no serious repercussions.

"You may go!"

Akitada rose, suppressing a twinge of pain, and withdrew.

31

The Unwelcome Guest

Akitada felt ambivalent about his report to the prime minister. Leaving aside the fact that he had angered the man, a man who held his life and future in his hands, he had no idea if Tadanobu's victims, any of them or all, would indeed be compensated in whatever fashion possible. But he knew he had at least done what he could to right the wrongs. And perhaps he had even caused the prime minister to regard his brother's behavior with revulsion. He had made the usual apologies for what Tadanobu had done, but Akitada had the distinct feeling that the prime minister had been shocked by some of the details. If so, perhaps Tadanobu could be restrained in the future.

The man was fifty years old. If he was made to remain in the capital under his brother's eye, he might not do more damage.

*

At home the following day, good news reached him. Not only had Miyagi's trial not taken place and Miyagi had been released from jail, her cell was now occupied by Doctor Kagehira.

Tora and Saburo both reported. They said Kobe planned to confront Ishikawa with Kagehira's accusation the next day.

Akitada nodded. "Good work, both of you. I suppose our work is done."

They looked at each other. Saburo said after a moment. "There was a problem with Miyagi, sir."

"What problem? She's a free woman."

Tora said, "She had no place to go and didn't really care where she went."

Akitada said irritably, "She can always go back to her old profession."

"No, sir. She won't."

"Well, surely there's the house she and Sato inhabited. She can live there until she makes up her mind. A woman with her looks and reputation will soon enough find a new lover."

They looked at each other again. Unhappily.

"The house has been closed up and offered for rent. And Miyagi's mourning, sir," Tora said.

Akitada frowned. "What is going on?"

Again they exchanged a look. "We brought her here, sir," Saburo said.

"We were afraid to leave her, because we thought she'd kill herself."

"You brought a woman from the quarter into my house?"

Before they could answer, there was a dry cough outside the door.

"Come in," Akitada called out.

Mrs. Kuruda entered, her hands tucked into her sleeves, her face determined. "Sir," she said, "I felt it my duty to tell you that these two have brought a very unsuitable person into this house."

Irritated with the woman's officious manner but aware that she was doing her job as she thought fit, Akitada said, "It is only for a short while."

She would have none of it. Looking him straight in the eye, she said, "Well, sir, in my day we didn't allow women of the street to share the quarters of our young daughters. Her ladyship would not approve. She said as much when she stopped by the other day. You had just left to visit your friend in the mountains."

Akitada felt himself flushing with anger. Yukiko had apparently discussed Aoi with Mrs. Kuruda.

Tora cried, "Miyagi is a very nice young person. And she just lost her husband. You need a softer heart, Mrs. Kuruda."

She sniffed. "My heart is soft enough for decent people. She's one of those who break up families. And if you ask me, she probably did her husband in to get his money."

"That's a lie," Tora snapped. "We just got the real murderer arrested. And you are a mean old woman."

Akitada swallowed his anger and interceded. "Thank you, Mrs. Kuruda. I'll look into it."

She bowed and waddled off.

Saburo muttered, "Sorry, sir."

Akitada frowned. "Did you put her in my daughter's quarters?"

"Sadako is looking after her," Tora said, flushing. "*She* has a very kind heart."

"Mrs. Kuruda is right. That is totally unsuitable. I will not have a woman from the quarter associate with my daughter or with a well-brought-up young woman under my care. Even if Sadako is too kind-hearted to turn anyone away."

He left them standing there and hurried to his daughter's pavilion. On the way, it occurred to him that he had no idea how to deal with this matter. He could not charge in like some ogre and drag the unfortunate Miyagi out of the pavilion to have her tossed into the street. He stopped in dismay.

In the end, he decided to see how the women were handling the situation.

He found them sitting together. All three looked up in astonishment when he walked in. Sadako and Miyagi rose. Miyagi, who was wearing clean clothes and had had her hair brushed, stood with her head bowed, clearly ill at ease. Akitada's daughter said brightly, "Father, only see what a lovely guest we have!"

This did not sit well with Akitada. He looked at Miyagi, a creature of the willow quarter where women sold their beauty for the highest price. She looked modest enough at the moment, quiet, pale, and deeply unhappy. But there was something new in her expression, something that had not been there when he last saw her in her cell. She looked firm and determined and her lips were compressed.

"Miyagi?" he said tentatively.

She met his eyes, nodded slightly, and said, "I shall not trouble you long, my Lord. I'll be returning to my home in the country as soon as my mother comes for me or I can arrange for the journey. But I am deeply grateful to you for freeing me and to your ladies for their kind and generous hearts. You are blessed in your family. May you also be blessed in all other things."

"Umm," he said, bereft of his righteous anger with the visitor. "No need to rush. I'm glad my ladies and the servants have made you welcome." He nodded to all of them, and retreated.

As he walked back to his study he wondered if her mother would immediately sell her again to another brothel. What about Sato's will? Could she get anything from the short time she had lived with him?

He was nearly at his study door, when he heard a soft step behind him and turned, Sadako stopped, looking embarrassed. She was, he thought, prettier than Miyagi, even though she was older.

"Yes, Sadako. What is it?"

"It's about Miyagi, sir."

He wondered if she was also about to object to Miyagi's bad influence and opened the door to his room. "Come in."

They sat, Sadako stiffly on her knees, her hands folded in her lap.

He remembered how she had walked in on him and Aoi and with embarrassment irritation rose again. "Well?" he asked brusquely.

She clenched her hands and burst into speech."Sir, I think Miyagi may be with child. That would make travel very dangerous. I have tried to talk her out of it, but she will not stay a day longer than she must. Could you urge her perhaps?"

His first reaction was shock: would he now be saddled with the cursed woman and her child forever? On second thought, however, there might be a solution to this dilemma. If the child was Sato's, she might have a claim on his property and a home for Sato's heir.

Sadako must have read the first expression on his face because she raised her chin and said, "We have talked a little. Her story is not unlike mine, poor girl. I was lucky; but she ended up in a brothel. I think one must make allowances for the fact that she had no choice in the matter. She was a mere child when her mother sold her. To be precise, I believe the man who bought her tricked her mother. What happened later is what happens to all the girls in that profession. They have little choice in the matter."

Given her expression, he took this for a reprimand. Clearly, she did not approve of his attitude toward Miyagi. He said coldly, "Miyagi's situation is regrettable, but my concern is for my daughter. I do not wish her to be exposed to the secrets of a brothel." Any more than he had wanted her exposed to the temptations of life at the imperial court. Less in fact.

Sadako bowed her head. "I understand, sir," she said sadly. "Miyagi will not speak of such things. I came because she insists on leaving here and returning to her mother. In her condition, I think that would be dangerous. But it shall be as you direct. She can be given a room elsewhere and wait for news there."

Akitada bit his lip. Now she made him look like a heartless ogre. No, he would not have it. He said, "Very well."

Sadako rose, bowed, and walked out.

*

He felt depressed after that encounter, but his ill humor had disappeared and was replaced by a wish to make up for the way he had acted. Miyagi could not stay, but he could help her make a new life. He summoned Tora's wife Hanae and explained the problem, including Miyagi's possible pregnancy. Hanae immediately offered to take her into their house.

"Poor girl," she murmured. "I've known such stories when I still worked in the quarter. They did not turn out well. This one may. She lost the man she loved, but she'll wish to raise his child. Leave it to me, sir."

Hanae had never been a prostitute herself, but she had been a dancer, a profession that would have led to the same work if Tora had not fallen in love with her. Akitada left the Miyagi problem with her, and sent for Saburo.

"Saburo," he said, "I want you to gather evidence of Sato's marriage to Miyagi. Talk to Sadako and Miyagi and see if there is any documentation. Get a statement from Miyagi's maid. Search the city archives for evidence. Whatever you can find will help. We must claim Sato's property for Miyagi's child."

"She's having a child?" Saburo grinned. "How very nice for her. The maid swears they were married. I've kept up my contact with the clerk in the city administration. Both Sato's manageress and a distant cousin have put in a claim. I doubt they will prevail against Sato's own child."

Saburo gone, Akitada rubbed his hands in satisfaction. He would get someone in the Ministry of Justice, where he still had old friends, to draw up a claim for Miyagi. It would be a busy day.

*

It was after the midday rice, when he emerged from the *Daidairi,* having successfully dealt with Miyagi's claim. He ate at a small stand just outside the main gate to the *Daidairi* where one of the many street vendors did a good business selling snacks and noodles in broth to the clerks and scribes working in the government offices. Today he had the unpleasant feeling that he was being stared at. Perhaps his visits to the prime minister had caused this interest. He glanced about. Upper level officials rarely mixed in this crowd and he saw no familiar faces. But a moment later he was joined by the prime minister's secretary.

As they stood together, slurping noodles and vegetables and sipping the hot, spicy broth, they renewed their acquaintance, and the secretary said, "His Excellency speaks highly of you, sir. He has been very busy doing good on behalf of his brother and it seems there is an improvement already."

"I'm gratified," Akitada said, his good mood heightened by this news.

Having parted from the secretary, he next went to see Kobe. The cases against Ishikawa and the Fujiwara captain were still open, and Kobe's determination to arrest the men would bring trouble.

Trouble, it seemed, had preceded him. He walked into a confrontation. Kobe sat behind his desk, looking stubborn, his sergeant stood stiffly beside him, and in front of both, two high-ranking officials were taking turns berating them. Akitada knew the two officials. The bigger and fatter of the two was Fujiwara Morozane, currently minister of the Treasury. The smaller one was Minamoto Yoritoshi, a major controller of the Council of State.

"I cannot imagine what possessed you to arrest a relative of the prime minister and one of the empresses," shouted Morozane, the stiff ribbons on the back of his court hat quivering with his rage.

"And Secretary Ishikawa! Isn't anyone safe from your madness?" squeaked the controller, a shorter version of the first.

Kobe's eyes fell on Akitada. "Hem," he said, "Perhaps this isn't a good time, Akitada. I'll speak to you later."

Akitada ignored this and joined the group. "Are you trying to deprive me of some of the recognition for bringing two criminals to justice?" he asked lightly, nodding and smiling at the two officials, who had turned to stare at him.

Morozane recognized him. "Sugawara, isn't it? What? So you're behind this. I might have known."

Kobe closed his eyes and groaned.

Akitada nodded to the fat man. "Minister Morozane. Good to see you again, sir. The two men that were arrested are respectively guilty of ordering a murder and of assisting in it. My career in the department of justice has taught me that it is the government's duty to administer the laws of the land. Superintendant Kobe consulted me in this case. Since there are, as you both point out, ranking members of the nobility involved, he thought it safer. My answer was that the emperor expects all of us to do our duty and follow the prescribed laws. Now, according to the *Taiho* code . . ."

The minister waved his hands to stop him. "You have no official standing in this matter, Sugawara."

Akitada raised his brows. "But Superintendent Kobe has. Besides, I doubt that His Excellency, the prime minister, will see my involvement as an excuse to sweep murder under the *tatami.* However, if you insist, I can ask him later. I have an appointment."

The controller caught his breath. The minister goggled. Silence fell.

Then the minister asked, "You have reported this to the prime minister?"

"Not yet, but I shall. Do you wish me to tell him about your interest in the matter?"

They both started to object. Morozane yielded the honor to Minamoto Yoritoshi.

"Let's not be hasty," Minamoto said. "As you say, this is a tricky business. If these charges are indeed correct, we must find a way of dealing with them in such a way that no blame falls on the administration. I'm quite sure the prime minister would agree."

Kobe frowned. "What do you propose?"

The two officials exchanged glances. Minamoto said, "The minister and I shall discuss how this is best handled. Perhaps you'd better release the two men for the time being."

Kobe shook his head. "Out of the question. They stay here until they face a trial."

The minister of the treasury urged, "This can be handled internally, Superintendent. We'll appoint a council of nobles who will hear the charges."

Kobe nodded. "When I have been assured that justice will be served, I'll have both men brought before whatever judge you appoint."

Akitada said with a nod, "There has been precedent for this. I believe it can be done quickly and when found guilty both men can be removed from the capital to avoid much publicity."

The two officials looked at each other again and then nodded. Minamoto said to Kobe, "We shall let you know."

When they were gone, Kobe sighed with relief. "That was quite brilliant, Akitada. Thank you."

Akitada smiled and asked hopefully, "Does that mean you'll withdraw your resignation?"

"No. Never. I'm done. Give me peace, my friend. I have earned it."

There was a pause, then Kobe asked, "What about Miyagi? She was released. I worry about her."

"She is at my house. Tora and Saburo took her there."

"I might have known. You're a kind man, Akitada. I cannot imagine another nobleman taking a woman from the quarter into his household. What are her plans?"

Akitada flushed, remembering his anger when he discovered that Miyagi had become his personal problem. He said, "We must try to prove her marriage. She seems to be having Sato's child." In his mind, he was not at all sure that the child was Sato's . It could have been fathered by any of her earlier clients.

Kobe smiled and clapped his hands. His joy for Miyagi was quite touching, given that he had not smiled for many months now. "How fortunate! If ever anyone deserved another chance, it's Miyagi."

Kobe had thought the same when he had taken to wife the blind shampoo girl Sachi. Only, he had thought himself the fortunate one.

Akitada said, "Well, I'd better get started. There will be paperwork to be sorted out and witness statements to be gathered."

32

The Trouble with Women

Akitada spent the rest of the day on Miyagi's problem. He called her to his study with Saburo and Tora by his side. She appeared with Sadako, who seemed to be in protective attendance. This irritated him, but he said nothing.

The women knelt before his desk. His retainers sat on either side of him. It looked uncomfortably like a hearing.

Akitada nodded to Miyagi and said, "I understand you have been made comfortable in Captain Tora's home?"

Miyagi nodded. "They are very kind."

"Good. Sadako tells me you are with child."

Miyagi flushed a deep red. She hung her head. "It is a blessing to me, sir, even if it delays my departure. I apologize."

Akitada waved that aside. "No matter. It occurred to me that the child may have a claim on Sato's estate."

Still flushed, she raised her head to look him in the eyes. "This child is Sato's. There is no other possibility."

This did not necessarily prove his paternity, but Akitada said nothing. Instead he pointed out the need to gather evidence of the marriage. Miyagi calmed down and revealed that Sato had indeed filed documents and also mentioned entering her name as co-owner of the house they had lived in."

Saburo asked quickly, "Did he list you as his wife?"

"Yes."

Saburo looked at Akitada. "We should find sufficient proof and file a claim, sir. And then there is the business."

Miyagi said, "I don't want anything but the little house. We were very happy there."

"Unless there are other heirs listed in a will," Akitada said, "your son will claim the rice dealership and whatever other properties Sato owned. I understand he was a rich man. Don't reject such a future for your child."

Tears had come to her eyes, but she still looked at him defiantly. "Yes. The child is his child."

Akitada dismissed the women and set his retainers to their tasks. Saburo would search the city files, and

Tora would find everyone who could testify that there had been a marriage between Sato and Miyagi.

It was night time by then. Satisfied with these accomplishments, Akitada decided to visit Aoi.

*

He left his house wearing only a light silk robe and short jacket. It was probably inadequate for the weather, but Aoi was not far away. The sky was still overcast, and there was a strong wind so that he had to catch hold of his hat from time to time. It had become uncomfortably warm, and that was bringing on a storm. Thunder rumbled in the distance, and over the western mountains lightning lit up the sky. It did not matter. His errand was important and would end pleasurably. It would be his chance to set his life straight. Tonight he would ask Aoi to be his wife. Perhaps, when the storm broke, they would be making love–the "wind and the rain," appropriate names f or their passion.

The marriage had much to recommend it. They were close in age and background. She was intelligent and well-educated. He enjoyed conversing with her as long as she stayed away from matters of exorcisms and communications with the dead. Aoi would know how to keep his household in order. There would be no more calls on him to argue with Sadako about unwelcome guests.

Aoi, being related to the senior branch of the Fujiwara, could also be counted on to bring at least a decent dowry. This would be helpful in case there were more children. After all, the divorce from Yukiko meant returning the rich properties he had gained from that marriage. On second thought, Aoi might well be too old to bear a child. Akitada did not mind this at all. He was content with his own two.

And best of all, Aoi was a wonderful lover. His whole body warmed simply thinking about bedding her.

Thus having solved most of his problems as he walked, he had missed the fact that he had been followed for a while. But when he stopped outside the Oimikado palace, the man turned down a side street and vanished. Reassured, Akitada arrived at Aoi's door a little wind-blown but with a smile on his face and a hunger in his belly to make love to this enigmatic woman, to possess the tigress.

Aoi was dressed in white and had been performing some service before a small Shinto shrine. He had surprised her, and she was at first distracted. But she took off the formal, stiff white gown and the white head dress and came to him wearing only a thin silk undergown. To his delight, he could see her body clearly outlined against the light of the candles. It was voluptuous and faintly rosy, and totally irresistible.

With a growl in the back of his throat, he embraced her, picking her up bodily, and carrying her to the bedding that had been spread out already.

She laughed a little and tugged at his clothes. "So passionate, my beloved?"

He answered this by kissing her and pushing the undergown off her shoulders to caress her breasts.

She gasped. "Oh, Akitada! Take me! Again and again."

He still said nothing, being occupied with shedding his own clothes.

Neither bothered to remove her undergown completely. It ended up, torn, and tangled between their legs, fetters that tied them to each other. And so they made love again. It was as good as it had been before. And outside the wind shook the building and the thunder came closer. She bit his neck and cried out, and he worked furiously until he, too, gained his pleasure and collapsed, burying his face between her breasts.

When sense returned, he found that there was no rain yet, but the night was still young, and he hoped to repeat his performance.

He rolled on his side, becoming aware of the tangle of silk that bound them together. It was an omen. He bent to kiss her and murmured, "My wife!"

She looked up at him, her eyes still soft and dreamy. "Yukiko? What has she done now?"

He tossed aside the remnants of the undergown and kissed her belly. Already desire stirred again. "Nothing. I have divorced her."

She sat up. "I heard a rumor. They are saying she is furious. You have made an enemy, Akitada."

He laughed and traced circles around her nipples with his finger. "I don't care. It's all been decided. Kosehira came and suggested that he adopt her child."

She took his hand and kissed it. "You must be careful, my love. Yukiko cannot bear being shamed, and you have shamed her. Everyone wonders if the child is yours. Now they will know it isn't."

"Good! She has made my life a misery." He took her head between in his hands and kissed her lips. "I love you, Aoi. You will be my wife. We shall live together until the end of our days. That's the way I want it."

She made a small protesting sound, but he stifled that by kissing her again.

"No, no," he said after they parted to catch their breaths, "don't make difficulties. It will be simple and wonderful. We will make love like this every night, and perhaps during the days also. You are the woman I want to spend the rest of my life with."

She touched his face and sighed. "Oh, Akitada." Then she got up and went behind a screen to remove the traces of their lovemaking and to put on clothes.

He was disappointed by this reaction. Somehow the "Oh, Akitada," had not sounded as joyous as he had expected. And clearly there was to be no more "wind and rains" even if the first heavy drops were now hitting the roof. Akitada stepped into his trouser skirt with a frown on his face. She had almost sounded irritated. He had laid open his soul and offered her his life, and she had not found the prospect to her taste.

But perhaps he had misheard. Heslipped his undergown over his head with only a minor twinge from his ribs, and asked, "Has my proposal come at an awkward time? Is there someone else? Or are you perhaps already married?"

She reappeared from behind the screen, fully dressed in a green gown and white trouser skirt. Looking sadly at him, she twisted her long hair into a knot. "In a way, Akitada, I am married, but not in the way you think."

"What does that mean?" he demanded, becoming irritated.

"I chose to serve the gods many years ago when I was a mere child. They have blessed me by giving me certain powers. I am bound to their service with bonds stronger that those of marriage or a love affair. For me, there is only one life, a life of worship and of communion with the gods."

He stood dumbstruck. All his past reservations and prejudices returned, and he felt an utter fool for having fallen for her. He glared. "Then what was this? Why this passion, this hunger for love-making, these protestations of love for me? Were they easy lies so you could slake your lust? Am I just one of many you choose to lie with when desire is upon you? You have lied to me, Aoi, and you have used me."

"No, Akitada!" With a cry of grief and shock, she ran to him, hands stretched to touch him. He stepped away.

She stopped, very pale now, and he saw tears welling up in her eyes. Her hands fell to her side, and she stood before him, weeping.

It nearly broke his heart. "Why, Aoi?" he demanded hoarsely. "I love you."

"I love you, too, Akitada. I shall always love you. I'll be your lover whenever you want me, but I cannot be your wife."

Furious at this second rejection, he snarled, "Aren't you afraid that all that lovemaking will leave you polluted? Won't the gods object to your service when you approach them contaminated by our lust?" He heard the bitterness in his voice and wished his pain were not so obvious.

She said, "The gods love life. The joining of man and woman is a celebration of life, not something dirty. I knew you did not approve of my work, but I thought you respected the ancient gods of our nation. They have given us justice, order, and their blessings. You, who devote your life to bringing about justice should understand. Have I been so wrong about you?"

He said nothing, turning his back to her. She was right about his respect for the ancient gods. But why could she not understand his need?

She asked in a small voice, "Must we part?"

He said, "For now, yes. I cannot speak to the future. I seem to have none at the moment," and left, without looking at her.

*

Outside the rain hit him in gusts as he emerged from the Oimikado Palace. The guards had sheltered in the gatehouse and dashed out to open the gate. They recognized him by now. He wondered what gossip they were passing around. Surely, his affair with Aoi was by now an open secret. What would they make of his departure in the middle of a storm?

Perhaps people already speculated about marriage. Such events were of enormous interest to courtiers because they signaled changes in the power structure. Aoi, though without immediate family support, was as highly connected as Yukiko had been. This had not mattered to him because he had wanted Aoi. He still wanted Aoi. He needed Aoi. Without her, he felt abandoned to a long, lonely, dreary bachelorhood. And the rejection hurt badly.

In his present mood, he welcomed the thunder and lightning, the blowing rain that molded his thin robe to his body, the wind that blew away his hat. He had no need for them.

She had rejected his offer, and he knew her well enough to know that he could not change her mind. He was beginning to feel anger on top of disappointment.

It was not far to his residence, but his mind was in turmoil and he could not face going home and to bed as if nothing had happened. He turned his steps southward and walked the wet, dark streets under trees tossed by the wind and eaves that poured a deluge on him as he passed. He thought about Aoi, about Yukiko, about the children, about Miyagi, and Tadanobu. They had all been his failures. He had proved helpless dealing with each of them. Briefly, Aoi had given him hope and strength, and now he no longer could cope.

The streets were empty. It was very dark, and only occasionally a light glimmered behind a garden wall.

Once he saw a man hurrying home with a lantern, the back of his robe pulled over his head. Akitada's eyes were accustomed to the dark, and he had no trouble following the streets or crossing one of the canals by its small bridge. Now and then he thought he could hear footfall behind him, perhaps of another solitary wanderer, but it might have been his imagination. Thunder still rumbled overhead though the storm was receding.

He thought he might leave the capital and live in the country this summer. With Kobe gone and his relationship with Kosehira newly awkward over the divorce and adoption, he would be happier there. He would take the children and remove his daughter from the dangerous influence of court life in the capital.

He was about to cross another canal when he became aware of the footsteps again. They seemed closer and more hurried. He turned his head and saw a big figure, dressed in black and with a black hood over its head.

His absentmindedness had nearly cost him his life. Even now, his brain did not signal danger right away. He puzzled at this stranger but thought he had nothing to do with him.

But then the man was upon him, his arm rose, and a long knife descended toward his chest before Akitada could react.

At the last moment, he flung himself aside. The knife ripped through his full sleeve. He fell against the railing of the bridge and almost tumbled over into the water below. His half-mended ribs responded with a surge of pain so agonizing and sharp that he cried out.

His assailant perhaps took a step back, but the knife had become entangled in Akitada's silk sleeve and he pulled at it in vain.

Knowing himself at the killer's mercy, Akitada fought for the knife by clamping both hands around the man's wrist. They struggled for a moment, a frightening and painful struggle with a faceless assailant who looked more like a demon than a human being and who had a free hand to fight back. He was using it to punch him wherever he could. Akitada tried to pry the other man's fingers loose and managed to bend one of them backward.

With a shout of pain, the attacker released the knife and flung himself bodily on Akitada, carrying him backward down to the ground. They both lay in the mud gasping and struggling. Akitada belatedly shouted for constables, though he knew there was not much chance of finding one in this quiet residential quarter.

The rain still fell and Akitada's clothes clung to him moistly, hampering his movements. With one hand he defended himself against his assailant, with the other he attempted to free the knife. In the present struggle it was as much a danger to his life as the man on top of him.

The pain in his side and the weight on his chest made it difficult to breathe. Akitada was quickly wearing out. He attempted another shout for help, then finally got the hilt of the knife in his hand and turned the blade against his attacker just as the man got both of his hands around Akitada's throat.

There was a grunt and he was free. The assassin rolled off him. Akitada grasped the knife, drew in a breath, and braced himself for the pain of getting to his feet and fighting again.

To his surprise, he managed to stand. The other man stayed where he was. Akitada gave him a kick with his foot. Nothing happened. He looked at the knife and saw that the long blade was covered with black blood. And more blood spread out from under the man's body to mix with the rain puddles.

It was an unreal scene. Lightning flashed from time to time, and after feeling his side to see if he had broken his ribs again, and then his arm to check for a knife wound, Akitada bent to feel the man's neck. He was dead. Akitada peeled back the hood, and with the next flash of lightning saw the face of a young stranger.

Finally footsteps approached and a moment later two constables reached them. Since it was clear who stood, holding the bloody knife, and who lay bleeding at his feet, this could have been troublesome to explain. But Akitada's clothes marked him as one of the good people, while the dead man's proved him to be an assassin.

Still, it was nearly dawn before Akitada got home, and by then he no longer grieved over having lost Aoi. It was a new day, the storm was past, and the sun was rising again.

33

Tadanobu Dies

Akitada's good mood was entirely due to a rumor that reached him just as the police concluded their questioning and confirmed that he had merely defended himself.

It was not clear who brought the news to police headquarters, but such matters tend to reach the police rather quickly. The prime minister's brother had died during the night, surprisingly so since his health had improved markedly, even to the point that he had been seen walking in his garden.

Akitada wasted no thought on what might have brought about this reversal. He had all along wished

Tadanobu dead for the crimes he had committed in the fifty years of his despicable life. So he walked homeward with a lighter step.

There he found Tora, Saburo, and Genba waiting for him with frowns on their faces.

"What's the matter?" he asked cheerfully in spite of the long night and an empty stomach.

"How could you go off unarmed again?" Tora growled.

Saburo added, "We were agreed that the danger wasn't past, sir. Tora and I could have come with you."

Genba merely looked at him accusingly.

It was a measure of the love his people had for him that they greeted him in this fashion, but he did feel rather like a child being reprimanded by his parents.

"The idea of taking you two with me on a visit to a lady hadn't occurred to me," he said, and headed for the house and his room.

They followed him.

"You went to see Lady Aoi?" Tora asked, interested.

"None of your business."

"Was that wise, sir?" Saburo asked. "Lady Aoi is closely related and allied with certain powerful people you have managed to offend."

It was true, but Akitada snapped, "Lady Aoi is my business."

"Have you heard? Lord Tadanobu has died," Genba offered, perhaps to emphasize the danger surrounding Akitada's recent activities.

"I've heard." Akitada walked into his study, where he found Sadako and his daughter.

Yasuko jumped up and ran to him. "Are you hurt? Did the killer wound you? Oh, Father, we have been awake all night, worrying. Why must you keep going out and getting into trouble?" She threw her arms around him and buried her face in his shoulder.

Akitada was moved by this concern and also surprised to find how much his daughter had grown. His eyes went to Sadako, who had risen and looked at him searchingly.

"I'm unhurt," he told Yasuko. "But I'm wet and muddy because I got caught in the storm last night and, er, slipped and fell at one point. I appreciate everyone's concern, but right now I'd like to change out of these clothes, take a bath, and eat my morning rice."

They left him then.

The prime minister's emissary arrived as Akitada was finishing his bowl of rice gruel and wondering if he should take a short nap before dealing with the day's duties.

The emissary was rather carelessly dressed, his rank ribbon crooked, his sash belonging to another outfit, his starched hat crooked, and his face unshaven. He practically shot in, when Tora opened the door to announce him.

"Sir, you are to come immediately," he shouted.

Akitada put down his bowl and regarded him in surprise. "I don't see what else I can do for His Excellency. I understand his brother had died. Please convey my–"

"You don't understand." The emissary, Akitada did not recall his name, stood before him, fluttering his hands in an agitated manner, and looking over his shoulder to see if they were alone.

Tora had closed the door behind the visitor, but Akitada knew well he would be outside trying to catch whatever news the messenger had brought. "What is it?" Akitada asked, irritably.

The man leaned closer and whispered, "Lord Tadanobu has been murdered."

"Murdered?" Akitada cried.

"Ssh!" The emissary put a finger to his lips and glanced anxiously toward the door.

Akitada took up his bowl again. "Do I take it that His Excellency did not manage to appease all of the persons his brother has injured?" he asked in a normal tone.

The emissary looked shocked at Akitada's lack of proper respect. "Er, His Excellency expects you," he said stiffly.

Akitada sighed and put down his bowl again. He got up, considered whether he should change into a court robe and hat and decided not to. The truth was that he was heartily tired of the prime minister's concerns after another night attack on his life.

They walked to Tadanobu's residence without speaking. The emissary's face was rigidly disapproving.

The prime minister was pacing in the reception room. With him was Tadanobu's major domo, familiar to Akitada from his previous visit. The servants they had passed had looked frightened. The major domo was so upset that his hands were shaking.

"Ah, there you are," the prime minister cried. "Did he tell you?" The nod was toward the emissary.

"I was told that your brother has been murdered, that's all," Akitada said.

His Excellency nodded. "Come," he said and strode off.

Akitada noted that the prime minister had not looked grief-stricken. Mostly his expression had been thin-lipped and angry. He followed the great man through several corridors to Tadanobu's private quarters. An imperial guard stood at the door. He bowed and opened it.

The room was in half-light because the shutters were closed. But several candelabra flickered in the draft and revealed a figure lying on rich bedding.

When Akitada stepped closer, he saw blood, a great deal of it. This surprised him. Given Tadanobu's past bouts of illness he had wondered about poison; it had seemed to him the most likely weapon for a murderer to have used. But this killer had used a knife. And Akitada thought immediately of the man who had attacked him.

He bent over the dead man for a brief examination. The silken quilts had already been pulled aside. Tadanobu was wearing only his white undergown, which was now soaked in blood. The murderer must have been in a frenzy to make certain Tadanobu would die. He found at least eight wounds in the man's belly and chest, plus a slashed throat. Most likely the attack had occurred while Tadanobu had been sleeping.

Straightening up, Akitada asked, "You have the killer?"

"No."

"You surprise me. I would have thought this could only have been done by someone in Tadanobu's household. Was he seen? Do you suspect who did this?"

"No. I know nothing. That's why you are here."

Akitada shook his head. "I work with the police. I take it you haven't called them."

"No police. We'll announce that his illness returned and he succumbed."

Akitada considered this. Whoever had done it had done them all a favor. The police were obligated to arrest and charge the person. Chances were good that the guilty person had good reason to take this revenge. The violence of the attack proved as much. But in the end, he could not do what he was asked to do, that is condone a murder or deliver the murderer to the Fujiwara sort of justice.

He looked the prime minister in the eye and said, "No. It would be best if you called in the police, but if you don't, I will."

The prime minister stared at him. He seemed to swell with anger. "Are you mad? I just told you how it will be done. If you say one word of this to anyone, you'll go straight to Kyushu and I'll make sure you're never heard of again."

So much for the passing moments of respect he had felt for the prime minister in the past. Akitada said nothing. But he did not look away. The hair at the back of his neck stood up.

The prime minister broke the staring contest first. He brushed a shaking hand over his eyes. "I loved my brother," he said in a broken voice. "He was my true brother. We had the same mother. When she died, she asked me to look after Tadanobu. Dear Heaven, how could I have prevented this?"

Akitada wisely did not answer this. His own belief in *karma* meant that Tadanobu had brought his criminal tendencies with him from an earlier life and that he was now headed to another life which would punish him for his deeds. But his murderer lived, and that was his own problem now.

After a long while to allow the prime minister to compose himself, he said, "It is likely that the killer is or was in this house and that someone here was aware of him. Or her."

His Excellency looked up. "A woman? You think a woman could have done this?"

"It looks as if your brother was asleep. Yes, a woman could have done this easily."

"But it is vicious. Women don't do such things."

Akitada almost laughed. "I have known several murderous females in my past of investigating crimes."

The prime minister sat down on one of the cushions. Not being invited to do so also, Akitada remained standing.

"What should I do?" the prime minister asked. He sounded so helpless, that Akitada had to suppress his surprise.

"I cannot speak for Your Excellency," he said, "but I have always found that the truth cleans falsehood from the minds of the common people and lets them be easy in their humble lives."

His Excellency nodded slowly. "Yes," he muttered as if to himself, "yes, that is true, but the gods . . . have been offended. His Majesty has been offended. Our sacred nation has been offended."

"Yes. For too long. It is time to make a change, Your Excellency. Too many crimes have been covered up. Too many offenses have been allowed to remain in the memory of the people."

"I tried. I tried to make amends. They forgave him."

"Not all, Excellency." Akitada nodded toward the blood-stained corpse.

The other man looked at him uncertainly. "How can I toss the memory of a beloved brother to the vilification by the people?"

"I think it is too late to worry about that."

The prime minister flinched. "How can this be?"

"I found out about Lord Tadanobu's deeds, and I did so quickly. The people do not forget so easily."

The prime minister sagged. "Very well. Do what must be done. But do not involve me."

It was not what Akitada wanted. It left him open to retaliation at a later time. But he nodded. "As you wish. The police and their doctor will arrive shortly. Please accept my sincere regrets for your sorrow, sir. Have you seen your brother's family members?"

"Only his first lady accompanied him to the capital. She is on a pilgrimage." He paused. "She is fond of pilgrimages, it seems."

"Well, that clears her of suspicion. It leaves only servants and visitors."

The sagging figure shuddered and covered his eyes with a hand. Akitada walked out.

*

Akitada found the prime minister's secretary waiting outside. When he saw Akitada, he hurried over.

"What are we to do?" he asked.

"Send for the police and let them handle it."

"The police?" The secretary looked shocked. "Are you sure?"

Akitada nodded.

The secretary went to the door, clearing his throat. After a moment, he opened it and cleared his throat again. Apparently His Excellency asked him to enter for he went in, closing the door behind himself. Akitada waited.

The secretary appeared again in a moment. He nodded to Akitada and said, "I shall go myself. His Excellency says you are free to talk to anyone you wish to question."

"Thank you."

They walked out of the building together. The secretary hurried off to summon the police, and Akitada headed for the service yard where Tadanobu's stables, storage houses, and kitchen were located. He noted that Tadanobu's household was well regulated. There seemed to be plenty of servants, stable hands, and laborers about to keep the master and his family comfortable. He made for the kitchen, trying to remember what Saburo had reported about his interview with Tadanobu's cook and the Harada woman. Two families who worked for Tadanobu had been on Aoi's list of his victims. The Haradas were the parents of the child Tadanobu had run down with his horse. They had been "paid off" by being given a property in the city and by continued employment in their former master's household. Especially interesting was the fact that Mrs. Harada and her daughter worked regularly in the house and in the kitchen, while the son delivered food stuffs and other supplies to the household. Tadanobu's old cook was the widow of Isaburo, the servant who had accidentally spilled wine and been punished by being tied up outside on a freezing night, a punishment that cost him his life.

It had become obvious to Akitada that Tadanobu's murderer had been a member of the household, or someone who had ready access to Tadanobu's room. And that had led him to wonder about Tadanobu's long and puzzling illness. Who more likely to have produced the symptoms of such an illness than one who was free to come and go, or a cook?

*

The kitchen was large, larger and better equipped than his own, and it was full of servants. None was very busy. The shock of their master's murder had thrown them into various states of anxiety. They stopped talking when he entered.

"I'm Lord Sugawara," he said, looking around at all the faces. "As you have heard, your master has been murdered. The police will be here shortly and ask you questions to find out if any of you have seen or heard anything that will help us find the killer. There is no need to be afraid as long as you obey them."

They reacted in various ways. Most bowed to him and nodded. Some shook their heads, some muttered their shock and grief or called on the Buddha. Eventually, they fell quiet and looked at him expectantly.

He had tried to read their expressions, but gave up quickly. There were too many of them, women of all ages and a few men. Presumably the men carried water or firewood for the three huge rice cooker ovens. Or perhaps they were stable hands who had walked in to talk about their master's death or get news from house servants who might be there.

A number looked anxious, but this did not necessarily imply guilt. The death of a master meant reorganization of the staff when a successor took over. Akitada wondered who Tadanobu's heirs were. In view of the man's recent illness, it seemed to him remarkable now that he was still only with his senior wife. The others, along with his children, had remained on his country estate. Perhaps it was a measure of his past cruelty that they had felt safer at a distance.

As for his senior wife, the current one was a cousin and Tadanobu's age. His scandalous marriage to Nobuko, an imperial handmaiden, had ended with his young wife taking refuge in a nunnery.

These thoughts passed through his mind as he looked at them and eventually focused on an old woman who was seated on a chair. This was unusual when everyone else was standing or kneeling.

"Ah," he said, walking up to her, "I think you may be Mrs. Isaburo."

"I'm the cook," she rasped.

Akitada saw that she was not only old, but quite ill. Her eyes were red-rimmed in a waxen face, and her arms and hands shook uncontrollably.

"But you are also Isaburo's widow?"

She nodded and raised a knotted fist as she tried to say something. But she choked, and bent forward in a paroxysm of coughing that shook her frail body. A young woman stepped forward and said, "Grandmother is very ill. Please do not trouble her, sir."

Akitada saw that the sleeve the old woman had held to her face was stained red with blood. It was clear that the woman was dying. He nodded to the younger woman and said, "Forgive me. Will you speak for her?"

She hesitated, then nodded, putting an arm around her grandmother.

The old woman croaked, "He's cursed him . . ." She gasped and clutched her granddaughter's arm.

The granddaughter bent to her and said, "Do not speak, Grandmother. It's bad for you."

The old woman took a shuddering breath, then grinned toothlessly. "It's done." She spoke quite clearly and nodded several times.

"What does she mean, 'he's cursed him' and 'it's done'?" Akitada asked.

"Nothing. Her mind wanders. It means nothing, sir." The girl was pretty, even with that stubborn look on her face.

"Isaburo cursed him," the old woman muttered.

There was a moment's silence, then Akitada asked, "Are any of the Haradas here today?"

The granddaughter looked across the room. Akitada's eyes followed hers and saw a middle-aged woman and a tall young man standing near the door.

"Thank you," he said, and walked across to them. They moved apart and seemed to want to leave, but he called out, "Mrs. Harada?"

She stopped, but the young man slipped out.

When she turned, he saw something like terror in her face.

"You are Mrs. Harada?"

"Yes. How did you know?"

"Oh." He smiled at her consternation. "I sent my clerk to talk to you. He pretended to be from the city administration, I believe."

The terror turned to resignation. She had turned pale, but she said nothing, waiting for him to speak first.

"I assume you know the cook?" She nodded, her face expressionless. "Did you also know her husband?" She nodded again. "You have both lost someone close to you because of Fujiwara Tadanobu's actions, and yet you don't seem to be angry at him, or happy that he is dead. Why is that?"

She looked down. "He paid us."

"Blood money?"

"We looked at it as that."

"But it wasn't enough, was it?"

She raised her head and glared at him. "No it wasn't. Not when he dismissed my husband after he and his father had served them all their lives." Her voice shook. "My husband was a warrior. He was someone who would give his life for his lord. But he turned him out just like that."

All at once Akitada understood her rage, and that of her whole family. What had happened to the Haradas was that they had been forced to exchange warrior status for that of low-class merchants, people even more despised than peasants, though frequently much richer than even noblemen. It was a perception of lost rank and must have hurt very much. And it would go on hurting, reminding them daily of what they had been and what they had become. And yet, she and her son had continued to come to the nobleman's house to do menial jobs.

He asked gently, "Your husband is dead?"

Her eyes flashed when she said, "He killed himself. With his sword. He shoved it into himself. Because he could not bear the shame. I pray for his courage."

That piece of information had been missing from Aoi's account. Her details on what had happened to the servants of Tadanobu had been significantly short. No doubt she had felt a later suicide of the father of the murdered boy was immaterial. But he was profoundly shocked by Mrs. Harada's last words. They amounted to a confession.

"I grieve for you and your family," he said. "Perhaps something could have been done to reinstate your sons, but now it is too late."

She nodded.

"You helped, didn't you?"

She looked away and shook her head.

"I don't blame you. What was done to your family was horrible. But the law must prevail."

"I did nothing," she finally muttered.

He nodded. "Very well. The police will find out."

She paled and reached for the door jamb to support herself. The police would use whips to get their answers. "My son, he knew nothing. He's innocent."

Akitada nodded again and walked out of the kitchen and into the service yard. He had heard the commotion of the arrival of the police. His heart was heavy.

The constables were everywhere, herding people into groups and keeping an eye on the gates. Akitada found Kobe about to climb the stairs to the main house and hurried to join him.

"Ah, there you are," Kobe said with a tight smile. "Trust you to be in the middle of this thing."

"Not my fault." Akitada held up his hands. "I had a look, being sent for by the prime minister. He wanted to handle it discreetly, whatever he meant by that. I argued for the police."

"Thanks a lot." Kobe grimaced.

They had reached the murder room and walked in. Kobe went quickly to the body, once again covered with a quilt. Pulling this back, he bent to study the wounds, and whistled softly. "Someone was very angry with him," he commented. He straightened and looked about him. "This must have been done by someone who had access to him."

"Yes. As it happens, the relatives of two people he killed are servants here."

Kobe's jaw sagged. "Dear heaven!"

"Yes. Let me tell you about them." He quickly outlined what he knew about who had access to Tadanobu and then told him of the Isaburo and Harada backgrounds. "It is possible, even likely, that they worked together," he added.

Kobe grimaced. "I'm going to hate this."

Akitada nodded. "Isaburo's wife, the cook, is dying, I think. She has probably been poisoning Tadanobu for a long time. I expect your men ought to search her room and question the kitchen staff. I think she must have put the poison in his food."

"Poison? He's been stabbed."

"He has been deathly ill for a long time. I think he was given some sort of poison on several occasions in the past. Since it did not kill him, someone decided to make sure this time."

"Surely not the dying cook?"

"No. But there is also the Harada family. And the cook has a young and strong granddaughter."

"I'm going to hate this," Kobe said again, shaking his head.

34

Yukiko

Akitada returned to his home, feeling very uneasy. The prime minister had sent word that he was to leave matters to the police and that he, the prime minister, would deal directly with the superintendent.

It signaled, of course, that Akitada had incurred the anger and distrust of His Excellency, but it also suggested that the prime minister expected to have an easier time convincing Kobe to suppress the investigation.

As for himself, he returned to his own life, albeit gradually. For one thing, Tora and Saburo awaited him full of questions. He sat down behind his desk and tried to answer them. Saburo was very upset.

"I talked to the widow of Isaburo and to Mrs. Harada, he said. "They showed no sign of resentment. In fact, they didn't seem to be grieving the deaths very much. Everything was about how good Tadanobu had been to them and how the boy and the old man had both deserved it by disobeying and being careless."

Akitada nodded. "I believe you, but let it be a lesson to you. People who are plotting something will lie to hide their true intentions."

Saburo hung his head. "I should have been more suspicious. Sorry, sir."

"Well, I didn't suspect them either until I realized that the murderer had to live in the Tadanobu residence or was a family friend."

"What about his wife?" Tora asked.

"Luckily away on a pilgrimage. It seems she goes on these a lot. Probably to get away from her husband. I did wonder that she should have gone even when he was so sick."

Saburo looked up. "Are you suspecting the cook of tampering with his food?"

"I'm certain of it. Kobe and his men will find proof. As it is, the old woman won't live long enough to go to trial. She practically admitted she was glad Tadanobu was dead."

Saburo frowned. "Really? She wasn't very chipper when I talked to her, but I didn't think she was dying."

"She's coughing up blood. But clearly she was in no condition to do the stabbing."

"Well," said Tora, "that leaves the Haradas. What did they say?"

Akitada frowned. "I don't know. I don't even know how many were involved. Saburo, who were the ones who worked at or visited Tadanobu's residence?"

Saburo scratched his head. "The mother certainly. And a daughter. And one of the sons made deliveries. They could all be involved."

"Yes. And then there was also the cook's granddaughter, a strapping young girl. Any of them could have used a knife to murder him."

"A knife from the kitchen?" Tora asked. "What granddaughter? Is she pretty?"

"No idea about the knife. The granddaughter is pretty. Quite young, too. I'd guess sixteen or seventeen."

Tora shook his head. "Hope it isn't her."

Akitada said, "I don't want it to be any of them. They've suffered enough."

Tora slapped his knees. "Well, at least you're out of danger. Kobe will lock them all up in his jail."

There was a brief silence. Akitada got to his feet. He said heavily, "No. It could not have had anything to do with Tadanobu. None of those servants could have known about my visits to Nakatoshi or Lady Aoi."

They gaped at him.

Tora said, "But then who?"

Akitada smiled a little. "I don't think you'll have to worry about it any longer. It was a personal matter. And now I have an errand."

*

He had never visited the part of the imperial palace that gave access to the women who served their majesties. It was a complicated matter, somewhat eased by the fact that he was or had been married to one of them. After following a servant down many hallways, some covered galleries, and up and down staircases between pavilions, he was left in a large bare room that contained only a dais with some silk cushions on it. Here he waited.

She came eventually, beautiful and haughty as ever, and with two spots of angry color burning in her cheeks.

"You!"

He nodded. "You look lovely, Yukiko, but then you always do. My compliments on that particularly stunning embroidered coat. Red always suited you."

She glared. "What does that mean? If you think you can come with sweet words to apologize after the scandal you have caused, forget it."

"The scandal *I* caused?"

"Yes. You let it be known that you have divorced me and that has ruined my reputation."

Akitada did not want to quarrel, but in justice he said, "Are you sure that it wasn't ruined already by your affair with Lord Okura? And by the fact that you conceived his child while we were separated?"

She flushed. "It could have been yours for all anybody knew."

"No, Yukiko. It was always known, at least here in the palace. I did my best to cover for you, but you have not tried to hide the affair subsequently."

She turned away. "That is over."

"Well, the damage is done."

She flared up, "And you? What about you? You keep a woman in your own house under the eyes of your young daughter! Oh, yes, Yasuko has told me all about it. And now you have added a very public seduction of Aoi to your list of love affairs."

He bit his lip. He would not get angry again. "There is nothing between Sadako and me. If Yasuko said there is, she has lied. And Aoi is none of your business. You are no longer my wife."

She was silent, then asked, "Why have you come, Akitada?"

"I have spoken with your father. He wants to adopt your child."

"And that will make everything all right?" she snapped.

"In a way. It is the best solution. Keep in mind that I, too, am the subject of gossip. The betrayed husband rarely fares well with those who take an interest in such things."

She walked to the dais and sat down angrily. "My father hates me. He despises me, his daughter. He only loves you. You cannot imagine the things he has said to me. He has called me a slut and a whore and told me that there was a special hell just for women like me. I hate you, Akitada. You have taken everything from me."

Astonished by this outburst, Akitada said, "I have come to realize it, but you are wrong about your father.

He loves you very much. Kosehira has a strong sense of loyalty to his friends and he wanted this marriage, so he feels responsible. He also has a strong sense of honor and was proud of you until this happened."

She thought about it. Then, in a small voice, she said, "It was I who wanted this marriage." She covered her face with her hands. "Oh, I wanted you so much. I idolized you. I thought you loved me. What a fool I was! You cannot love anyone. You only love your work."

Akitada winced. He was tempted to tell her that he, too had been a fool, that he, too had wanted her, and that in the end they just were not suited. He said nothing of the sort, for he knew now that Yukiko had not only betrayed him with another man, she had done much worse.

"You asked why I have come. The answer is that I've had enough of your murderous attacks on me."

Yukiko jumped up. "What? What murderous attacks?"

"You know very well what I mean. "Mrs. Kuruda told you I'd gone to visit Nakatoshi. Perhaps those three yokels you sent after me did not mean to kill me, though they did me enough damage, but the second man who waited for me outside Aoi's certainly meant to kill me. You've had me followed for days now."

She turned pale and swayed on her feet. The temptation was great to let her fall, but Akitada went to steady her. She clutched at his arm. "Are you sure?"

Akitada noted that she did not deny it. "Yes, he had a knife and meant business."

She turned away. "Okura had you followed. You hurt me, Akitada. When you took up with Aoi, you must have known I would find out. And so did everybody else. You cannot imagine how they looked at me. It shamed me and I was out of my mind with misery. And then you divorced me." She covered her face again. "I didn't want this but I told Okura how much I hated you."

Akitada was disgusted. "So you blame the attacks on him? Very well. Tell your lover to stop hiring assassins or I'll bring charges. The man he sent after me is dead, but he has been identified. No doubt he belongs to his household."

It would have been a fine revenge to bring charges, he thought, but he just wanted peace. He turned to leave.

She ran after him. "Wait, Akitada. I didn't mean it to get serious. You must believe me. I . . . you made me suffer and I wanted to make trouble for you. I broke up with Okura when I found out. Oh, Akitada, I was so upset about Aoi, I went to talk to you, but Mrs. Kuruda said you'd left to visit Nakatoshi. I'm sorry."

Revenge.

He stopped and turned. She looked genuinely miserable. In a gentler voice he said, "We both made mistakes, Yukiko. Remember, your father loves you. I hope you'll find happiness in your future.

*

At home he went to speak to his children. Yoshi was in the stable yard. He came, out of breath, his eyes shining, and cried, "Father, I beat Tora! At stick fighting. What do you think of that?"

It made Akitada sad. Tora was aging and he had problems with his head. Serious headaches troubled him and sometimes he lost his balance. But he smiled and congratulated his son. Yoshi was not surprised or curious about the divorce. He had never been close to Yukiko. He had another matter on his mind. He wanted to attend the university with his cousin, Akiko's son. Akitada told him he would think about it.

Yasuko was with Sadako. They seemed to be sorting through his daughter's summer clothes. Yasuko said impatiently, "I shall need some new clothes if I visit Yukiko at court. What is it that you want to tell us, Father?"

Akitada looked at her a little uncertainly, not sure how she would take the news. He decided she was old enough to know what had been going on.

"You must have wondered why I have not been around much lately," he said. "There was a case—no, two cases, though you know about Miyagi—that have taken all my time."

Yasuko snapped, "Yes, and you have been attacked twice and you have a new woman."

Sadako hissed. "Yasuko! Your manners. Don't speak to your father that way."

Akitada sighed. This would not be easy. "You're right, Yasuko. Let me tell you about the other case first.

It concerned the brother of the prime minister, Fujiwara Tadanobu."

Sadako gasped, then clamped a hand over her mouth.

Akitada decided to ignore this. "Dealing with the matter was dangerous for several reasons, but it is over now and has been resolved. I shall have time for both of you. I had decided that we would go on a long visit to your aunt Yoshiko. It is time you met those cousins. But Yoshi is thinking of attending the university here."

Yasuko said, "I'm staying, too. Yukiko has invited to visit her."

He saw that he had distracted them from his affair with Aoi, but had not yet finished his news. Sadako was silent. He said, "There is something else you should know, Yasuko. I have divorced Yukiko. She will henceforth reside with her father, Lord Kosehira, when she is not serving at court."

This was greeted with stunned silence. He saw tears rise to Yasuko's eyes. She wailed, "Why, Father? I thought you loved her. She's very beautiful and everyone loves her."

"She is much younger than I. We were not well suited. Her life and mine are very different."

Yasuko made a face. "Yes. She enjoys all the excitement at court and you hate company. What about little Akiko?"

He swallowed. "She will remain with her mother and grandparents."

"Can I visit?"

"Yes, but perhaps later on."

Yasuko was not mollified. "So, I suppose you'll marry this other woman now."

Sadako hissed her warning again.

Akitada said, "No," and left.

When he was alone again, he grieved having lost his daughter's love and respect. Yoshi simply did not seem to care. He had his own interests.

Akitada felt that his home had become joyless. They used to have such good times together, making music and watching the seasons change.

No more.

*

He was sitting at his desk, pondering where he had gone so wrong, where he had taken a wrong turn on the path of his life and ended walking stony and treacherous ground. Someone cleared her throat at the door. He frowned, not wanting any company at the moment. "Who is it?"

"It's me. Sadako."

She sounded almost timid.

"Come in."

He had a chance to look at her more closely. Yes, she had a pretty face and her hair was quite lovely. Sadako must be in her mid thirties, he thought

He asked, "How old are you?"

She flushed. "Thirty-nine years, sir."

"Ah. You look a mere girl." He smiled at her.

This seemed to make her even more nervous. She approached slowly. "I've come to ask you something, sir. You mentioned Fujiwara Tadanobu earlier."

"Yes. He was very ill and I was supposed to find out what troubled him. I failed. He died last night."

She bowed her head. "Buddha be praised," she said with such fervor that he did a double take.

"Yes. He was an evil man. Did he harm someone you knew?"

She nodded.

"Will you tell me about it?"

She gave him an uncertain look. "I have been forbidden to talk about it. By pain of death. But I think I can trust you."

Akitada's eyebrows rose. "By pain of death? What in the world happened?" And then a memory surfaced and suspicion rose. "You told me once that you grew up in the north. By any chance was that in Rikuchu Province?"

She gasped, "How did you know?"

"Are you related to Tanaka Juntaro?"

She nodded. "Tanaka Juntaro was my father."

"Great heavens! You should have told me."

"I couldn't. We were all made to swear never to mention what happened to anyone. You mustn't tell. Please!"

Akitada frowned. "I can see where Tadanobu and his officials would have used such a method to suppress news of what had happened. But it's all over now. Over for good. Your family is to be reinstated. The prime minister has so ordered." He smiled at her confusion. "It's good news, Sadako. "

She brushed away some tears. "It has been such a long time. There was nothing, no money and no place to take refuge. There seems no point in it now. Everything is gone."

"You have no news of your family?"

"In the beginning I sent a letter now and then, and I heard from them. They were very poor. My brother had left to serve as a soldier. My sister worked as a maid. My mother was not well enough to work. Then the letters stopped coming." She twisted her hands and wept.

. Akitada rose and went to her, putting an arm around her shoulder. "Don't cry. I'll look into it and see what we can find out."

She nodded, muttered her thanks, and left.

Akitada looked after her and considered the fact that, being well-born, she had suddenly become very eligible woman.

*

Kobe came that night to join him for his evening rice again. Akitada was pleased and hoped it would become a habit.

"How are things going?" he asked after they had been served their food.

"Well." Kobe ate some noodles in broth. He seemed hungry, and Akitada did not press him. But when his bowl was empty, Kobe set it down, sighed, and said, "You have a good cook. My meals have been odd and irregular.

"That's why your coming gives me such pleasure. That and having my curiosity satisfied.

Kobe smiled. "The Fujiwara captain has been released. He will probably pay a fine for making false accusations. He claimed to have made a mistake of identifying the wrong man."

Akitada nodded. He had expected something of the sort. .

"Ishikawa will go to trial next week. I was relieved to find that his colleagues and friends don't like him much. The doctor will testify against him. His property will probably be confiscated, but he'll be allowed to join a brother in Shinano Province."

Akitada nodded again. "I got the feeling that Kagehira had a small side business poisoning people who got in someone's way."

Kobe frowned. "We would have come across him and we haven't. He may have had some plans of the sort, but I think this experience has taught him a lesson."

It was probably as much as could be expected. "What will happen to Ishikawa?"

"Exile. And he'll pay blood money."

"I see."

They sat silently, thinking about the case.

Kobe asked, "What about Miyagi? She'll have some money after Ishikawa's trial unless there is another heir."

Akitada smiled. "There may be another heir. Miyagi expects Sato's child."

Kobe's craggy face broke into his first smile in weeks. "Is she? How nice! Any chance of claiming Sato's business?"

"We think so. Saburo has found documentation of a marriage, and there is her maid who lived with them after Sato brought her to his house. She remembers buying dumplings."

"How nice!" Kobe said again and helped himself to a large bowl of fragrant rice.

A brief silence fell while they finished their meal.

When Mrs. Kuruda had removed the dishes, Akitada refilled their cups. "So? What about the Tadanobu matter?

35

Penalties

Kobe suddenly looked old. He sighed. "I knew it would be hard. The worst part is that there was no right thing to do. Justice demands prosecution of violent acts. And we dealt with two of these, involving at least three people, all of whom tried to bring justice to their world because we did not."

Akitada nodded. "Yes. I don't know the answer either. The old woman has been poisoning Tadanobu all along?"

"Yes. We searched her room and found dried mushrooms. There were several sorts, all potentially fatal, some causing madness, according to Doctor Hori. She never denied it. Kept saying "Buddha be praised!" with a happy smile whenever I referred to the death of

Tadanobu. Her granddaughter tried to protect her, claiming her grandmother was dying and didn't know what she was saying. Pointing out that Tadanobu hadn't died from poison. Even saying that her grandmother was too frail to cook and that she, the granddaughter had prepared the food. I think she was willing to confess to the poisoning if we had let her."

"Remarkable young woman."

"There is nothing we can do to the old woman. She will die before she can be tried, and I have no mind to charge the granddaughter."

Akitada nodded and said nothing.

After a moment, Kobe continued, "It's different with the Haradas. They both confessed."

"Both?"

"Yes, mother and son. They may have acted together. The mother worked as a maid and had access to the living quarters, but I suspect it was the son who brought the knife. It was one from the kitchen, by the way."

"And their motive?"

"Well, that surprised me. It wasn't the death of the child. They felt they had been compensated for that. No, it was the shame of having been dismissed from serving the family. Of having lost their warrior rank and been forced to live as commoners, low class commoners. Theirs is a warrior family, they said."

"I suspected as much. What will happen to them?"

Kobe shrugged. "We have charged both. If we cannot clear up who did what, they'll both get the maximum penalty."

"I suppose nothing can be done. A pity. The Harada son would have made a fine soldier."

*

If Akitada had hoped to leave the capital with its bad memories behind for a healing visit with his favorite sister in the country, he was disappointed. The prime minister was not done with him.

But this time the news was good—or at least not bad—Akitada was being appointed to serve as assistant minister of justice. He was returning to his old job with a promotion. But this required his presence in the capital for several weeks, and he sent Yoshiko his regrets with a promise to visit before year's end.

To his additional surprise, the prime minister commuted the Harada son's sentence from exile at hard labor to exile to the northern front. Mrs. Harada was fined as an accessory. The family lost their property and moved north.

Akitada, though busy with his new duties, was deeply unhappy. It seemed to him that the older he got the more he lost. Kosehira was busy raising his little granddaughter and felt too guilty to invite Akitada or visit him. Kobe had retired to the country. He had promised to write, but that was not the same. Yoshi attended the university where he had made many new friends, and rarely came home. Yasuko had paid a visit to the baby and returned quiet. She barely spoke to him. She, more than anyone, made him feel a failure. Tora was getting old. Their practice bouts at stick fighting, now that Akitada's ribs were healed, lacked their former passion.

But then he was also aging; it was not fair to blame it on Tora. And Aoi, the woman he loved, had rejected him. He did not flatter himself that she was willing to welcome him to her bed. No, she had rejected *him*, had not wanted to share his life, to be with him into old age.

Meanwhile spring was in full flower, and the sweet scent of the blooming azaleas hung over his garden. The cherry tree was flowering, and the birds filled the air with their voices. More and more frequently, Akitada's thought turned to Tamako, and the old grief returned.

One night, feeling especially lonely, Akitada pushed aside his paperwork. He took out his flute and went to sit cross-legged on the veranda.

He played, tentatively at first, then letting the melodies carry him along. He played all the sad songs of losing loved ones, and then he played the songs of parting from friends and lovers, and finally the exile's songs of longing for a faraway home. When he was done, he put down his flute and looked up at the moon.

He was startled when there was movement beside him and a small figure crept close, putting her arms around him.

"Yasuko?"

"Yes, Father." A sob.

"What's wrong?" He pulled her closer.

"Sadako is leaving us. She's going home to her family. Oh, Father I shall miss her so."

"How do you know she's leaving?"

"She had a letter. From her older brother. She's to come home."

Yes, he should have expected it. The Tanaka family had regained their patrimony and was calling back their lost children. He should be glad, but he, too, grieved Sadako's departure.

"It will be just you and me now, Father," said his daughter in a small voice. "And I have not been a good daughter." Another sob. "I have also been unkind to Sadako. No doubt she's leaving because she hates me."

"No, Yasuko. She wants to see her family again. And yes, you and I shall have each other. I hope you'll come to me whenever you feel lonely."

She hugged him a little more tightly and nodded her head.

Smiling, Akitada took up the flute again and played her favorite tune.

HISTORICAL NOTE

The year is 1034. We are at the height of the Heian Era (794-1185). Japan had a centralized government under an emperor and with an administration by senior nobles. The system followed loosely that of Tang China. It worked reasonably well, because the many provinces were administered by senior nobles who served as governors and were appointed by the central government. They brought.their own staff. The provincial police was also under a man sent from the capital. A network of excellent roads connected the provinces to the capital. But the central government could not muster military support and had to rely on local families to quell rebellions and defend against enemies. This weakness eventually produced the warlords of the samurai period and ended the imperial rule

The capital, following Chinese precedent, was designed with a grid of north-south and east-west streets, protected from evil influences by mountains to the north, and embraced by two rivers. The rivers brought water into the city via a web of canals to allow for beautiful gardens and avenues of willow trees as well as for the daily needs of the inhabitants. The government complex (*Daidairi*) with the imperial palace was in the northernmost sector with the homes and palaces of the court nobles to either side. *Suzaku Avenue* bisected the city from the central gate of the *Daidairi* in the north to the famous *Rashomon* at its southern end. *Rashomon*, however, had already disappeared by this time. The city was not walled. It had two sides, with two markets, two city administrations, and two jails each.

We know a good deal about the lives of the nobility because their activities are chronicled in their own writings and in books by such great female authors as Lady Murasaki and Sei Shonagon. However, very little is known about the common people. Some information may be gleaned from later collections of "Tales" and from history books that describe trade, crafts, religions, art and architecture, festivals, education and other aspects of the Heian culture. While we are not yet in the age of the warlords, there were career warriors (*samurai),* and sword-making had already reached a high level of skill. The noble owners of vast estates had retainers, and the city nobles lived in great style in walled and gated compounds. The common people worked for them or for the government and shopped at the two markets. Everybody lived in fear of sudden fires and of earthquakes, epidemics, failed rice crops, and other disasters. Both Shinto and Buddhism flourished, as did all sorts of superstitious practices. The capital, may not have had a "willow quarter," but prostitution existed, particularly in the towns along the Yodo River where such amusement quarters did a lively business. Some of the details in the novel about how these businesses were conducted come from later Japanese sources.

The capital's law enforcement was in the hands of the capital-imperial police, a semi-military force that engaged in arrests, investigations, and prosecutions. Judges and jails were part of the system. In addition, each city ward also had wardens who kept order in their own areas. In spite of this, crime flourished in the city and on the highways, possibly because there were frequent amnesties to ward off some disaster and the death penalty did not exist, since Buddhism forbids the taking of life. Exile and forced labor in a remote province was the most serious form of punishment.

Relationships between men and women differed from those in the West and from later Japanese customs. They were both more casual and more formal. A nobleman usually had several wives, ranked by family background or by whether they had produced heirs. Marriages could be dissolved on the husband's word. However, elaborate arrangements between the families of bride and groom, involving dowries, generally protected women from being casually discarded. Women also could and did own property. The wives of ordinary men generally did not have to contend with secondary wives. Their worth to the husband came in the form of their labor and the women derived a certain respect and freedom from this. The women of the nobility were generally not expected to leave their homes, though exceptions were made for service in the palace and religious pilgrimages.

The education of the children of the nobility began early and in the household. The boys had tutors or were taught by their fathers; the girls by their mothers, or sometimes their fathers. The boys had to learn to read, speak, and write Chinese, the language of government. The girls rarely had such instruction, though a few, like Lady Murasaki or Sei Shonagon knew and used the language, hiding their accomplishment because it was frowned upon. In their early teens, the boys generally went on to the imperial university where they studied under professors and took examinations. Final examinations influenced their future positions in the government and thus their ranks. There were also provincial schools for the children of the landed gentry and provincial officials. Within the capital, some great families, like the Fujiwara clan, established their own family schools, and one school was founded by a Buddhist monk and accepted students from all walks of life. The subjects taught were Confucianism, the Chinese classics, law, poetry and music, and mathematics and medicine.

The exorcisms in the case of *ikiryo*, that is possession by an angry spirit of an offended person, are well attested in the literature of the time. The most famous case was that of Sugawara Michizane, whose unjust punishment led to his death and was thought to have brought disasters in subsequent reigns. The Fujiwara-led court deified him to appease his anger. In their diaries, both Lady Murasaki and Sei Shonagon have described exorcisms carried out at court to protect ailing persons or women in childbirth against the evil spirits of those who might have been offended or merely jealous. The novel *Genji* contains such a scene in "The Heart Vine" chapter. A medium, usually female, played a major role in such practices. They were essentially Shinto, but Buddhist readings and prayers were carried on simultaneously. Both living and dead spirits could haunt their enemies.

About the Author

I. J. Parker was born and educated in Europe and turned to mystery writing after an academic career in the U.S. She has published her Akitada stories in *Alfred Hitchcock's Mystery Magazine,* winning the Shamus award in 2000. Several stories have also appeared in collections, such as *Fifty Years of Crime and Suspense* and *Shaken.* The award-winning "Akitada's First Case" is available as a podcast.

Many of the stories have been collected in *Akitada and the Way of Justice.*

The Akitada series of crime novels features the same protagonist, an eleventh century Japanese nobleman/detective. *Ikiryo: Revenge and Justice* is number seventeen. The books are available as e-books, in print, and in audio format, and have been translated into twelve languages. The early novels are published by Penguin.

Books by I. J. Parker

The Akitada series in chronological order

The Dragon Scroll

Rashomon Gate

Black Arrow

Island of Exiles

The Hell Screen

The Convict's Sword

The Masuda Affair

The Fires of the Gods

Death on an Autumn River

The Emperor's Woman

Death of a Doll Maker

The Crane Pavilion

The Old Men of Omi

The Shrine Virgin

The Assassin's Daughter

The Island of the Gods

Ikiryo: Revenge and Justice

The collection of stories

Akitada and the Way of Justice

Other Historical Novels

The HOLLOW REED saga:

Dream of a Spring Night

Dust before the Wind

The Sword Master

The Left-Handed God

Contact Information

Please visit I.J.Parker's web site at
www.ijparker.com
You may contact her via e-mail there. This way you will be informed when new books come out.

The novels may be ordered from Amazon or Barnes&Noble as trade paperbacks. There are electronic versions of all the works. Please do post reviews. They help sell books and keep Akitada novels coming. Thank you for your support.

44909715R00244

Made in the USA
San Bernardino, CA
23 July 2019